W9-CZA-690

Possessed . . .

Neil stiffened as he saw his son Toby sitting up in bed, staring at him. His small face was white, white as the silvered light from the moon, and his eyes were intense and glittering. He wasn't smiling. He wasn't frowning. His expression was calm and controlled and, because of that, even more frightening. *Eight-year-old boys grin, or cry, or show some feeling,* Neil thought. *Why is he staring at me like that?*

Toby's eyes sparkled with malevolence. His features seemed to shift and change in the moonlight, one transparency laid over another, until he looked like someone else altogether. Someone older, someone infinitely older . . . and someone infinitely evil.

The boy rose slowly from the bed and seemed to glide toward Neil. He stood only a few feet away, and then he spoke in the voice of Misquamacus, in that hollow distant voice that echoed of eons of ancient time.

"You have spoken to the white magician Erskine. He will come, along with my treacherous blood brother Singing Rock, and I shall show them that my manitou is indestructible, and that my vengeance spans fifty thousand moons."

Neil said steadily, "You must let Toby go. I want you to get out of my son!"

Toby smiled, a slow laconic smile. "You are powerless to prevent me. . . ."

By Graham Masterton, from Pinnacle Books

The Manitou
The Djinn
The Sphinx
Charnel House
Devils of D-Day

WRITE FOR OUR FREE CATALOG

If there is a Pinnacle Book you want—and you cannot find it locally—it is available from us simply by sending the title and price plus 25¢ to cover mailing and handling costs to:

PINNACLE—Book Mailing Service
P.O. Box 1050
Rockville Centre, N.Y. 11571

____Check here if you want to receive our catalog regularly.

REVENGE
OF THE
MANITOU
GRAHAM MASTERTON

PINNACLE BOOKS • LOS ANGELES

This is a work of fiction. All the characters and events portrayed in this book are fictional, and any resemblance to real people or incidents is purely coincidental.

REVENGE OF THE MANITOU

Copyright © 1979 by Wieslawa, Inc.

All rights reserved, including the right to reproduce this book or portions thereof in any form.

An original Pinnacle Books edition, published for the first time anywhere.

First printing, February 1979

ISBN: 0-523-40446-8

Cover illustration by Paul Stinson

Printed in the United States of America

PINNACLE BOOKS, INC.
2029 Century Park East
Los Angeles, California 90067

Ye *Wampanaug* wise Man *Misquamacus* affirm'd ye Daemon had ye Name *Ossadagowah*, which signifys ye child of *Sadogowah*, ye which is held to be a Frightful Spirit spoke of by antients as come down from ye Stars. Ye *Wampanaugs* and ye *Nansets* and *Nahrigansets* knew how to draw It out of ye Heavens but never did so because of ye exceeding great Evilness of it.

—H. P. Lovecraft

REVENGE OF
THE MANITOU

ONE

He woke up during the night and he was sure there was someone in his room.

He froze, not daring to breathe, his eight-year-old fingers clutching the candy-striped sheet right up to his nose. He strained his eyes and his ears in the darkness, looking and listening for the slightest movement, the slightest squeak of floorboards. His pulse raced silently and endlessly, a steeplechase of boyish terror that ran up every artery and down every vein.

"*Daddy*," he said, but the word came out so quietly that nobody could have heard him. His parents were sleeping right down at the other end of the corridor, and that meant safety was two doors and thirty feet away, across a gloomy landing where an old grandfather clock ticked, and where even in daytime there was a curious sense of solitude and suffocating stillness.

He was sure he could hear somebody sighing, or breathing. Soft, suppressed sighs, as if they meant sadness, or pain. It may have been nothing more than the rustle of the curtains, as they rose and fell in the draft

1

from the half-open window. Or it may have been the sea, sliding and whispering over the dark beach, just a half-mile away.

He waited and waited, but nothing happened. Five minutes passed. Ten. He lifted his blond, tousled head from the pillow, and looked around the room with widened eyes. There was the carved pine footboard, at the end of his bed. There was the walnut wardrobe. There was his toy box, its lid only half-closed because of the model tanks and cranes and baseball gloves that were always crammed in there.

There were his clothes, his jeans and his T-shirt, over the back of his upright ladder-backed chair.

He waited a little longer, frowning. Then he carefully climbed out of bed, and walked across to the window. Outside, under a grayish sky of torn clouds and fitful predawn winds, a night heron called *kwawk*, *kwawk*, and a wooden door banged and banged. He looked down at the untidy backyard, and the leaning fence that separated the Fenners' house from the grassy dunes of the Sonoma coastline. There was nobody there.

He went back to bed, and pulled the sheets almost over his head. He knew it was silly, because his daddy had told him it was silly. But somehow tonight was different from those times when he was just afraid of the shadows, or overexcited from watching flying-saucer movies on television. Tonight, there was someone there. Someone who sighed.

He lay there tense for nearly twenty minutes. The wooden door kept banging, with mindless regularity, but he didn't hear anything else. After a while, his eyes began to close. He jerked awake once, but then they closed again, and he slept.

It was the worst nightmare he had ever had. It didn't

seem as though he was dreaming at all. He rose from his bed, and turned toward the wardrobe, his head moving in an odd, stiff way. The grain of the walnut on the wardrobe doors had always disturbed him a little, because it was figured with foxlike faces. Now, it was terrifying. It seemed as if there was someone *inside* the surface of the wood, someone who was calling out to him, trying desperately to tell him something. Someone who was trapped, but also frightening.

He could hear a voice, like the voice of someone speaking through a thick glass window. ". . . *Allen . . . Allen . . . for God's sake, Allen . . . for God's sake, help me . . . Allen . . .*," the voice called.

The boy went closer to the wardrobe, one hand raised in front of him, as if he was going to touch the wood to find where the voice was coming from. Dimly, scarcely visible except as a faint luminosity on the varnish, he could make out a gray face, a face whose lips were moving in a blurry plea for mercy, for assistance, for some way out of an unimaginable hell.

"*Allen . . .*" pleaded the voice, monotonously. "*Allen . . . for God's sake . . .*"

The boy whispered, "Who's Allen? Who's Allen? My name's Toby. I'm Toby Fenner. Who's Allen?"

He could see the face was fading. And yet, for one moment, he had an indescribable sense of freezing dread, as if a cold wind had blown across him from years and years ago. There was a feeling of *someplace else . . .* someplace known and familiar and yet frighteningly strange. The feeling was there and it was gone, so quickly that he couldn't grasp what it was.

He banged his hands against the wardrobe door and said, "Who's Allen? Who's Allen?"

He was more and more alarmed, and he screeched at

the top of his high-pitched voice, *"Who's Allen? Who's Allen? Who's Allen?"*

The bedroom door burst open and his daddy said, "Toby? Toby—what in hell's the matter?"

Over breakfast at the pine kitchen table, bacon and eggs and pancakes, his daddy sat munching and drinking coffee and watching him fixedly. The *San Francisco Examiner* lay folded and unread next to his elbow. Toby, already dressed for school in a pale-blue summer shirt and jeans, concentrated his attention on his pancakes. Today, they were treasure islands on a sea of syrup, gradually being excavated by a giant fork.

At the kitchen stove, his mommy was cleaning up. She was wearing her pink gingham print apron, and her blond hair was tied back in a ponytail. She was slim and young and she cooked bacon just the way Toby liked it. His daddy was darker and quieter, and spoke slower, but there was deep affection between them which didn't have much need of words. They could fly kites all Sunday afternoon on the shoreline, or go fishing in one of the boats from his daddy's boatyard, and say no more than five words between lunch and dusk.

Through the kitchen window, the sky was a pattern of white clouds and blue. It was September on the north California shore, warm and windy, a time when the sand blew between the rough grass, and the laundry snapped on the line.

Susan Fenner said, "More coffee? It's all fresh."

Neil Fenner raised his cup without taking his eyes off Toby. "Sure. I'd love some."

Susan glanced at Toby as she filled her husband's cup. "Are you going to eat those pancakes or what?" she asked him, a little sharply.

4

Toby looked up. His daddy said, "Eat your pancakes."

Toby obeyed. The treasure islands were dug up by the giant fork, and shoveled into a monster grinder.

Susan said, "Anything in the paper this morning?"

Neil glanced at it, and shook his head.

"You're not going to read it?" Susan asked, pulling out one of the pine kitchen chairs and sitting down with her cup of coffee. She never ate breakfast herself, although she wouldn't let Neil or Toby out of the house without a good cooked meal inside them. She knew that Neil usually forgot to take his lunch break, and that Toby traded his peanut-butter sandwiches for plastic GIs or bubble gum.

Neil said no, and passed the paper across the table. Susan opened it and turned to the Homecraft section.

"Would you believe this?" she said. "It says that Cuisinart cookery is going out of style. And I don't even have a Cuisinart yet."

"In that case, we've saved ourselves some money," said Neil, but he didn't sound as if he was really interested. Susan looked up at him and frowned.

"Is anything wrong, Neil?" she asked.

He shook his head. But then he suddenly reached across the table and held Toby's wrist, so that the boy's next forkful of pancake was held poised over his plate. Toby said, "Sir?"

Neil looked at his son carefully and intensely. In a husky voice, he said, "Toby, do you know who Allen is?"

Toby looked at his father uncomprehendingly. "Allen, sir?"

"That's right. You were saying his name last night,

5

when you were having that nightmare. You were saying 'I'm not Allen, I'm Toby.' "

Toby blinked. In the light of day, he didn't remember the nightmare very clearly at all. He had a sense that it was something to do with the wardrobe door, but he couldn't quite think what it was. He remembered a feeling of fright. He remembered his daddy putting him back to bed, and tucking him in tightly. But the name "Allen" didn't mean anything.

Susan said, "Was that what he was saying? 'I'm not Allen, I'm Toby'?"

Neil nodded.

"But kids say all kinds of silly things in their sleep," she told him. "My younger sister used to sing nursery rhymes in her sleep."

"This wasn't the same," said Neil.

Susan looked at Toby and then back to her husband. She said quietly, "I don't know what you mean."

Neil let go of his son's wrist. He dropped his eyes toward the table, at his scraped-clean plate, and then said, "My brother's name was Allen. Everybody used to call him Jim on account of his second name, James. But his first name was Allen."

"But Toby doesn't know that."

Neil said, "I know."

There was an awkward silence. Then Susan said, "What are you trying to say? That Toby's having nightmares about your brother?"

"I don't know what I'm trying to say. It just shocked me, that's all. Toby's room used to be Allen's. Jim's, I mean."

Susan put down her cup of coffee. She looked at Neil and she could see that he wasn't pulling her leg. He did, sometimes, with fond but heavy-handed humor which

6

he'd inherited from his Polish mother. Good old middle-European practical jokes. But today, he was edgy and disturbed as if he'd had a premonition of unsettled days ahead.

Susan said, "You think it's a *ghost*, or something?"

Neil looked serious for a moment, and then gave a sheepish grin, and shrugged. "Ghost? I don't know. I don't believe in ghosts. I mean, I don't believe in ghosts that wander around in the night."

Toby piped up, "Is there a ghost, Daddy? A real ghost?"

Neil said, "No, Toby. There isn't any such thing. They come out of storybooks, and that's all."

"I heard some noises in the night," Toby told him. "Was that a ghost?"

"No, son. It was just the wind."

"But what you said about Allen?"

Neil lowered his head. Susan took Toby's hand and said softly, "Daddy was just saying that you must have had a very special kind of dream, that's all. It's nothing to get frightened about. Now, are you going to finish that pancake, because it's time for school."

Neil drove Toby in his Chevy pickup as far as Bodega Bay, and dropped him off at the schoolhouse. The bell was ringing plaintively, and most of the kids were already in the building. Toby climbed down to the road, but instead of running straight into school, he stood beside the truck for a moment, looking up at his father. His blond hair was ruffled by the Pacific wind.

He said, "Daddy?"

Neil looked at him. "What's the matter?"

Toby said, "I didn't mean to upset you or anything."

Neil laughed. "Upset me? You haven't upset me."

7

"I thought you were. Mommy said I mustn't talk about Jim."

Neil didn't answer. It was still difficult for him to think about his brother. He no longer got those terrible, clear pictures in his mind. He'd managed, with time, to blur them beyond recognition. But there was still that sensation of breathless pain, like jumping into the ocean on a December day. There was still that helplessness, still that desperation.

Neil said, "You'd better get into school. The teacher's going to be worrying where you are."

Toby hesitated. Neil continued, "Go along, now," and Toby knew that his daddy meant it. He swung his books and his lunch pail over his shoulder and walked slowly across the gray, dusty yard. Neil watched him go into the battered pale-blue door, and then the door swung shut. He sighed.

He knew that he ought to be straight with Toby, and tell him about Jim. But somehow he couldn't, not until he could get straight about Jim in his own mind. He'd begun, a couple of times, to try and tell Toby what had happened; but the words always came out wrong. What words could there possibly be to describe the experience of watching your own brother being slowly crushed to death under an automobile? What words could there possibly be to describe the knowledge that it was your fault, that you'd accidentally released the jack?

He could see Jim's hand reaching out to him even today. He could see Jim's pleading, swollen face, with the blood running from his mouth and his nose. How do you tell your eight-year-old kid about that?

He drove down to Bodega Bay and parked the Chevy in the parking lot outside the Tides Restaurant. Then he walked out along the gray wooden planks of the jetty to the *White Dove*, a sailboat he was fixing up for a client. Gulls turned and fluttered in the wind, and the tackle and rigging of all the boats tied up in the bay clattered and clanked.

Bodega Bay was a small, shallow bay, enclosed in a hook of land that came out from the Sonoma coast like a beckoning finger. The beaches all around were gray and littered with burnt wood and beer cans, but beyond the beaches were green, rounded hills and quiet farms. The tourists had all gone home now, and the coastline was foggy and silent, except for the *meep-meep* of gulls, and the slopping of the sea on the piers of the jetty.

Neil clambered down onto the *White Dove*'s salt-bleached deck and walked aft. The owner had used the boat all summer, and it needed painting, varnishing, and cleaning. Neil glanced up at the mast and saw that several of the lines were frayed and loose.

He was just about to go below and see what repairs were needed in the small cabin when he thought he heard someone speak. He looked up, but there was nobody around, except for old Doughty, Bodega Bay's Ancient Mariner, who was sitting on a lobster basket thirty or forty feet away.

Neil paused for a couple of seconds, but then he decided he must have made a mistake, and he bent his head to go below.

A voice whispered; *"Allen."*

Neil froze. For no reason that he could possibly explain, he felt frightened in a way that he had never felt before. He couldn't move for a moment, as if the whispered voice had drained him of all energy. Then he turned around, his eyes wide, his face white.

There was nothing there but the foggy bay, the dim, gray Pacific, the swooping gulls. No other sound but the

9

creak of the ropes and timbers as the *White Dove* rose and dipped in the swell of Bodega Bay.

Neil took a deep breath, and went down into the boat's cabin. There were three narrow berths, still covered with rumpled blankets and sheets. In the center of the cabin was a varnished table, littered with Dixie cups and empty bottles of bourbon, and burned by cigarette ends. It disgusted Neil to see people treat boats this way. Even the simplest boat was a crafted creation which protected men from the sea, and he believed in treating every vessel, however humble, with care and respect.

He took a look around, and then turned to go back up the companionway. The voice whispered, "*Allen, help me . . . Allen, please help me . . .*"

Totally scared, he turned around. For one ridiculous moment, he was sure that he saw someone looking in at the dim forward porthole, but then the face instantly reassembled itself into a pattern of coiled ropes and clips.

Shaken, he climbed out of the cabin and stood back on the deck. He didn't know what to think or what to feel. Maybe Toby's dream was just getting under the skin of his imagination. Maybe he was overworked. He took a couple of steady breaths, and then walked forward, back to the jetty, to collect his tools and his cans of varnish.

In school, with the sunshine sloping across the desks, Mrs. Novato, a young dark-haired woman with a hairy mole on one cheek and a taste for billowing Indian dresses, announced a class excursion in one week's time. It would cost a dollar-thirty-five, and every pupil would have to bring a packed lunch. They were going to

10

drive up to Lake Berryessa, in the Vaca Mountains, for nature study and maybe some swimming, too.

Toby was sitting next to Petra Delgada, a serious little girl who never spoke much and always went to mass on Sundays. Mrs. Novato had placed him there because he giggled and talked too much whenever he sat next to his best friend, the coppery-haired Linus Hopland. Linus was in the front row now, his hair shining in the sunshine like the Point Arena lighthouse. Toby whispered to Petra, "Are you going up to the lake? Will your folks let you?"

Petra shrugged, and pursed her lips demurely. "I don't know. I've been sick for the past four days. Mommy may not let me."

"You've been sick? You mean, you've puked?"

"You mustn't say puke. It's disgusting."

Toby colored a little. He didn't like Petra to think that he wasn't grown-up and sophisticated. Petra, after all, was nearly nine, and next in line for class president. Toby said: "Well, what do you mean? You got the measles?"

"As a matter of fact, I have insomnia," said Petra.

"Is that catching?"

"Of course not, stupid. Insomnia is when you can't sleep. Can't you see these rings around my eyes? Mommy says it's due to hypertension in prepuberty."

Toby frowned. He didn't like to admit that he didn't have the faintest idea of what Petra was talking about. He'd kind of heard of "puberty," and he knew it had something to do with growing hairs on your doodad— which is what his grandpa always used to call it—but that was about the extent of his knowledge. Like most children to whom the most important things in life are

11

skateboards, Charlie's Angels, and Captain Cosmic, he'd been told, but had quickly forgotten.

"What do you do all night if you don't sleep?" asked Toby. "Do you walk about, or what?"

"Oh, I sleep some of the time," explained Petra. "The trouble is, I keep having bad dreams. They wake me up, and then it takes me a long time to go back to sleep."

"Bad dreams? I had a bad dream last night."

"Well, I'm sure your bad dream wasn't as bad as *my* bad dreams," said Petra. "My bad dreams are simply *awful*."

"I dreamed there was somebody stuck in my wardrobe," said Toby. In the sunlit classroom, it sounded pretty lame. The cold terror of seeing that gray face in the walnut door had been vaporized by the warmth of the day.

Petra tilted her nose up. "That's nothing. I keep dreaming about blood. I keep dreaming about all these people covered with blood."

Toby was impressed. "That's *real* frightening," he admitted. "People covered with blood—that's *real* frightening."

"Mommy says it's prepuberty fears," said Petra, airily. "She's says it's a woman's fear of her natural function brought about by men's lack of understanding of what a woman is."

Mrs. Novato called; "Petra? Are you talking? I'm surprised at you."

Petra gave Toby a sharp look, and said, "I'm sorry, Mrs. Novato. I was trying to explain something to Toby."

The class of twenty boys and girls, all between the ages of eight and ten, looked around at them. Mrs. Novato said, "If there's something you don't understand, Toby, you can always ask me. That's what I'm paid for. Apart from that, I'm a little better informed than Petra on most subjects."

Linus Hopland was grinning at Toby and pulling faces. Toby couldn't help smirking, and he had to bite his tongue to prevent himself from laughing out loud.

Mrs. Novato said; "Stand up, Toby. If you've got a question to ask, if there's something you don't understand, then let's share your problem. That is what a class is for, to share."

Toby reluctantly stood. He kept his eyes fixed on his desk.

"Well?" asked Mrs. Novato. "What was it that you wished to know?"

Toby didn't answer.

"It was so important that you had to discuss it with Petra in the middle of nature study, and yet you can't tell me what it was?"

Toby said, in a small, husky voice, "It was Petra's dreams, Mrs. Novato."

"Speak up," insisted his teacher. "I didn't hear you."

"It was Petra's dreams. Petra's been having bad dreams, and so have I."

Mrs. Novato blinked at him. "Bad dreams? What kind of bad dreams?"

"I've been dreaming about a man stuck in my wardrobe calling for help, and Petra's been having dreams about people covered with blood."

Mrs. Novato walked slowly down the aisle toward them. She looked first at Toby and then at Petra. On the blackboard behind her was the chalked message: "Trees in the Petrified Forest were turned to stone by *minerals.*"

13

Mrs. Novato said, "Have you told your parents about these dreams?"

The children nodded.

"Yes, Mrs. Novato."

Mrs. Novato smiled. "In that case, I'm sure you're both going to be fine. Maybe a little less cheese at bedtime, and those dreams are sure to disappear. Now, forget about what goes on in dreams and let's have your attention on something that's real. The trees in the Petrified Forest."

Toby sat down again. Petra, annoyed at having been scolded by Mrs. Novato, pinched him hard on the leg.

During lunch recess, in the hot, dusty school yard with its chain-link fence, Toby sat on a split-log bench and ate his peanut-butter-and-jelly sandwiches. Today, despite Ben Nichelini's entreaties to trade a sandwich for a live lizard on a piece of string, he felt hungry, and he ate everything his mother had prepared for him. He carefully saved his Baby Ruth bar until last.

Andy Beaver, who was the envy of the class because his uncle had taken him to see *Star Wars*, was doing a passable imitation of R-2 D-2, while Karen Doughty was breathing in and out very loudly and panting: "I'm Darth Vader! I'm Darth Vader!"

Daniel Soscol, one of the youngest boys in the class, came across the school yard and sat down next to Toby, watching him eat with silent interest. Daniel wasn't very popular because he was so young and so quiet. He had thin arms and legs, and big dark eyes. His father was a plumber in Valley Ford, and his mother had died in May.

Toby continued to eat. When he had finished, he took out the square of kitchen towel that his mother had neatly folded under his sandwiches, and wiped his mouth.

Daniel said, "I heard you say about the dreams."

Toby looked up. "So?" he said, acting a little tough because Daniel was the class runt. He wouldn't have liked Andy Beaver to see him being too nice to Daniel, in case Andy Beaver's gang started to treat him the same way. Leaving thumbtacks on his seat, hiding his books, things like that.

Daniel said, "I had bad dreams, too. Real scary ones. I dreamed I was walking through this forest and suddenly all these things came dropping out of the trees."

"What's scary about that?"

"What's scary about somebody stuck in a wardrobe?"

"Well, it was scary at the time," said Toby.

"So was mine."

They sat in silence for a moment. Toby unwrapped his Baby Ruth and started to chew it. A coolish breeze from the west raised dust on the yard, and in the distance a cock began to crow.

Daniel said, "We're not the only ones. Ben Nichelini had a bad dream too. He dreamed he was running and running and all these fierce people were trying to catch him."

"Everybody has dreams like that," said Toby.

"Well, I guess so," admitted Daniel. "I just think it's funny all these kids having bad dreams."

Andy Beaver came up, burbling and warbling like R-2 D-2. Daniel didn't bother to stick around. When Andy was in a playful mood, it usually meant that Daniel was going to get his hair twisted or his shorts pulled down. Daniel said so long to Toby, and ran away across the yard and into the classroom.

"Have you been talking to teacher's pet?" asked

Andy. He was blond and pugnacious, and would probably spend most of his adult life watching baseball and
drinking Old Milwaukee.

Toby screwed up his eyes against the sun. "What if I
have?"

"You just don't talk to teacher's pet, that's all. He's a
sissy."

"His mom just died. Maybe you'd be a sissy if your
mom just died."

"I wouldn't be a sissy for nothing. What were you
talking about?"

Toby finished his chocolate bar and screwed up the
paper. "What's it to you?"

Andy Beaver grabbed his hand and bent his fingers
back. Toby yelped in pain, but Andy was much
stronger, and he couldn't get free. A couple of the other
kids came over, yelling, "Fight! Fight!" Toby and
Andy fell to the dusty ground and rolled over and over,
kicking and grunting and punching.

At last, Andy held Toby down on the ground, his
knees pressed against Toby's arms. Both of them were
flushed and grubby, and there were tears in their eyes.

Andy said, "Okay—what were you talking about? I
want to know!"

Toby coughed. "We were talking about those bad
dreams, that's all. Nothing that *you'd* understand."

"Oh yeah?"

Toby pushed him off and struggled to his feet. His
shirt was hanging out at the back, and his pants were
ripped. He took out his handkerchief and wiped his
face.

"You're so smart, you think you're the only person
who ever had dreams," Andy said.

"So when was the last time *you* had a bad dream?"

16

demanded Toby. "The last time your mother cooked spaghetti, I'll bet."

"It was not!" said Andy, hotly. "I had bad dreams last night, and the night before."

"*You* had bad dreams?" asked Toby.

"I did too. Nightmares."

"You shouldn't have gone to see *Star Wars*," said Ben Nichelini. "You're not man enough to take it."

"Will you shut up?" said Andy. "I had bad dreams about people having all their hair torn off of their heads. Dozens of 'em. All screaming and shouting, because somebody was tearing the hair right off of their heads."

"Gee, that's scary," put in Debbie Spurr. She was a thin, mousy little girl in a brown gingham print-frock and her hair in bows. "That's worse than my bad dream."

"What is this?" asked Andy. "Just because Toby and Petra and me had bad dreams, that doesn't mean everybody else has to say they had one too."

"David had one," said Toby. "That makes four."

"I *did* have one," insisted Debbie. "I thought I was awake, but I wasn't. I heard someone calling out. It was terrifically scary. They kept on calling and calling, and I didn't know what to do. It was a woman, and she sounded awful scared."

Toby looked at Andy, and for the very first time in their lives they looked at each other as people, not as classmates or as children. Their young faces were sober and expressionless, as if they had both recognized that what was happening was unusual and dangerous. Then Andy broke the spell by smirking a little, and saying, "That was nothing compared to *my* dream. Some

17

woman calling out? I'll put a thumbtack on Mrs. Novato's chair, then you'll hear some woman calling out."

Just then, Mrs. Novato came to the schoolhouse door and blew her whistle to signal the end of the lunch recess. The talk about bad dreams broke up as they drifted back to the classroom, and Andy Beaver started on his R-2 D-2 impressions again, colliding with the girls and making burbling sounds. Toby walked back to the school door alone, and he was the last to go in. At the door, some feeling made him pause, and he looked back at the schoolhouse fence.

Under the windy sun, a tall man was standing, only about three or four feet beyond the gate. His eyes were shaded by a wide, dusty hat, and he was dressed in worn, dusty clothes. His lips appeared to be moving, and Toby was sure that he could hear the whispered word "*Allen . . .*"

Right in front of his horrified eyes, the man began to fade in the afternoon heat, like a photograph. In a moment, he had vanished, and there was nothing to see but the rounded hills of Bodega, and the hot blacktop leading westward to the beach.

A scuffling noise right behind Toby made him jump. He looked up and it was Mrs. Novato. She said, with patronizing patience, "Are you deigning to join us, Mr. Fenner, or are you going to spend the rest of the day admiring the landscape?"

Toby was pale, and his face was sweaty. Mrs. Novato, instantly regretful of her sarcasm, asked, "Toby—are you all right?"

Toby felt as if his face was being pressed into a pillow. There was a terrible lack of air, a terrible closeness. He felt his legs turning black, and the blackness

18

rose up in him and engulfed his brain. Mrs. Novato caught him as he fell in a dead faint.

That evening, as he lay tucked up in bed, his mother came upstairs with a bowl of Philadelphia pepper pot soup and a plate of crackers. He was feeling much better already, but Doctor Crowder had insisted that he should rest. He had finished a jigsaw of the *Monitor* and the *Merrimac*, and snapped and unsnapped a snap-together model of a Cadillac Eldorado, and now he was reading a Doctor Strange comic.

His mother sat down on the side of his bed, and set his soup and crackers on his bedside table. Outside, the sky was dusking up, and there was a smell of eucalyptus from the row of trees which separated their plot from the MacDeans next door.

Susan Fenner said, "How's it going, tiger?"

Toby smiled. "I guess I'm okay now."

"You want to talk about it? You didn't want to talk to Doctor Crowder."

Toby turned his head away. He knew just what everyone would say if he told them about the man by the school fence. They'd say he had heat stroke, or too many peanut-butter-and-jelly sandwiches. It seemed like every weird thing that ever happened, adults attributed it to something you ate. His mommy waited patiently while he kept his head turned away, but he wished she wouldn't, because he really didn't want to tell her what had happened.

Eventually, his mommy took his hand. In a soft voice, she said, "Is it because you don't think I'll believe you? Is that it?"

He still didn't turn back, but he swallowed and said, "A little bit."

"Well," she said gently, "you don't have to. You're entitled to keep anything private that you want to. But you were real sick at school today, and because I love you, and because I care about you, I'd like to know what it was."

Toby bit his lip. Then he looked back at his mommy, and his face was so crumpled and so distressed that she felt the tears prickle her eyes. She held him close, and hugged him, and they both wept a little, until at last he felt better, and he sat up straight in bed and smiled at her with two trails of tears down his face.

"You're a silly, wonderful boy," she chided him. "You know you can tell me anything you want. Anything."

Toby swallowed, and nodded. The he began, "I was going into school after lunch. I turned around, and I saw a man. He was standing over by the fence."

Susan frowned. "A man? What was he doing?"

"He wasn't doing anything. He was just standing there."

She softly brushed back his tousled hair. "Are you sure?" she asked him. "I mean, he wasn't—well, undressed or anything?"

Toby shook his head. There was a long silence while Susan stroked his hair, and tried to think what it was that could have scared Toby so much. Eventually, she said, "What was he like, this man? Did he looked frightening?"

Toby screwed up his eyes as he thought. Then he told her, slowly and very carefully, "He wasn't frightening like a monster or anything. He wasn't going to chase me. But he wanted me to help. He wanted me to *help*, and I didn't know how to."

Susan said, "I don't understand. What sort of help did he want?"

Toby looked up at her anxiously. "I couldn't help him," he said, in a small voice. "I didn't know what to do."

"But Toby," asked Susan, "what sort of help did he want? What did he want you to do?"

Toby was silent for a moment, and then he said, very quietly, "I don't know."

Susan squeezed his hand. Maybe Toby was just going through some kind of imaginative stage in his life. Maybe it was all that ridiculous stuff he saw on television and read in his comic books. She knew that some mothers censored what their children read and watched, but Neil had always insisted that a childhood of Superman and Captain Marvel had never done *him* any harm, and so they had always allowed Toby to see any trash that he wanted to. As it had turned out, he usually preferred quality programs and good books anyway, but maybe Doctor Strange and the Incredible Hulk had gotten his eight-year-old mind out of gear . . .

Toby said, "He wasn't alive."

Susan, astray with her own thoughts, murmured, "What?"

"The man I saw. He wasn't alive."

"But Toby, you said he was standing up by the fence. How could he stand up if he wasn't alive?"

Toby lowered his eyes. "I don't know. But he wasn't alive."

Susan reached for the soup bowl, and handed it to him. "You listen," she said, in a quiet, firm voice. "Just forget about what you saw today. It was nothing to worry about. Eat your soup and your crackers, and in a little while Daddy will come up and read you a story.

21

Then you can get a good night's sleep, and in the morning you won't think anything about it."

She left his bedroom door ajar and went downstairs. Neil has come in a half-hour ago, and was sitting at the kitchen table drinking a Lite beer and reading the paper. He looked up when she came in.

"How is he now?" he asked her.

She went over to the range and stirred the big black iron pot of vegetable soup. The fragrance of fresh-cooked carrots and leeks filled the kitchen. She said, "He's a little better. But he says a man frightened him."

Neil put his paper down. "A man? What man?"

"He doesn't know. It wasn't like an indecent assault or anything. The man was just standing by the school fence, and Toby said he scared him somehow. The man wanted help and Toby didn't know how to help him."

"Help? What kind of help?"

Susan shook her head. "I don't know. It worries me. I hope he hasn't picked up some sort of illness. I mean, he talks as though he's suffering from fever."

"Did Doc Crowder check his temperature?"

"Sure. It's normal. He said there was nothing wrong."

Neil rubbed his chin. For some reason, he kept remembering that moment on the *White Dove*, the strange whisper of "*Allen*." He stood up and walked to the window. It was dark outside now, and he saw his own thin reflection staring back at him from a ghostly reflected kitchen.

Susan continued, "He kept insisting he wasn't alive."

"Who?"

"The man by the school fence. Toby said that he wasn't alive."

22

Neil turned around. "Did he say what he meant by that?"

She shrugged. "I guess he meant it was a ghost."

Neil let out a long, resigned breath. "A ghost. That means it was my fault. All that talk about ghosts at breakfast."

"Well, it could have been," said Susan. "But don't you think you ought to call Mrs. Novato, and find out if they've had any bums hanging around the school?"

Neil nodded. "Let me go talk to Toby first."

He went up the narrow stairs onto the wood-paneled landing, and across to Toby's room. Toby had almost finished his soup and his crackers, and there was a little more color in his cheeks than before. Neil pulled a bentwood chair across and straddled it, looking at his son with affection.

"Hi," he said gently.

"Hi," said Toby.

"How was the soup?" asked Neil.

Toby put the empty dish back on his bedside table. "It was good. I feel better now. Maybe I could get up and watch the flying robot."

"Maybe you could stay in bed and have a rest."

"I'm not sick, Daddy. Honest. I just fainted a little."

Neil grinned. "A little faint is plenty."

Toby showed him the snap-together Cadillac. "That's neat, isn't it? You don't have to have glue. It just snaps together."

Neil admired it. "When I was a kid, you had to carve the pieces out yourself, out of balsa wood," he said. "You had to sand 'em smooth, and stick 'em together, and do it all from scratch."

"That sounds like hard work," said Toby, sympathetically.

Neil smiled, but didn't answer. Instead, he said, "Toby, that man you saw. Can you tell me what he looked like?"

Toby lowered his eyes.

"It's pretty important, Toby," Neil told him. "The point is, if there really was a man there, and he's been prowling around the schoolhouse, then the police ought to know."

Toby was silent.

Neil reached over and took his hand. "Toby," he said. "I want you to tell me what the man looked like. This isn't a game. This is for real."

Toby swallowed, and then he whispered, "He was tall, and he had a hat like a cowboy, and one of those long white coats that cowboys used to wear."

"A duster, you mean."

Toby nodded. "He had a beard, I think. A kind of a light-colored beard. And that was all."

Neil said, "Mommy told me you thought he wasn't alive."

"He wasn't."

"What makes you think that?"

"He just wasn't. I know he wasn't."

"Was he a ghost?"

Toby lowered his eyes again. He fidgeted with his small fingers, and there was a hint of high color on his cheeks. He didn't say anything, but then he didn't know what to say. The man at the schoolhouse hadn't been a ghost in the way that most people think about ghosts. He hadn't come to haunt anybody. He had to come to ask for help, some terrible kind of help that Toby couldn't even begin to understand. The feeling of need that came from the man in the long white duster had been so strong that Toby, just before he fainted, had felt

24

that the man was real and that he, Toby, was a ghost, nothing but a shade of a boy.

Neil said, "I think it's time you got some sleep now, don't you? When you wake up in the morning, you'll have gotten over all this."

Toby said, "He won't come again, will he? You see, I don't know what to do when he comes. I don't know how to help him."

"He won't come again. At least, I don't believe so."

Toby snuggled down in bed, and Neil tucked him in. He took the empty soup dish, and stood there for a while, looking down at his son's mop of sun-bleached hair, at those eyes screwed up in a conscientious attempt at sleep, at those cheeks that were still soft and chubby.

He knelt down beside the bed and touched Toby's forehead. Then he whispered, "If you do see that man again, you call me, you hear? You call me loud and I'll come running."

Toby opened one eye. "Yes, sir," he said, in a husky voice, and then began the long dark slide into sleep.

He was awakened by the sound of the shed door banging. It was dark, very dark, and there was a rippling wind blowing from the sea. The drapes rose and fell like a huge beast breathing, and it sounded as if every loose floorboard and doorknob in the whole house was being rattled by cold, inquisitive drafts.

He lay there a while, listening. He wished very much he could go back to sleep again. He wished it was morning, and he wished his parents' room wasn't so far away, and more than anything he wished he was anyplace else but alone in this bed in the middle of this black breezy night, with the house stirring and shifting as if it had come to life.

He thought he heard a sound. A slow, deliberate creak, like a heavy foot pressing on a stair tread. He held his breath until he was almost bursting, listening, listening, but he didn't hear the noise again. The drapes rustled and swished, and outside in the night the shed door banged and paused and banged again.

The voice whispered: "*Allen . . .*"

He didn't want to hear it. He buried his head under the bedclothes, and lay there in hot darkness, his heart pounding, almost stifling under the blankets and quilted comforter. He lay there for almost five minutes, but then a terrible thought occurred to him. Supposing, while he was hiding under the bedclothes, the man in the long white duster had come into the room, and was standing over him?

Toby came struggling up from the blankets like a diver coming up for air. He raised a flushed face from the bed, ready to encounter any kind of terror. But the room was still empty, and the curtains were still rising and falling, and the only sounds were those winds that shook the sash windows and persistently tried the doors.

He was scared now. Really, desperately scared. In a tiny, inaudible voice, he called, "Daddy."

There was no reply. The house was as dark and noisy as before. But he was sure he could hear footsteps somewhere. He was sure the tall man in the wide-brimmed hat and the long duster was coming up the stairs. He was trembling all over, but he didn't know what to do.

"*Allen, for God's sake . . .,*" whispered the voice.

Toby whimpered no and tried not to look toward the foxy whorls of wood on the wardrobe door, but his fright was so compelling that he couldn't look away. The whorls twisted, and that gray shadowy face began to materialize, that tired anguished face in its prison of polished wood.

"*Allen,*" pleaded the voice, monotonously. "*Allen . . . help me . . . for God's sake, Allen, help me . . .*"

Toby sat up in bed, rigid and white. The face was looking his way, and yet it didn't appear to see him. It was gaunt and bearded, and it had the silvery quality of a photograph. Yet its lips moved as it spoke, and its eyes opened and closed in slow, regular blinking movements.

"I'm not Allen," said Toby, in a small voice. "I'm not Allen, I'm Toby. I can't help you. I'm not Allen at all."

"*Allen, help me . . .*" insisted the gray face.

"I *can't,*" wept Toby. "I don't know what you want. I *can't.*"

"*Allen . . . ,*" moaned the voice. "*Allen, for the love of God . . . bring them up to the peak . . . bring them up, or we're lost . . .*"

Toby cried, "I can't! I can't! I don't know what you mean!"

It seemed at that moment as if the face truly opened its eyes at last. It stared at Toby, and as it stared, Toby felt as if he was being blown by a wind that came from far away and long ago, as if he was standing somewhere out in the open, but under a sky that was a hundred years gone. He had the eerie, terrifying sensation that the face on the wardrobe was real, and that the wardrobe wasn't a wardrobe at all. He could hear someone calling far off to his left, but for some reason he was incapable of turning his head. The gray, bearded face kept him transfixed.

"Allen," said the face, in a voice that sounded normal and very close. "Allen, I can't hold out much longer without you."

Toby found himself slurring an answer. His own voice seemed to echo and reverberate inside his head, as if he was speaking to himself from another room.

"I'll do what I can," he said slowly. "Just you hold out the best way you know how, and I'll do what I can."

He turned and looked down to his left. He knew there was a valley down that way, and he knew that there was help if he could only make it in time. The sun was three hours above the far mountains, and he wasn't sure that was going to give him long enough. He reckoned his best bet was to ride along the creek, but even then they might run into some nasty surprises.

He said, "Give me till sundown. I'll do my level darndest."

Neil came along the landing, tying up his bathrobe. He was sure that he'd heard Toby calling out a few moments ago, although everything seemed quiet now. He'd had a hard day on the *White Dove*, blow-torching off the discolored paint and the varnish, and he'd been deep in a bottomless sleep. As for Susan, you could have danced a rumba on the bed and she would never have stirred.

As he walked past the grandfather clock, ticking slowly and steadily in its dark coffin, he thought he heard voices. Deep, gruff voices, with a strange twang to them. He paused, listening, and then he went on tiptoe to Toby's half-open bedroom door.

He peered through the crack in the doorjamb, but he couldn't see anything. Then he heard one of those gruff voices again, a voice that said, "I'll do what I can. Just you hold out the best way you know how."

28

Neil hesitated. What the hell was going on? He pushed open Toby's door, and there was Toby, kneeling up on the comforter in his striped pajamas, looking away across the room. It seemed unusually cold and windy, and Neil shivered.

He said, "Toby?" and Toby turned around.

It took Neil seconds upon horrified seconds to realize what he was looking at. Instead of Toby's round young face, he was looking into the lined, weatherbeaten face of an old man, a man whose expression was as tough and cold and self-sufficient as a snake's.

He jerked involuntarily. But then he stared at this grotesque apparition of an old man's face on his young son's body, and he whispered, "Who are you? What's happened to my son? *Where's Toby?*"

The old face nodded, as if it hadn't even heard him. It looked back across the room with its faded, crow's-footed eyes, and said, *"Give me till sundown. I'll do my level darndest."*

TWO

Neil was shaking and shaking Toby as if he wanted to shake that terrible head right off him. But then, through the blindness of his fright and his anxiety, he heard Toby crying "Daddy—*daddy!*" and he stopped shaking and looked down at his son in bewilderment.

The face, the image of a face, had vanished. Toby was just Toby, and there were tears in his eyes from being battered so hard. Neil couldn't say anything, couldn't speak at all, but he held Toby close, and stroked his head, and rocked backward and forward on the bed to soothe him.

Susan came into the room, bleary with sleep. "Neil— what's *happening*?"

Neil's throat was choked with fright and tears. He just shook his head, and cradled Toby closer.

Susan said, "I heard somebody shouting. It didn't sound like you at all. Neil—what's happening? What's going on here?"

Neil took a deep breath. "I don't know. It just seems crazy."

31

"But what was it?"

Neil ran his fingers through Toby's hair, and then sat his son up straight so that he could take a look at him. Toby was tired, with plum-colored circles under his eyes, and he was pale, but otherwise he looked all right. All trace of that lined, hard-bitten face had vanished.

Neil said, "There's something going on here, Susan. I don't know what it is, but it's not a bad dream and it's not Toby's imagination."

"What do you mean—'something'? What kind of a something?"

"I don't have any idea. But I heard voices coming out of this room tonight, and when I came in here, Toby was different."

"Different?"

"Well, I don't know," said Neil. "It looked as though he was wearing some kind of a mask, only it wasn't a mask at all. He looked like an old man."

"An old man? Are you kidding me, Neil?"

Neil held Toby close again. He could feel the boy's heart beating against his own heart, a birdlike flutter. He said, dryly, "I wouldn't kid you, Susan. You know that. I came in here and Toby had his back to me. He turned around and there he was, with this lined old face."

"But I don't understand. What do you mean, a lined old face?"

"For Christ's sake, Susan, I don't understand, either. But that's what it was. He looked like an old man."

Susan bent down and stroked Toby's smooth, pale cheek. "I'm calling Doctor Crowder," she said. "There's something wrong here, and I want to know what."

Toby said softly, "I'm all right, Daddy. I'm really all right."

32

Susan took Toby from Neil's arms, and cuddled him. He seemed so thin and bony and vulnerable in his blue-striped pajamas. She whispered in his ear, "Was it the bad dream again, honey? Is that what it was?"

He nodded. "I heard the man saying Allen again. I saw the face in the wardrobe. It was the same man that was by the school fence."

"You mean the man you dreamed about was the man you saw at school? The same man?" asked Neil.

Toby, drowsy and heavy-lidded, mumbled, "Yes."

"He had a beard and a hat?"

Toby said, "Yes." His eyes were beginning to close now, and his head was resting heavily on Susan's shoulder. After the emotional excitement of his nightmare, he was seeking refuge in deep sleep. Neil said, "Toby—Toby—don't go to sleep—" but Susan shushed him, gently laid the boy back in his bed, and covered him with his comforter.

Neil looked at Toby for a while, and then went across to the wardrobe and gingerly touched the polished surface.

"I don't know what the hell's the matter," he said. "Maybe it's some kind of silly hysteria. Maybe Toby's transmitting it to me. But I can tell you something, Susan, *I* saw that face tonight. I saw that face for real."

"Did it look like anyone you knew?"

He shook his head. "I never saw anyone like that in my whole life."

They switched off Toby's light, but they left the door ajar and the light burning in the passage outside. Then they went downstairs to the kitchen, and Neil poured them both a glass of red wine. It was the only liquor they had in the house.

"I'm really worried," said Susan. "It seems to be getting worse. And it doesn't seem to sound like the usual kind of nightmare at all. I mean, he saw this man in the *daylight*."

Neil took a large swallow of wine, and grimaced. "If you ask me, it's a ghost. Or a poltergeist. Or whatever they call those damned mischievous spirits."

"You're not serious."

"I don't know what the hell I am. But all I know is that I walked in there and saw this old man's face right on top of Toby's body. It had wrinkles around the eyes, and a little black mustache, and those deep-lined cheeks that some old folks have. It was so *clear*. If I saw the old guy again, I'd know him at once."

Susan sipped her wine and sighed. "I don't know what to say. I believe you, Neil, and I believe Toby. But maybe it just isn't what it seems."

"Then what could it be?"

"I don't know. But I think we ought to call Doctor Crowder in the morning. *And* Mrs. Novato."

Neil sat down at the kitchen table and took her hand. "Right now, I feel more like calling a shrink."

Susan stroked the back of his fingers, briefly touching the worn gold wedding band. "You don't need a psychiatrist. If you ask me, Toby's had a recurring nightmare, and because you love him so much, you're kind of identifying with it. Taking the fright onto yourself, because you want to protect Toby."

"I don't know. Is there any more wine in that bottle?"

They drained the Pinot Noir, and then they went back to bed. It was almost dawn, five o'clock, and Neil lay there for the rest of the night without sleeping, staring at the ceiling. The Pacific wind began to warm, and the lace curtains stirred themselves, casting flowery patterns across the room. Could that really be true—that he was trying to take Toby's nightmares onto himself? Or was there something really inside that wardrobe, and had that old-timer's face really superimposed itself on Toby's features?

At six, he almost fell asleep, but he jerked awake again. He went downstairs and made himself a pot of strong black coffee, and drank it looking out over the grassy wasteland that led to Schoolhouse Beach and the ocean.

The next morning, he parked the Chevy pickup outside the school gates and walked Toby up to the classroom door. Mrs. Novato smiled when she saw him, and they shook hands.

"Mr. Fenner," said Mrs. Novato. "How are you?"

"I'm fine," said Neil. "I just thought I'd come along to make sure Toby was okay."

Toby saw Linus, and tugged his hand away from Neil to run after him. Mrs. Novato smiled, and said, "They're a couple of menaces, those two, when they get together."

Neil gave her a quick, uncertain smile in reply.

"Mind you," said Mrs. Novato, "I prefer boys with spirit. It's the spirited ones who always do the best. Did you know that Senator Openhauer went to school here? He was one of the most disobedient pupils we ever had, or so the principal says."

"Mrs. Novato," put in Neil, uncomfortably, "I'm kind of worried about Toby. He says he saw a man here yesterday, out by the school fence, and whatever happened, that man scared the living daylights out of him."

"He saw a man? Here?"

"Just before he fainted, he told us. Some man in a

long, white old-fashioned duster coat, and a beard, and a broad-brimmed hat."

Mrs. Novato frowned. Behind her, in the classroom, the children were running around and flicking paper pellets. She turned around for a moment, and called: "Class! Let's have some silence!" Immediately, the children were hushed. Mrs. Novato always meant what she said, and if you disobeyed you got to write out the Pledge of Allegiance ten times.

She turned back to Neil. Thinking very carefully, she said, "I know Toby's a truthful boy, Mr. Fenner. I never knew him tell him a lie. But I was out there when he fainted, and there wasn't anybody in sight."

"He couldn't have run off?"

Mrs. Novato pointed toward the fence. "You can see for yourself. It's wide open for two hundred, three hundred feet. If there had been a man there, I would have seen him for sure."

Neil rubbed the back of his neck and looked out across the hills. "I don't know. It just doesn't seem like Toby to make things up. He was sure that he saw this man, and he dreamed about him last night."

Mrs. Novato laid a reassuring hand on his arm. "I shouldn't worry about it too much, Mr. Fenner. A lot of the children have been having bad dreams of late. I think it's become the class craze to have nightmares. Children are very psychologically suggestible, and I think they've gotten themselves into what you might call a state of, well, very mild hysteria."

Neil looked across the porch toward the classroom. The children all looked normal enough. They were giggling and playing around just like ordinary kids, and they certainly didn't seem to be suffering from any kind of collective breakdown.

"Have you talked to the school doctor about them?" he asked Mrs. Novato. "I mean, as far as Toby's concerned, I wouldn't like things to get any worse."

"I can call the doctor if you like," agreed Mrs. Novato. "But I think he'll simply confirm my opinion that this is some kind of passing fad."

Inside the classroom, the children were playing cowboys and Indians, and pretending to shoot at each other with their fingers. Neil grinned, and said, "I shouldn't bother, Mrs. Novato. It looks as though they're pretty healthy to me. Mind you, I don't know how you manage to keep control."

"It comes with practice—and iron discipline," laughed Mrs. Novato.

Neil said, "Okay. If you could just keep an eye on Toby for me, I'd appreciate it."

"Sure thing."

He had just turned to leave the porch when he heard one of the children calling above the hubbub of the classroom—calling something in a high, piping voice that penetrated the shouting and laughing and pseudo "gunfire." It wasn't Toby. It was one of the other children—a small dark-haired boy in a green T-shirt.

He was calling, *Where's Allen gone? Where's Allen gone? Did Allen go for help?*

Neil felt a chill, prickling sensation around his scalp and wrists as if all his nerves were shrinking. He turned back to Mrs. Novato and barked, "Mrs. Novato—*Mrs. Novato!*"

The teacher blinked at him uncertainly. "Yes, Mr. Fenner? Was there something else?"

Neil could hardly find the words. He was breathing in tight, suffocated gasps, and there seemed to be something pressing on him. Too much gravity, too much air.

And all the time, over the noise of the classroom, the boy was calling: *"Has anyone seen where Allen went? For the love of God, where's Allen?"*

"Mrs. Novato," said Neil, "could I speak to your children for just a couple of minutes?"

Mrs. Novato's helpful expression tightened a little. "I'm afraid we have to start class in just a moment, Mr. Fenner. I really can't—"

"Mrs. Novato, I think it would help them. I think this, whatever it is, this hysteria—well, I think it's a little more than hysteria. I think I should talk to them, just for a few minutes."

Mrs. Novato's smile had now faded altogether. She was standing in the classroom door with her hand on the doorknob and Neil could see that she was quite prepared to close it in his face if he became too insistent.

"You'll really have to talk to Mr. Groh, the principal," she told him. "I'm not authorized to let anyone speak to the class, unless they're a qualified lecturer or teacher."

"Allen!" shouted the boy. *"Where did Allen go?"*

Neil's hands were shaking, and there was sweat on his upper lip. He wiped his mouth against his sleeve, and he said to Mrs. Novato, "One minute, and that's all. I promise you. And if I start to say something you don't like, you can throw me out."

Mrs. Novato looked more bewildered than anything else. Neil said, "Please," and at last she sighed, as if she were really allowing this against her better judgment, and as if she couldn't understand why all the complicated things in life had to happen to her.

She led him up to the front of the class, onto her small plinth, and she raised her hands for silence. Neil felt unexpectedly embarrassed in front of all these expectant childish faces. He looked for Toby, and spotted him at last near the back of the room, sitting next to a pale girl with dark hair. Toby was openly pleased to see his daddy standing up there, but puzzled too. The boy sitting in front of Toby was obviously asking him, behind his hand, what his pop was up to, standing nervously in front of the eight-year-olds at Bodega schoolhouse, his mind crowded with fears and dreams, and Neil wished he could have answered that question himself.

Mrs. Novato rapped her ruler on the desk for silence, and said, "Class, I want your attention for a moment. Mr. Fenner here, Toby's father, wants to speak a few important words to you. It's about the bad dreams that some of you have been having, so I believe you ought to pay close attention."

Neil coughed, and found himself blushing. "Thank you, Mrs. Novato. It's kind of you to let me speak. All I want to say is, Toby's been having some pretty unpleasant nightmares lately, and Mrs. Novato tells me that some of the rest of you have, too. Would you be kind enough to put up your hand if you've been having nightmares?"

There was a silence. The children stared at Neil, expressionless. Mrs. Novato gave a twitchy little smile, and said, "Come on now, children. You know that one or two of you have. Petra, how about you?"

Petra, the little girl sitting next to Toby, raised her hand. So did Toby. Then, one by one, others raised their hands. Ben Nichelini, Andy Beaver, Debbie Spurr, Linus Hopland, Daniel Soscol. Every child in the class of twenty-one.

Mrs. Novato glanced worriedly at Neil, and said, "I had no idea that *all* of them—"

39

Neil looked around the class. Twenty-one young, serious faces. They may have been normal, well-adjusted, boisterous kids, but they weren't putting him on. There was no sniggering or whispering. They were all sitting there with their hands raised, and not one of them smiled.

"Okay," said Neil, hoarsely, "you can put your hands down now."

Mrs. Novato said, "This is most upsetting, Mr. Fenner. I can't imagine what's going on."

"That's why I wanted to speak to them," Neil told her. "I believe that something's happening here that's more than bad dreams."

He turned to the children, and he tried to speak as reassuringly and quietly as he could. "I don't want to take up too much of your time," he said, "but I'd like you to think about these dreams as a kind of a class project. The more we find out about them, I think the better chance we have of discovering why you've been dreaming them, and what they are. I'd like you all to spend a few minutes at home tonight, and write or draw what you saw in your dream. Think hard, and remember whatever you can. If you can think of any names you heard in your dreams, jot them down. What you write or draw doesn't have to make any particular sense. Just put down whatever comes into your mind."

Mrs. Novato said, "I'm not at all sure that Mr. Groh is going to approve of this, Mr. Fenner."

"Why not?"

"Well, he doesn't want to antagonize the parents. Some of them are pretty touchy about nonstandard projects, you know."

Neil took in the class with a wide sweep of his arm. "Mrs. Novato, did you see how many hands went up?

Twenty-one out of twenty-one. Don't you think we ought to make just a minimum effort to find out what this is all about?"

The classroom was quiet, except for sporadic coughs and the shuffling of sneakers. Then Mrs. Novato said, "All right, Mr. Fenner. I'll give it just one try. But I don't think the children ought to do this at home. They can draw their dreams right here in the classroom, this afternoon, during their drawing lesson. It should improve the results, too. Not all of them have crayons and paper at home."

She lifted her hands toward the class, and clapped them once, briskly. "Now then, children," she said, "I want you all to say good morning to Mr. Fenner, and then I want you to open your geography books to the big color map of northern California, which is on page twenty-five."

The children sang, "Good morning, Mr. Fenner," and Neil said "Thanks" to Mrs. Novato and left the classroom. On his way out, he gave Toby a quick, secret wink.

Outside in the school yard, it was growing hot. The weather was unusually warm for September, way up in the high seventies and the low eighties. Through the dusty glare, Neil glanced across at the fence where Toby had seen the man in the long white coat, but the scrubby grass was deserted. Neil could see why Mrs. Novato hadn't believed anyone could have been standing there. The fields were wide open for hundreds of feet, and the first patch of cover was a sparse group of thorn bushes, at least three minutes' hard running away.

He walked over to the fence and examined the ground. It was hard clay, too rough to show any footprints. He believed that Mrs. Novato hadn't seen anybody, but he also believed that Toby was telling the truth. Tough little boys didn't go fainting for no reason at all—and come to that, unimpressionable fathers didn't go imagining old men's spectral faces for no reason at all, either.

He went slowly back to his pickup truck, and sat behind the wheel for a while, thinking. He had a feeling that something wasn't right—the same feeling you get on a warm day, when a storm's beginning to build. He looked in his rearview mirror a couple of times, half-expecting to see the man in the white duster standing by the fence, but nothing appeared. After a few minutes, he turned the key in the ignition and drove off toward the bay, and another day's work.

Although it was warm and clear in the valleys, there was a foggy chill out on Bodega Bay, and Neil wore his windbreaker while he finished off varnishing the *White Dove*'s afterdeck and cabin doors. Old Doughty wasn't far off, smoking his pipe and watching the coast-guard cutters from under his peaked nautical cap, and over by the gift shop a party of Japanese tourists were proudly having their picture taken in front of Bodega Bay's well-worn collection of whales' jaws and sharks' teeth.

As Neil put the last licks of varnish on the doors, Doughty got up off his perch and came strolling along the jetty. He paused by the *White Dove*'s berth, and stood watching Neil for a while, puffing and gurgling at his pipe.

"I reckon you've got yourself a few good hours' work in that beaten-up tub," he remarked. "I never saw anyone handle a craft so badly, the way that Mr. Collings knocked her about. I was damned surprised he never drowned himself."

42

Neil shrugged. "It's his funeral," he said, noncommittally.

Doughty grunted. He was nearly eighty, with a big, wrinkled face that was weatherbeaten to a dull red color. He wore the same navy-blue reefer jacket that he had worn the first time Neil's father had brought him down to the jetty twenty years ago and hefty fisherman's rubbers. There was a time when he had operated a fishing fleet of his own, but that was long before most people could remember.

"I don't know why you bother fancying that boat up so nice," Doughty said. "You know that he's going to knock her about just as bad next summer."

"I do it because he pays me," replied Neil.

Doughty sighed. "You're not like your father. Nor your grandfather, for that matter."

"I never said I was. And from what I've been told about my grandfather, he drank a bottle of rum a day, and smoked five cigars before breakfast."

"What's wrong in that?" Doughty wanted to know.

Neil laughed. He slicked varnish across the bottom of the cabin door and set down his brush.

"They always used to tell stories about the Fenner family on the wharf here," said Doughty. "I remember when I was round about ten years old, my pa pointed out your great-grandfather Jack Fenner to me, and told me not to displease him, on account of he'd thrown three fishermen into the bay for offering him undersize lobsters."

"I've heard all the stories," said Neil, tidying up his paint cans. "I freely admit that I'm the most colorless Fenner that ever lived."

"You're not the worst, though," said Doughty, tapping out the dottle of his pipe against a wooden upright.

"So I suppose you've got something to be thankful for."

"Oh, yes? And who do you reckon was the worst?"

Doughty fumbled in his pocket and brought out two pieces of saltwater taffy. He tossed one to Neil, and unwrapped the other one himself. He said, "I have to suck these slow, you know, otherwise they get themselves snarled up in my dentures."

Neil came forward and clambered up onto the jetty. "You still haven't told me who was the worst Fenner of all. I bet he wasn't as bad as the worst Doughty of all."

"Oh, he sure was," said Doughty, shaking his head. "The Doughtys was clergy originally, from Plymouth, England. Highly peaceable folk. But the Fenners were tough farmers, tough settlers, and vigilantes. The Fenners did more to settle Napa Valley than George Yount, and most folks say that George Yount was the father of Napa Valley."

Neil and Doughty walked side by side to the parking lot, where Neil let down the back of his pickup and heaved out three coils of fresh rope.

"The worst Fenner of all was called Bloody Fenner, and I'm surprised your pa never told you about him," said Doughty.

"I think he did, when I was younger. An Indian fighter, wasn't he, back in the 1830s? They called him 'Bloody' Fenner because he collected ears and scalps."

Doughty nodded. "That's right. But the story goes that he did worse than that. Back when the white men were fighting the Wappos up in the mountains, he used to fight on one side or another, according to how it took his fancy. If the Wappos offered him a couple of square miles of good farming ground, he'd set traps for the white men; and if the white men were ready to pay him enough, he'd bushwhack the Wappos. Nobody never

44

proved nothing, of course, so he never came to trial, but the stories went around for years that Bloody Fenner was responsible for some of the worst of the Indian massacres, and it took a good few years before the Fenner family wasn't shunned no more."

Neil hefted the ropes back to the *White Dove*, and heaved them onto the deck. "That's something I *wasn't* told," he said to Doughty. "I guess Bloody Fenner was someone my family preferred to forget."

Doughty stuck his pinkie up inside his palate to dislodge a sticky lump of taffy. "If you really want to know about the old days, you ought to take a trip across to Calistoga and talk to Billy Ritchie—that's if he's still alive, but I haven't heard different. Billy Ritchie's grandpa was a friend of Robert Louis Stevenson, and a lot of folks say he was the model for Israel Hands in *Treasure Island*. They were a tough lot, in those days, but they say that Bloody Fenner was the toughest of all."

Neil climbed down onto the *White Dove* and started to uncoil one of the ropes. The day was warming up now, out here on the bay, but the gray fog was even denser, and he couldn't even see as far as the harbor's inlet. A fishing boat chugged past like a gray ghost.

"Here," said Neil. He reached in his pocket and handed Doughty a five-dollar bill. "Why don't you go set them up in the bar? As soon as I'm through here, I'll come join you."

It was a gentle way of buying Doughty a free drink. The unwritten code of behavior on Bodega wharf was that you let Doughty bend your ear for a while, and then you slipped him a little money to make life a little easier for him.

Doughty said, "Don't forget to come along, mind. I'll

45

set you up an old-fashioned." Then he tipped his nautical cap, and swayed off along the boardwalk as if he were on the deck of an old-time clipper.

Neil grinned to himself and went back to his painting and tidying up. Although the *White Dove* was superficially battered, it wouldn't take much to bring back her glamour, and she wasn't going to need a major overhaul this year. Neil reckoned to have finished her off by the end of the week. Then he could get back to his small yard across the other side of the wharf and complete work on a fishing boat he was refitting.

It was almost eleven o'clock in the morning, and the fog was at its densest. The sun was a pale yellow disk, and the wind had stilled. Neil found that he was sweating as he sorted and tied the new ropes, and he felt for a moment as if he could scarcely breathe.

He glanced out toward the bay and frowned. He was sure he could see something out there in the water. He screwed up his eyes against the yellowish haze of the fog; whatever it was, it was too far away to distinguish clearly. It was tall and pale and upright, like a drifting buoy, or the sail of a small weekend dinghy.

It was only when the fog stirred that he began to understand, with an overwhelming sense of dread, that the shape wasn't a sail at all, nor a buoy. *It was a man. A man in a long white coat, standing silent and unsupported in the middle of the bay.*

Biting his lip with uncertainty, Neil rose to his feet. The fog passed in front of the figure in veil after veil, but there was no question at all. It was a man, or the ghost of a man. He wore a dark broad-brimmed hat and a duster, and he stood on the water as if it was dry land.

Neil shouted, "Hey! You!" but his voice sounded

flat and weak in the fog, and the man took no notice at all.

Panicking, Neil turned back to the wharf and called: "Doughty! Doughty! Come take a look at this! For Christ's sake! Come take a look at this!"

A voice whispered, *"Allen . . . please, Allen . . ."*

"Doughty!" yelled Neil.

The door of the cocktail bar opened, and Dave Conway from the fish stall came out, a tall red-bearded man with a well-known line of sarcasm. "Anything wrong there, Neil?" he called out.

"Dave, do you see something out there in the bay or am I crazy?" Neil shouted.

Dave peered out at the fog. It was now so thick that the man had almost disappeared. There was just a fading trace of his white coat.

Dave said, "Sure, I see something. You're not crazy after all."

"Tell me what you see! What is it?"

"Well," said Dave, "I wouldn't like to stick my neck out, but I'd say that's fog."

Neil, tense, let out a sharp, exasperated breath.

"Did I say something wrong?" asked Dave. "It's not fog? It's gray lint? It's cotton candy maybe?"

Neil shook his head. "Forget it. It was just an optical illusion."

Dave strolled up toward him. "You really thought you saw something out there? What did you think it was?"

"I don't know," said Neil. "It looked so weird I just wanted a second opinion."

"You can tell me," Dave encouraged him. "I won't laugh at you for longer than a half-hour."

47

Neil turned away. "I guess it was just my imagination. Forget it."

"You didn't tell me what it was, so how can I forget it?"

Neil put down his ropework. "All right," he said, "I thought I saw somebody, a man, standing out there in the bay."

"*Standing?*"

"That's right. Standing on the water, just the way you're standing on that jetty."

Dave pulled a face. "Well, you told me it was crazy, and you're right. Are you sure you haven't been reading the Bible too heavily lately?"

"Dave," asked Neil, "will you just forget it? It was a trick of the light."

"Maybe he was surfing and you didn't notice the surfboard in the fog," suggested Dave. "Or maybe he was standing on top of a submarine."

"Dave, please forget I ever told you," said Neil. "I'm not in the mood for jokes."

"Nor would I be, if I'd seen a guy standing on the water in the middle of the bay," said Dave, with weighty mock seriousness. "Nor would I be."

That afternoon, Toby brought home a large yellow Manila envelope from school, along with a note from Mrs. Novato. While Toby went out to play with his toy bulldozer, Neil took the package into the parlor and sat down at his old rolltop desk. Susan came in from the kitchen in her apron and slippers, and said, "What's that?"

Neil looked at her, and gave a wry little smile. "It's an experiment, I guess."

48

Susan wiped her floury hands on her apron. She'd been making apple cookies, and she smelled of fresh cooking apples and butter. "An experiment?" she asked him. "You mean, something to do with school?"

He nodded. "You remember Toby kept on about Allen in his nightmares? Well, this morning, when I took him to school, I heard one of the other kids talking about Allen, too, so I asked Mrs. Novato to let me talk to the class for a couple of minutes. I asked them if any one of them had dreamed dreams like Toby."

"Well? And had they?"

Neil opened the envelope. "There are twenty-one kids in that class, honey, and every single one of them put up a hand to say yes."

Susan looked confused. "You mean—they'd all had the same nightmare? Surely they were just pulling your leg, acting like kids."

"I don't know *what* nightmares they'd had. But I asked them to draw what they'd seen in their dreams, and Mrs. Novato agreed to let them do it during their art lesson. Here's a note she sent along."

Susan took the note and scanned it quickly.

It read:

Dear Mr. Fenner,

I am sending you the drawings the children made this afternoon in the hope that they might put your mind at rest. It seems to me that my first opinion of mild collective hysteria is the correct one. I am sure that these nightmares will pass once a new craze starts. There are already signs that Crackling Candy is talking hold! By the way, if Toby wishes to join our little expedition to Lake Berryessa next

Wednesday, please give him $1.35 to bring to school tomorrow.

Yours,
Nora Novato

Neil rubbed his cheek. "Well," he said slowly, "that doesn't sound too promising, does it?"

"I think it sounds marvelous," said Susan. "The sooner Toby stops having those awful dreams, the better."

"Susan, it's not just dreams. It's waking visions as well. What about that old man's face I saw on Toby last night? What about the man in the white coat that Toby saw? What about the guy standing on the bay?"

Susan stared at him. "*What* guy standing on *what* bay? What are you talking about?"

He glanced at her, and then he lowered his eyes. "I'm sorry. I was meaning to tell you, but I didn't know how. It was just something that happened today. Or rather it was something I *thought* happened today."

She leaned forward and put her arm around his shoulder. "You didn't know how to tell me? But Neil, I'm as worried about all this as you are! I'm your wife. That's what I'm here for, to confide in."

He said, huskily, "Sure, honey, I know. It's just that it's kind of hard to admit to yourself that you might be flipping your lid, or suffering from some kind of kids' hysteria."

"Don't be so ridiculous! If you saw something, you saw it. Maybe there's a natural explanation. Maybe it was some kind of mirage. But if you saw it, that's it, I believe you."

He shrugged. "I'm glad you've got some confidence

50

in me. I'm not sure that I've got much confidence in myself."

Susan kissed his hair. "I love you," she said simply. "If there's something making you worried, then it worries me, too. Don't forget that."

Neil reached inside the Manila envelope and took out a sheaf of brightly colored drawings. Susan drew up a chair beside him, and they looked through them, one by one.

The drawings, although they varied in style and color, were strangely alike. They showed trees, mountains, and struggling figures. Some of them depicted twenty or thirty stick people, their arms all flung up in the air, with splashes of scribbled red all around. Others showed only one or two people, lying on their backs amid the greenery. There were arrows flying through the air in about a dozen drawings, and in others there were men holding rifles.

Only about eight or nine children had written names or words beside their pictures. Toby had written "Allen, help." Daniel Soscol had written "Alun" and then crossed it out. Debbie Spurr had put down "Allen, Allen, didn't come back."

There were some odd names, too. "Ta-La-Ha-Lu-Si" was written in heavy green crayon on one picture. Another bore the legend "Kaimus." Yet another said "Oweaoo" and "Sokwet."

Susan and Neil spent twenty minutes going through the drawings, but in the end they laid them down on the desk and looked at each other in bewilderment.

"I don't know what the hell it all means," admitted Neil. "It just doesn't seem to make any kind of sense at all."

"It's strange that they all have the same kind of pic-

51

ture in their minds, though," said Susan. "I mean, how many other groups of twenty-one different people would all have the same nightmare? Look at this one— this is Toby's. His drawing is almost the same as everyone else's."

Neil pushed back his chair and stood up. Outside, through the cheap net curtains, he could see Toby in the backyard, shoveling up dust with his Tonka bulldozer. Neil felt such a wave of protectiveness toward him that the tears prickled his eyes. What on God's earth was Toby caught up in? Were these really just nightmares, or were they something arcane and dangerous?

Susan suggested, "Maybe we ought to talk to Doctor Crowder again. Perhaps it's some kind of psychological sickness."

Neil slowly shook his head. "Toby's not sick, and neither are the rest of those kids. Nor am I, if it comes to that. I feel it's more like something from outside, something trying to get through to us, you know?"

"You're talking about something like a séance? Like a spirit, trying to get through?"

"That's right, kind of. I just have the feeling that there's *pressure* around, something's *pressing in* from all around us. I don't know what the hell it is, but I can feel it. It's there all the time now, night and day."

"Neil—" said Susan, guardedly.

He turned away from the window. "I know. It sounds nuts. Maybe it is nuts. But I feel just as sane as I did last week. And if I'm nuts, then all these school children are nuts, too, and I don't believe they are."

He picked up one of the drawings, showing a fierce battle between men in big hats and men with long black hair. There were green-and-gray mountains in the background, and the sky was forested with huge arrows. The

52

arrows were all tipped with black, carefully and deliberately drawn with black crayon.

"What would you say this was?" asked Neil, showing it to Susan.

She looked at it carefully. "It seems pretty obvious. A fight between cowboys and Indians."

"Who's winning?"

"The cowboys?"

"Why do you say that?"

Susan looked again. "Well, there's one cowboy in the middle there and he seems to be standing up shooting his pistol and looking very happy about it."

"That's true," said Neil, "but look at the other cowboys. Most of them seem pretty upset. And a whole lot of them are lying there with arrows sticking out of them. It's the same in this next picture, and this one. It seems like the Indians are definitely getting the best of this fight."

Susan skimmed through nine or ten more drawings, and then nodded. "I think you're right," she said. "But what does it mean?"

"I don't know. Maybe it just means that all the kids in the class read about the same battle, or went to see the same movie. Can you remember a movie that Toby might have seen on television or something, with this kind of a battle in it?"

She ran her hand through her loosely tied blond hair. "They had a movie about Custer about a month ago."

"Then maybe that is what this is all about," said Neil. "This grinning cowboy standing here could be General Custer, and maybe this is the Little Big Horn."

"There's no river, though, is there?" Susan pointed out. "The Little Big Horn didn't take place up in the mountains, and all these drawings have mountains. I'd say this looks like someplace up in the Sonoma or the Vaca Mountains, wouldn't you?"

"Could be," admitted Neil.

He took a last shuffle through the drawings and was about to slide them back into their envelope when something caught his attention. He peered closer at Ben Nichelini's drawing, and right at the back of a crowd of blood-splattered white men, he saw what looked distinctly like a childish rendering of a man in a white duster coat, with a beard and a wide-brimmed hat. There was a large arrow sticking out of the man's back.

He went across to the parlor window and opened it. He called: "Toby—c'mere a minute, will you?"

Susan asked, "What is it? Have you seen something?"

"I'm just guessing," Neil told her. "Wait and see what Toby says."

Toby came running in through the kitchen, still clutching his bulldozer. "What is it, sir?"

Neil held up the drawings. "You know what these are, Toby?"

"Sure do. They were all the dreams you asked us to draw. That's Ben Nichelini's, isn't it?"

"That's right. Did you look at it before?"

"No, sir. Mrs. Novato said we weren't to. She said we had to draw the pictures all by ourselves, without copying or anything."

Neil handed the drawing over. Very softly, he said, "I want you to look at that picture really closely, Toby, and I want you to tell me if you see anything that you're familiar with. Is there anything there that reminds you of someone or something you've seen before?"

Toby scrutinized the drawing with an intent frown. While he did so, Neil glanced across at Susan, and raised a finger to tell her that he would explain every-

54

thing later. Susan watched her son worriedly, her flour-white hands clasped together in the lap of her apron.

Eventually, Toby handed the drawing back. He said in a small voice, "There's a man who looks like the man I saw by the school fence."

"Is that him?" asked Neil, pointing.

Toby replied, "Yes. But there's something wrong with that picture."

"Something wrong?" asked Susan. "What do you mean, honey?"

Toby said, "Allen's not there. He should be there, but he's not."

"Allen? Then this man in the white coat—he's *not* Allen?"

"No, sir. Allen's this one."

Toby looked through the drawings until he found the picture of the smiling cowboy with the pistol, the one who was standing up looking happy while all the other cowboys fell to the ground around him, pierced by Indian arrows.

"That's Allen?" asked Neil. "How do you know?"

"I just do. That's what he looks like."

"But have you ever met him? Ever seen him before?"

Toby shook his head. "No, sir."

"Did you dream about him?"

"No, sir."

"Then what makes him Allen? How do you know this man isn't Allen, or the man in the white coat isn't Allen?"

"The man in the white coat is always asking Allen for help," said Toby, straight-faced. "So *he* couldn't be Allen. And anyway, Allen is just Allen. None of these other men are Allen."

Susan and Neil looked at each other for a while, and

then Susan said, "It looks like a dead end, doesn't it? Where do we go from here?"

"I don't know," answered Neil. "The whole damned thing is so meaningless."

Susan waited a while longer, but outside it was beginning to grow dusky. After a few minutes she touched Neil's hand and went back to her baking in the kitchen. Toby took his bulldozer upstairs to his bedroom, and Neil could hear him making motor noises all around the floor. The sweet aroma of apple cookies soon began to remind him that he hadn't eaten yet, and that he was hungry.

Maybe tonight would be a night without bad dreams. Maybe the man in the long white coat would vanish and never appear again. But somehow, depressingly, it seemed to Neil as if they were all caught up in a strange and mysterious event over which they had no control. He had a feeling of impending trouble, and it wouldn't leave him alone. He tapped his fingers on his rolltop desk and tried to think what all these signs and drawings and dreams could mean.

He wondered if it might be worthwhile taking Doughty's advice, and driving over to Calistoga to see Billy Ritchie. If Billy Ritchie knew about the old days in Napa and Sonoma, then maybe the name Allen would mean something to him. Maybe he'd heard tales of a notorious man in a white duster, and perhaps he could tell him what "Ta-La-Ha-Lu-Si" and "Kaimus" meant, too.

Susan called from the kitchen: "Do you want to try one of these cookies while they're still hot?"

"Sure thing," said Neil. He got out of his chair, but just as he closed the door behind him he heard a shriek

56

from upstairs that made him jump in nervous shock. It was a high-pitched, terrified shriek. It was Toby.

Neil ran up the stairs three at a time, bounded across the landing and hurled Toby's door wide open. The boy was standing in the middle of the room, still clutching his bulldozer, but staring in paralyzed terror at his wardrobe. There was an oddly nauseating chill in the room, a chill that reminded Neil of a butcher's cold storage. It must have been an illusion but the floor seemed to be swaying, too, as if there were slow, glutinous waves flowing under the carpet.

"Toby," Neil said shakily. "Toby, what's wrong?"

Toby turned to him with slow, spastic movements. There seemed to be something wrong with the boy's face. The outlines of it were blurred, almost phosphorescent and, even though his lips were closed, he appeared to be speaking. It was his eyes that frightened Neil the most, though. They weren't the eyes of a child at all. They were old, flat, and as dead as iron.

A deep, turgid groaning noise shook the room. It was a groan like a ship's timbers being crushed by pack ice. A groan like Jim had given when the Buick collapsed onto his chest, hugely amplified. Neil reached out his hand for Toby, but his son seemed to have shrunk miles and miles beyond reach, and there was a cold wind blowing that stiffened the father's limbs and slowed him down.

Neil turned and looked toward the wardrobe. What he saw then almost convinced him that he was going crazy, that his mind had finally let go. In the wood itself he could see a fierce, feral face, like a face under the surface of a polished pond. It stared at him with such viciousness and malevolence that he couldn't take his

57

eyes away from it. But far more uncanny and terrifying was that *a hand was reaching out of the flat walnut veneer, a hand that was made of shiny wood, yet alive.* It clawed toward him, sharp-nailed and vicious, and it ripped at his shirt as he lunged toward Toby and tried to pick the boy up in his arms.

He didn't look any more. If he looked, he knew that his strength and his sanity would break down. He lifted Toby over his shoulder, and blindly turned back toward the bedroom door, shielding his face from the sight of that wolfish face in the wardrobe.

Susan was halfway up the stairs toward them as Neil collapsed on the landing, and Toby rolled to the floor beside him. Neil screamed, *"The door! Close the door!"* and she quickly slammed it and turned the key.

"Toby! Neil! What's happening?" she said. "There was such a noise up here, I didn't—"

Neil held her arm. "It's in there," he told her. His voice was unsteady and feverish. "What Toby saw in his nightmare, it isn't a nightmare. It's real, and it's in there. There was a face, Susan. A goddamned face in the wardrobe. And a hand that came right out of the wood. Right out of the damned wood!"

He climbed to his feet. She tried to steady him, but he was too jumpy to be touched and he pushed her away. She knelt down beside Toby, who was shivering and quaking, and held him close.

"Listen," whispered Neil. "Listen, you can hear it."

They were silent. They heard a soft, peculiar noise, like a wind whistling across a mountain. Then they heard a sound that made Neil press his hands against his face, a sound so unnatural and frightening that they could scarcely bear to listen.

58

Across the floor of the bedroom, wooden feet walked. Stumbling, uncertain steps. And wooden hands groped across the walls, fumbling for the door.

THREE

After a few minutes, the noises stopped. They waited breathless on the landing for almost ten minutes, but there was silence.

Susan asked quietly, "What was it? Neil, what was it?"

He was very drawn and pale. He felt as if his brain had been given a severe electric shock. His lips and his tongue didn't seem to coordinate properly, so that when he spoke, he jumbled his words.

"I don't know. It was like a devil. It came right out of the wood, and it must have been made of wood. A wooden devil, walking about."

"Neil—things like that just don't *happen*. It must have been the wind blowing the door or something. Maybe you saw your own reflection."

Neil, leaning against the wall, shook his head slowly and deliberately.

"Well, maybe it was some kind of hallucination," Susan suggested. "I mean, Neil, things like that just don't happen. They don't exist. A man made of wood step-ping out of the wardrobe door? It's insane."

Neil looked down at her sharply. She realized what she'd said, and she reached up to hold his hand, and squeeze it. "Oh, Neil, I didn't mean—"

He pulled away from her, and ran both hands through his hair. "You don't have to say you're sorry," he told her, hoaresely. "You're probably right."

"Neil—"

He turned back toward her. "How's Toby? He looks as though he's getting his color back."

Toby had opened his eyes now, and he smiled up at his daddy faintly. Susan stroked his forehead, and said, "It's all right, darling, you can sleep with us tonight, in our room. You won't have to sleep in that nasty room again."

Neil hunkered down beside Toby and touched him affectionately on the nose. "How are you doing, tiger?"

"Okay," said Toby. "I was scared, that's all."

"Can you remember what happened?" asked Neil.

"Neil—" protested Susan. "He's only just gotten over it."

Neil said, "Honey, we have to know what happened in there. It was out of this world. If we're going to have to fight some ghost or other, then I think we have to know what it is."

"I think we ought to go downstairs, calm down, and call Doctor Crowder," said Susan. "I'll put on the kettle and we can have some strong black coffee."

Neil said, "Toby—all I want to know is, what hap-pened?"

Toby's eyes flickered for a moment, and then he said softly, "I was just playing with my buldozer. Then I heard that man talking again. He sounded real scared. I saw his face in the wardrobe. Then it wasn't his face anymore, it was Allen's face. Then *I* was Allen, and there was somebody else there. He was terrible. He was very tall and he scared me, and he came right out of the wood."

"Do you know what he was? Or *who* he was?"

Susan said, "Neil, *please*, he's almost unconscious."

"Susan, we have to know," insisted Neil. "If we don't know, then we can't protect ourselves. Toby—who was it? Who was the man in the door?"

Toby's lower lip started to turn down, and tears filled his eyes. He said, "I don't know. I don't know," and then he shook with uncontrollable sobs. Susan held him close, and soothed him, and Neil slowly got to his feet.

"I'm going to call Doc Crowder," said Neil. "This is one time I don't believe we can help ourselves."

He helped Susan and Toby downstairs to the kitchen and lit the gas under the kettle to make coffee. Then he went into the living room and dialed the doctor's home number. He realized, as he dialed, how much his hands were shaking and, as he leaned back against his rolltop desk, waiting for the doctor to answer, he could see his face reflected in the glass of a desk-top photograph of Susan. He was white and haggard.

The phone rang for almost a minute before it was picked up.

Mrs. Crowder said, "Doctor's Crowder's residence. Who is this, please?"

"Emma?" said Neil. "It's Neil Fenner. Is the doctor home?"

"Why, Neil! How are you? It's been a long time since you came up this way. How's Toby?"

Neil rubbed his eyes. "It's—well, it's Toby I wanted to talk to the doctor about. We've got ourselves a problem here, Emma, and I was wondering if he could find the time to come down here."

"Is it really urgent? I know he's got a lot to do tonight. The Baxter sisters just came down with whooping cough."

"Emma—if it wasn't serious I wouldn't ask. I know how hard he works."

Emma said warmly, "Okay, Neil. I know that. He's going to call home when he's through at the Baxters, so I'll ask him to come on down to see you. It's nothing too bad, I hope?"

Neil didn't answer for a moment. He didn't know how to describe what had happened, or what to say about it. In the end, he said thickly, "No, no. It's nothing too bad. Nothing to get upset about."

He hung up and then went back into the kitchen to brew coffee. Toby was looking calmer now, but all three of them were still pale with shock. Neil went to the wooden door that led to the stairs and closed it, turning the key in the lock.

Susan said nervously, "You don't think it's still—"

Neil shook his head. "I think it's gone, or disappeared, whatever it was. But I'm not taking any chances. I'm going to let Doc Crowder take a look at that wardrobe, and then first light tomorrow I'm going to take it outside and I'm going to burn it to ashes."

Toby looked up at his father with wide eyes. He whispered, "You mustn't do that, daddy. You mustn't burn it."

Neil pulled out a chair and sat down beside him. "Mustn't? What do you mean, tiger?"

Toby licked his lips, and he began to pant a little, as if he were short of breath. "He says—he says that—"

"Who?" asked Susan. "Who says?"

Toby's eyes flickered, and then the pupils rolled upward, so that his naked whites were all that they could see. His small fingers, spread on the pine kitchen table, began to clench and scratch at the wood. Susan reached out for him, reached out to hold and protect him, but then he said in a hoarse, accented voice: "He says you mustn't disturb the gateway. He says you will die if you disturb it."

"Toby?" demanded Neil, leaning forward. "*Toby!*"

Toby opened his eyes, and for a fleeting second Neil saw again that dead, flat, menacing expression. There was a cold sourness about Toby's breath, and when he spoke it seemed as if a freezing, fetid wind blew from his mouth.

"You must disturb nothing. You must not interfere. You are dust in the storms of time. I care nothing for you, but if you interfere you will be destroyed, even as you destroyed my brothers."

Susan was screaming, but Neil hardly heard her. He took Toby by the shoulders and shouted, "Who are you? I want to know who you are! Who are you?"

Toby smiled. It was an uncanny, unnatural, poisonous smile. In the same grating voice, he said: "The prophecy that is still buried on the great stone redwood is about to come to pass. It is almost the day of the dark stars."

Neil said, "Prophecy? Dark stars? What are you talking about?"

But then Toby abruptly vomited Coca-Cola and half-digested cookies, and fell off his chair like a rag doll.

Doctor Crowder took Neil out onto the boardwalk veranda and lit up his brierwood pipe. It was almost ten o'clock now, and a cool wind was flowing in from the sea. Neil was calmer, as a dose of Valium began to take effect, and he sat down on the rail and faced the doctor with a serious, concerned face.

The old doctor puffed away for a while, listening to the night birds and the rustle of dry grass. He was a short, white-whiskered man with a bald, tanned dome and a bulbous nose. He'd been practicing in Sonoma County most of his life, except for a spell during the war when he served on Guadalcanal as a senior medical officer. He'd delivered Toby, but he didn't know the Fenners too well. They were a young, hardworking family, and most of the time they kept to themselves.

After a few minutes' silence, Neil said, "I get the feeling you don't believe me. You think I've been hallucinating."

Doctor Crowder studiously examined the bowl of his pipe. "I wouldn't say that. Not hallucinating, exactly."

"But you don't believe that what I saw was real? You don't believe that a wooden man came out of that wardrobe door?"

The doctor glanced at him. "Would you?" he asked. "If I told you that story?"

Neil scratched the back of his neck. "I guess not. The only difference is, it's true. I saw it as plain as I can see you now."

"That's what most people say, when they've seen an unidentified flying object—or a ghost. There used to be a woman who lived up at Oakmont, and she swore blind that she'd seen phantom riders crossing her backyard, not just once, but every once in a while."

Neil said, "Doctor, you have to admit that some of this is spooky. What about all these schoolchildren having the same nightmare? There has to be something in that."

"Well," said Doctor Crowder, "I think that Mrs. Novato put her finger on it when she talked about mild collective hysteria. Children are open to any kind of silly idea, and it wouldn't be out of the ordinary for a whole school to have the same kind of nightmare. Mind you, they could be pulling your leg. They may just have got together and cooked up this whole thing to scare you witless."

Neil looked at the doctor in disappointment. "You don't really think that, do you?"

"No, I don't," Doctor Crowder told him. "But you have to investigate every possibility before you start jumping off in all kinds of directions shouting about spirits and demons. In my book, Neil Fenner, spirits and demons don't exist. They're a figment of man's imagination, and the only way they'll ever take hold of a man, or a boy, is if that man or that boy allows his imagination to run away with him."

"What are you trying to tell me, doctor? You're trying to say that I'm getting hysterical, too?"

Doctor Crowder raised his hand in a pacifying gesture and firmly shook his head. "I'm not trying to tell you that at all. I wouldn't presume. But what I *am* saying is that if Toby's suffering from this kind of mild frenzy, then it's up to you to stay as stable and as rational as you possibly can, because otherwise you'll only make him worse."

Neil stood up, and took a few testy paces up and down the boardwalk. "Doctor," he said, "I'm as rational and stable as you are. I swear to you, deaf, dumb, and blind, that I saw that wooden man come out of the wardrobe, and what's more, Susan heard him. We can't both be wrong."

"You could have heard anything. A window banging, maybe."

"It was a wooden demon, dammit! That's what it was, and nobody can persuade me otherwise. I don't know why it was there, or what it really was, or what the hell was going on, but I saw it, and I heard it, and I was as scared as I've ever been in my whole life."

Doctor Crowder took his pipe out of his mouth and spent a long while staring out at the night sky. It was partly cloudy, and only a few stars sparkled above the Bodega valley. In the distance, the Pacific surf was as soft and persistent as breathing.

Eventually, the doctor said, "I don't know what else to say to you, Neil. You haven't convinced me that any of this is indisputable fact, and until you do, I can only treat it like a medical or a psychological complaint. You see my problem, don't you?"

"I guess so."

"I'm glad," said Doctor Crowder. "And I'll tell you this much. I don't believe you're going crazy, or anything terrible like that. I think you *may* be suffering from strain or hypertension, and I think that you owe it to yourself to look at your work situation and even your marriage situation to find out if that's true. It could be that you're feeling some kind of delayed shock, some kind of psychological ripple effect, from the death of your brother. It could be that you're just tired. But I'll grant that you believe sincerely that what you saw was real, and I'm even prepared to keep a little bit of my mind open—though not much, I'll tell you—just in case you can prove to me that wooden men really do step out of solid wardrobe doors."

Neil nodded. "Okay, doctor. I'm sorry if I sounded sore."

Doctor Crowder laid a hand on his shoulder. "You've got to look forward, Neil. You've got to think of the future, and what you can do to make your life better. Then I guarantee that you won't be bothered by the ghosts of the past."

Just then, Susan came out of the kitchen door. She said, "Toby's sleeping now. I tucked him up in our bed. Do you think he's going to be all right, doctor?"

"There's nothing to worry yourself about at all," Doctor Crowder told her, reassuringly. "He's a highly strung boy, and I think that things have gotten a little out of hand, that's all. It sometimes happens at this age, when their imagination begins to develop. They see monsters, pirates, devils, all that kind of thing. But it'll pass, and the next you know he'll be dreaming about girls."

Susan laughed, and it seemed like the first laugh for a long time. Neil took her arm and kissed her, and then reached out his hand to say good night to the doctor.

"You can call me any time," said Doctor Crowder as they shook hands. "Don't be shy. It's about time we got to know each other better."

They watched him walk across the darkened yard to his dusty black Impala. He gave them a wave, and then he drove off into the night, leaving the Fenners alone again with their fears, imagined or real. Neil scratched at his nose with the back of his hand, and then said, "I could do with a drink."

Susan put her arm around his waist. "I bought a bottle of Riesling at the store today. We were going to have it with dinner."

He nuzzled her hair. It smelled fresh and good. He suddenly realized how much he relied on her, and how much he loved her. If there was any hypertension in his life, it certainly didn't have anything to do with Susan. He took a last look out at the night, and then they went inside.

In the morning, after Neil had driven Toby to school, he came back to the house and went upstairs. He crossed the landing to Toby's room, and gingerly opened the door. He was pretty sure there was nobody in there. After all, he'd taken Doc Crowder up there last night, and showed him the wardrobe, and the room had been as empty and ordinary as ever. But he still pushed the door back with caution, and he still stepped in with his heart beating irregularly and fast.

The room was silent and empty. The wardrobe stood where it always had. It wasn't even a special wardrobe. Neil had picked it up for four bucks at a garage sale in Tomales, along with a bed and his rolltop desk.

He stood for a while looking at it and then approached it. He knew that it was stupid to feel frightened, but he did. He turned the small brass key in the door and jerked it open. Inside, there was nothing but Toby's T-shirts, neatly folded, his shorts, and his baseball outfit. No demons with wolflike faces. No men in white coats.

It seemed almost dumb to take the wardrobe out and smash it up. It was a perfectly good piece of furniture, and where was he going to find another one like it for the same price? New furniture was always so tacky.

But then he remembered the face again, and the terrible stumbling sound of the wooden man, and he remembered Toby growling, *"He says you mustn't touch the gateway. He says you will die if you touch it."*

He took out Toby's clothes and laid them on the bed. Then he locked the wardrobe doors, and began to shuffle and hump it across the bedroom. It was a heavy old piece, but all he was going to do was slide it out of Toby's bedroom window so that it dropped into the yard below.

Sweating and straining, he shifted the wardrobe across to the window, and then he stood it on its side while he opened the shutters. Outside it was a dull, warm day, typical north Pacific coast weather, and he could hear Susan's radio playing pop music through the wide-open kitchen window.

He was about to turn back to the wardrobe when he caught a glimpse of something out of the corner of his eye. He looked again across the dust-colored yard, and he saw the man in the long white coat standing in the grass by the fence.

A cold, unnerving chill went down his back. He closed his eyes and then looked again, and the man was still there. The man's face was hidden under the shadow of his broad-brimmed hat, but Neil could see that he had a tawny, light-colored beard, and that he was wearing a gun belt outside his coat.

The voice breathed, "*Allen, for God's sake . . . Allen, help me . . .*"

And the figure was beckoning. With wide sweeps of his arm, he was *beckoning*.

Neil felt stunned, as if he had been anesthetized with novocaine. He stood by the open window for a long, paralyzed moment, and then he turned and ran down the stairs as fast as he could, almost twisting his ankle on the bottom stair.

Susan called, "*Neil!*" but he was already out of the house and running across the yard, running hard for the fence. He could hear his own panting in his ears, and the sound of his feet on the hard dust. The morning of gray clouds and warm wind jumbled past his eyes as he ran.

He half-expected the man in the long white coat to vanish. But the figure was still there, tantalizingly close, a strange white specter on a humid and ordinary day. Neil reached the fence, clambered over it, and jogged across the rough grass to where the man was standing.

Even this close, it was difficult to make out the man's features. They were shaded so deeply by his hat that Neil could only just distinguish his dull, dark eyes.

The two of them stood ten feet apart, and the grass rustled around them. Crickets jumped and skirred, and the wind blew toward the ocean, the wind from the valleys of Sonoma and Napa and Lake counties, and the broad, harsh plain that led out to Sacramento.

Neil said, "Who are you? What do you want? You've been around here for days."

When he answered, the man's voice seemed curiously close, as if he were whispering in Neil's ear. His lips scarcely moved, if they moved at all.

He said, "*Allen?*"

Neil shook his head. "I'm not Allen. Who's Allen?"

"*Allen went for help,*" breathed the man. "*For God's sake, Allen.*"

"Who is Allen?" demanded Neil. "Tell me who Allen is and maybe I can help you."

From the house, he heard Susan call: "Neil? Neil?"

The man in the long white duster turned his head slightly. "*Allen went for help,*" he repeated, in a flat, desperate whisper. "*Allen went down toward the creek for help.*"

"But who is he?" asked Neil. "Who is he?"

"*They're all around us,*" said the man. "*They're all*

around us and they won't take prisoners. For God's sake, Allen. Help us, Allen."

Susan was running toward them. Neil turned, and he could see her bright apron in the dull morning sunlight. He turned back again, and in a curious way the man in the long white duster was fading. He seemed to be retreating from Neil, shrinking, yet at the same time vanishing into the air. In a few seconds, he had disappeared.

Susan reached the fence, panting for breath. Neil walked back toward her silently, and took her hands across the split-log fence.

She asked, "What are you doing here? What's happening?"

Neil looked down at her. "Didn't you see him?"

"Who?"

He turned, and pointed to the place where the man had been standing. "Didn't you see the man in the white coat? He was right over there. I was talking to him."

"You were *talking* to him? Where did he go?"

"He went—well, he just kind of *went*."

Susan frowned. "Neil," she said, "you're sure you're not—"

He stared at her. "Not what? Not nuts? Not ready for the funny farm?"

"Neil, you mustn't think that I—"

"Susan, he was there!" Neil shouted. "He was right there, right there by that patch of grass! I talked to him!"

She let go of his hands. He stood by the fence and watched her as she walked back across the yard to the house, with her head lowered. She climbed up the steps to the veranda, went into the kitchen door, and closed it behind her. He banged his fist against the fence railing

73

in frustration. Of all the damned, stupid, ridiculous things. He needed help and reassurance more than he ever had in his whole life, and everybody, including his wife, thought he was turning into a raving lunatic. He looked back at the grass where the man had been standing, and he felt confused, frightened, and helpless. Almost as helpless as the day that the jack had slipped, and Jim had reached out his hand toward him and begged for some miraculous salvation which Neil just didn't have the power to give him.

Neil climbed over the fence and trudged back to the house. In the kitchen, Susan was sitting at the table scraping carrots. The tears were running down her cheeks into the salad.

Neil put his arm around her. He said, "Susan?"

There was a moment when she tried to be strong, but then she burst into tears and clung to him, and for a long time they held each other close, her hot cheek wet against his; he was almost moved to tears himself.

At last she looked up at him, flushed and unhappy, her eyelashes stuck together with crying.

She said, "I don't know what to do. It's all so frightening."

He shrugged, "I know. I don't know what to do either. But I'm doing whatever I can."

She swallowed, and then she said, "You won't mind me asking this, will you? I know it sounds awful, but I have to ask it."

"Go right ahead."

"Well," she said uncertainly, "you're not—you're not going mad are you? You don't have madness in your family?"

He couldn't help smiling. "Not that I know of. I think my grandfather used to fly Chinese kites out on the point, and got himself a name for being quite an eccentric, but real madness . . ."

"Not even way back? I couldn't bear it if Toby—"

He squeezed her close. "Listen, I'm not going mad, and neither is Toby, and neither is anyone else. We just have one of those weird situations that nobody quite understands. It's like flying saucers, Doctor Crowder told me, or ghosts. All we have to do is find out what it is, and when we know, we'll be fine."

Susan dabbed at her eyes with her apron. "I'm sorry. I guess it's been a strain, that's all. I was sitting there thinking that you must have had a mad cousin in your dim and distant past, and that you and Toby were paying the price for it. I'm real sorry, Neil. I mean it."

Neil kissed her. "I'm glad you came straight out and asked. If I'd have been you, I would have been thinking the same thing. I'm happy to say, though, that there hasn't been *anybody* in my family's illustrious history who—"

He paused. She stopped in the middle of drying her tears and looked up at him. He gave her a quick, uncertain smile.

"What were you saying?" she asked him.

He shook his head. "It doesn't matter. It seems ridiculous. I guess I'm allowing this thing to get under my skin."

"You mustn't, honey," she said gently. "We'll work it out somehow."

"Sure," he told her, but he didn't feel very convinced. "Now, I'd better get upstairs and finish off that wardrobe."

"Do you really have to?" she asked him. "It seems such a pity, just breaking it up for the sake of it."

"Would *you* sleep with it in the room?" asked Neil. "Would you let Toby sleep with it in the room?"

"I guess not. But Doctor Crowder may have been right. It could have been Toby's window banging."

"So you think I'm imagining things, too?"

"Honey, I don't. I believe what you say. I heard the noises myself. It's just that, well, a wooden man? It could have been a freak kind of reflection, you know. A trick of the light."

Neil walked across to the other side of the kitchen, and stared for two or three minutes out of the window. He could see the grass waving on the opposite side of the fence, the grass where the man in the long white duster coat had been standing. Perhaps, after all, the man was nothing more than an optical illusion. Dave Conway hadn't seen him in the bay, and Susan hadn't seen him outside the yard. Perhaps he only existed inside Neil's mind. And Toby's, too, of course.

Neil said, "I think I'm going to go out for a few hours. I need to turn this thing over, get it straight in my head."

Susan came over and put her arms around him. "I love you," she said in a soft voice.

"I know," he told her.

"What are you going to do about the wardrobe?" she asked.

"I'll break it up when I get back. We'll have a bonfire in the yard. Maybe we can bake some potatoes. It's about time we tried to have ourselves a little fun."

"You won't be long, will you?"

He checked his watch. "It's eleven-thirty now. I'll be back in time to pick up Toby from school."

He gave her a light kiss on the forehead, and then he took the pickup keys from their hook by the door, and

76

left the house without another word. Susan watched him go. When the dust from the truck had drifted away, she went through to the living room and called her mother on the telephone. She had a feeling that what she had just felt was the first tremor of some kind of earthquake, and that before long she was going to need all the help she could find.

The phone rang and rang but her mother didn't answer. She hoped that wasn't a bad omen.

Neil drove through to Santa Rosa, over the winding rural road that took him through Sebastopol, and out onto 101 by the Shell gas station. Inland, it was sunny and hot, and he drove with what he always called his two-fifty air conditioning (two windows open at fifty miles an hour). He was sweating, and his shirt stuck to the vinyl seat, but he scarcely noticed the temperature. He turned left on 101 and headed north.

On the pickup's radio, Warren Zevon was singing *Werewolves of London*. He wasn't listening. He was looking for the turnoff to Petrified Forest Road, which would lead him over the redwood-forested Sonoma mountains to Calistoga.

He almost missed it, and when he jammed on his brakes and signaled a right, a lumber truck blared its five-tone horns at him, and the driver leaned over to mouth some unheard obscenity.

Along the twisting, climbing highway, it was peaceful and deserted. The pickup labored on the grades, but now Neil had made up his mind what he was going to do, he didn't feel the same desperate urgency. Through the forests of pines and cottonwoods, madrona, and red-barked manzanita, he climbed into the clear fragrant mountain air.

The Petrified Forest itself was just below the brim of the mountains that sloped down to the town of Calistoga. Neil had always promised Toby that he would take him there to see the giant petrified redwoods, but it was one of those trips that they'd never gotten around to taking. He drove past the wooden gates of the entrance with his pickup blowing out blue smoke.

In Calistoga's main street, a sleepy one-horse thoroughfare at the head of Napa Valley, Neil parked the pickup in the shade of an old flat-fronted hotel building and climbed out. It was way up in the high eighties, and he wiped his forehead on his shirt sleeve. Beyond the main street, there were only the dark-green, forested mountains, and the air was heavy with the scent of the trees. The sky was cloudless and inky blue.

He walked along the street until he found a drugstore. Inside, it was air-conditioned and smelled of menthol. He went up to the prescription counter and waited while the short, bespectacled druggist wrote the label for a large bottle of stomach pills.

"Can I help you?" the druggist asked him. His spectacles had such strong lenses that his eyes were hugely magnified.

"I'm looking for an old man named Billy Ritchie," said Neil. "I guessed, since he was old, he might come in here for prescriptions."

The druggist finished off his label. "Sure. I know Billy Ritchie. I'd like to know someone in town who doesn't. A real old character. Where are you from?"

"Out by Bodega Bay. I met a friend of his, an old sailor, and the sailor said I ought to drop by and see Billy if I was passing."

The druggist nodded. "Sure. If you cross the street here, and take the first on your right, that's Washington

78

Street, then take the fifth right again, that's Lake Street, you'll find Billy in the green-painted house on the left. You can't miss it, his name's on the mailbox.

"Thanks."

Neil left the store and crossed Lincoln Avenue in the shadowless midday heat. He walked as far as Lake Street, sweating and short of breath, and the house was right there. A small clapboard cabin, painted the color of lawn mowers. It was shaded by maples and firs and looked deserted. Neil went up to the door and knocked.

It took a long time, but after a while he heard a clattering sound inside, and the security chain was drawn back. The door opened, and in the dim hallway, Neil saw a wizened old man in an invalid chair.

"Are you Billy Ritchie?" he asked, quite loudly, in case the old man was deaf.

"That's me, sir. What do you want?"

"I'm afraid it's kind of hard to tell you in one breath. But I was talking to Doughty out on the jetty at Bodega Bay, and he said I should come see you. He said you could tell me some stories of the old days."

The old man nodded. He was bald, smooth-shaven, and toothless, and the only hairy thing about him was the black chinchilla cat which sat in his lap, and which he endlessly stroked.

"I can tell you stories, sure. What stories do you want to know?"

"I'd like to know about the Fenners, back in the days of the Wappo Indians, if that's convenient."

Billy Ritchie coughed. "Those were bad days. What do you want to know about them for?"

"A couple of reasons. For one, my name's Neil Fenner."

The old man laughed, and coughed some more.

79

"Sounds like as good a reason as any. Tell you what, I'll strike you a bargain. Get yourself back down the road there and bring me a six-pack of Coors and a pint of Old Crow, and that's all I ask in return. I can't tell stories on a dry whistle."

"You've got yourself a deal."

Ten minutes later, his hair dripping with sweat and his shirt soaked, Neil came back with the liquor. The old man had left the front door ajar, and as Neil walked up the path, the host called, "Walk straight in there, friend. Close it behind you, though. You never know who might come prowling to steal my valuables."

The little house was dark and cool, and surprisingly clean and well cared-for. Billy Ritchie, without his legs, had made his home his whole world, and it was wallpapered from floor to ceiling with color pictures cut from calendars and magazines. Every room was a patchwork of scenic views snipped from tourist brochures, close-ups of butterflies and flowers, religious scenes and snow scenes, cartoons and classic works of art, all interleaved with center spreads from *Penthouse* and *Hustler*.

"Most folks comment on every damn picture except the girls," said Billy Ritchie. "But what I say is, if an old gent can't admire some young flesh when he's past everything but spitting contests, then it's a sad world."

The old man was sitting in a shadowy corner of the room, his head silhouetted by the light from the half-closed venetian blinds behind him. Through the slats of the blind, Neil could see a tangled garden, overgrown with wild grass.

"There's glasses on the side there," Billy Ritchie said. "Pour me a beer and a stiff one, and whatever you want for yourself."

Neil went across to a low sideboard with a decorated glass front and laid out three glasses. He opened a beer for each of them, and poured out three fingers of bourbon for Billy Ritchie. Then he sat himself down in an uncomfortable, yellow-painted, basketwork chair, lifted his drink, and said; "Good health, Mr. Ritchie."

The old man raised his glass in return. "Same to you. But call me Billy, and don't worry too much about my health. I lost the use of my legs twenty years ago when I fell off a damn bad-tempered horse, and I've been fit as a damn drum ever since. I've seen a lot, though, and talked to a whole host of the old-timers, and there isn't much that's passed me by."

"What do you know about Bloody Fenner? That's what they called him, didn't they?"

"Oh, they sure did," said Billy. "Bloody by name and damn bloody by nature. But you have to judge a man like that by the days he lived in, and those days in the Napa Valley weren't easy. This was fine land, and the Indians weren't too happy about handing it over. If you wanted to survive, you had to be real tough, and ready to make the best of things. That was what Bloody Fenner was good at. Making the best of things."

Neil swallowed beer and wiped his mouth with the back of his hand. "I heard he was a traitor, of sorts."

Billy Ritchie pulled a face. "Not to himself, he wasn't. He did pretty well in the 1830s, made himself a fair pile of money, and owned a whole stretch of good land up along the Silverado Trail. Trouble was, the Fenner family lost most of their acreage in the late forties, after the year of the Bear Flag Party across at Sonoma, when the Californians declared independence from the Mexicans. Fenner had gotten along good with the Mexicans, on account of he was smart and wily, and willing to perform a service to any man who paid him.

But when the Bear Flag folks took over, they made life so damn difficult for the Fenner family they sold out and moved to the coast, and I guess the land they bought was where you're living now."

Neil nodded. "Part of it, anyway. My grandfather sold about a hundred acres during the Depression."

Old Billy Ritchie took a mouthful of Old Crow, coughed, and said, "A lot of folks did, especially around Napa. First, prohibition hit the wineries, then the Depression. They weren't good times."

"But what about Bloody Fenner?" asked Neil.

"Bloody Fenner?" echoed Billy Ritchie. "Bloody Fenner was the best damn brawler and fighter this side of the Sacramento River. He knew all the Indians by name, the Wappos and the Patwins, and there were plenty who said that he'd been initiated in a Wappo temescal. The stories say that he was a tall man, with a face as fierce as a bear, and that he could shoot a fly off of a horse's ass if he was blindfolded and standing on his head."

Neil grinned. "Sounds like that's one talent that's gotten bred out of the family."

"Just as well, if you ask my opinion," Billy Ritchie rejoined. "Bloody Fenner wasn't loved by nobody, except for his wife, and by all accounts she was twice as hard-bitten as he was."

Neil was silent for a moment, watching the old-timer sitting in his invalid chair, stroking and stroking that black, furry cat. Then the guest said softly, "Did you ever hear tell of a battle? A battle that Bloody Fenner might have fought in?"

"Sure. He fought in plenty. He fought for José Sanchez back in the early days, and the story goes that he helped Father Altamira round up Patwins and put them to work for the mission at Sonoma. That was back in the late 1820s, and times were raw then, I can tell you."

"I'm thinking of one battle in particular," said Neil. "A battle where the white men came off pretty badly, and the Indians did well."

"There were a few of those," said Billy Ritchie, shaking his head. "I heard tell of a massacre of ten white farmers and their families by the Wappos up at St. Helena, and there was an ambush of three white squatters by Wappos in York Creek. Maybe the worst, though, was the time they say Bloody Fenner took a league of land from the Wappo Indians in exchange for leading twenty settlers and their families into a trap set in the forest up at Las Posadas, close to Conn Creek. The settlers had trusted Fenner, you see, and paid him in gold to act as their scout and interpreter, so that they could lay out claims to farmland in Bell Canyon. But he took them slap-bang into a Wappo ambush, and they were all killed. Twenty farmers, and their twenty wives, and fifty-three young children."

Neil licked his lips. "Did anyone prove that it was Fenner who did it? Or was it just hearsay?"

"What proof did anyone have in them days?" asked Billy Ritchie. "The land was rough and the folks were rougher. You stayed alive if you were hard and dogged and used your gun without thinking twice. But the stories say that Fenner was the only white man who came out of that massacre alive, and that's suspicious in itself. He said that he left the settlers, and rode back along Conn Creek to bring help from his Mexican soldier friends, and there's nothing to say that he didn't. But if he *did* bring help, it was a sight too late to save anyone;

83

and what was oddest of all, the settlers' bodies were all scalped, and their ears cut off."

"What was odd about that?" asked Neil. "The Wappos were pretty fierce sometimes, weren't they?"

"Oh, they could be. But what they *didn't* do was take scalps, or ears, or genitalia, like some of the Indians did. It wasn't their style. They were diggers, not fighters, and all they cared about was protecting their good agricultural land from the white men. They weren't interested in trophies."

"You're saying that Fenner took the scalps? A *white* man took *white* scalps?"

"You don't have to look so shocked. It wasn't unusual in them days. In fact, some of the old-timers say it was white men who taught the Indians to take scalps in the first place."

"That's horrific," said Neil.

Old Billy Ritchie shrugged, and swilled some bourbon down with a mouthful of beer.

Neil said, "Did you ever see a picture of Bloody Fenner? An engraving or anything like that?"

Billy Ritchie shook his head. "The only drawings I ever saw of Napa Valley in them days were landscapes. Mainly forests, it was. But I don't think nobody ever took it into their heads to draw Bloody Fenner."

"There's something else," said Neil. "Did you ever hear of a prophecy connected with Bloody Fenner? Something that was supposed to be written on a stone redwood tree?"

Billy Ritchie thought about that, and then shook his head again. "No, sir, I can't say that I ever did."

"Then how about the day of the dark stars?"

Billy Ritchie lifted his head slowly and stared at him. For the first time since Neil had walked into the house, he stopped stroking the cat, and his old hand lay on her black fur like a dead, dried leaf.

"Did I hear you right?" he said, in a soft, unsettling tone.

"The day of the dark stars," repeated Neil. "That was all I said."

The old man quivered in his chair, as if a cold wind had blown across the room. But the air was still, and growing stuffy, and outside it must have been close to 100 degrees.

"Where did you hear about the day of the dark stars?" he asked Neil. "I lay my life I didn't believe I'd ever hear that phrase again."

"I don't know," said Neil, reluctant to tell the old man about Toby until he knew what the "day of the dark stars" was, and why the mention of it seemed to be so unnerving. "I guess I just kind of picked it up."

Billy Ritchie looked at Neil as if he knew that he was only telling him half of the truth, but then he piloted his wheel chair across the room, and silently poured himself another large shot of bourbon. As he screwed the cap back on the bottle, he looked up at Neil, and said: "The first and last time I heard of the day of the dark stars was from a trapper I met when I was a young man up in the Modoc Forest. This man was old and he was thin as a polecat, and he had scars on every spare inch of his body from fighting Indians and animals. We spent two nights and two days together, and then we went our separate ways."

"But what did he tell you?" asked Neil.

Billy Ritchie's eyes were rheumy and distant. "He told me all about the old days in Modoc country, just so that I could pass his stories on, so they wouldn't be lost. What he said was that once the Indians knew they couldn't hold back the white man any longer, they kind of bowed their heads and accepted their fate after a fashion, because they always knew that their gods would give them revenge. It was a Wappo belief, for instance, that for every Indian who died from cholera or smallpox, or was shot down by scalp hunters, a white man would die in return. They said that it might not happen in a month, in a year, or even in twenty years, but that one day the stars would go dark because they would call down the most powerful and evil Indian demons there ever were, the demons they didn't even dare to call down in their own lifetimes, like Nashuna and Pa-la-kai and Ossadagowah, and that the demons would slaughter a man for a man, a woman for a woman, a child for a child."

Billy Ritchie took another swig from his glass, and then he said, "The way I heard it, Nashuna was the demon of darkness, and Pa-la-kai was the demon of blood, and Ossadagowah was a kind of a beast-thing that nobody could even describe, a kind of a wild demon that scared everyone witless."

"You sound as though you believe it," said Neil, carefully.

The old man gave a wry smile. "I'd believe it before I believed some of the words I read in the Bible," he said, quietly. "Them Indians knew their lands, you see, and they knew their skies and their waters, and they knew all about the spirits and the demons that dwelled in those lands and those skies and those waters. The way that trapper told me, the day of the dark stars was going to happen before the twentieth century turned—he wasn't sure when, but that was what he was told."

Neil raised his eyebrows. "Sounds scary, doesn't it? But who's going to call these demons down? I've been to powwows at a couple of Indian reservations, and there's an Indian who comes down to Bodega Bay to fish, and it seems to me that there isn't much magic left in any of today's red people."

"It's not *today's* red people you've got to worry about," said Billy Ritchie. "It's the spirits of the red people from out of the *past*. What this trapper told me was that the greatest of all the medicine men, the twenty-two most powerful wonder-workers from all the main tribes, all of their spirits would come together, God knows how, and they'd call down the worstest demons they could, and get their revenge."

"You mean the ghosts of twenty-two old-time medicine men are supposed to be getting together to punish us? Come on, Billy. That's a tall story and you know it."

Billy Ritchie didn't look offended. "People have said that before," he said, philosophically. "But let me show you something, before you make up your mind that all those old Indian legends were nonsense."

He propelled himself across to a small bureau which stood in the far corner of the room and opened the top drawer. He shuffled through a heap of untidy papers and news clippings while Neil watched him silently and drank his beer.

"Here we are," said Billy Ritchie, after a while, and wheeled himself over. He gave Neil two black-and-white photographs, full plate size, and told him, "Take a close look at those."

One of the photographs showed a street scene in Calistoga. It was hard to tell when it was, because the town had hardly changed in fifty years. There were horses and buggies, and men in wide-brimmed hats, but it could have been taken any time between 1890 and 1920.

In the foreground of the picture stood a group of men with drooping mustaches, and just to their left, sitting on the edge of the boardwalk, was an Indian, in a dusty, black business suit. He was handsome and well-built, and around his neck he wore strings of necklaces and beads, which indicated that he was a medicine man.

The other photograph was taken in the woods someplace. Neil didn't recognize the scenery at all. A group of Indians were standing by a fallen tree, squinting at the camera as if they mistrusted it. Among them was the same medicine man, in a woolen robe this time, but wearing the same necklaces and beads.

"All right," said Neil, "it's two pictures of the same Indian. What's that supposed to prove?"

"Look at the dates on the back," suggested Billy Ritchie.

Neil turned the photographs over. One, the street scene in Calistoga, was marked 8/1/15. The woodland scene was marked August 5th, 1915.

"I don't get it," persisted Neil. "These were taken three days apart. What's so strange about that?"

Billy Ritchie cackled. "What's so strange about it is that the picture in the woods was taken by a photographer called Lewis Clifton, of Massachusetts, up by the Wampanoag settlement on the Miskatonic River in New England. These photographs were taken three days apart, sure. But they were also taken *three thousand miles apart*."

"That's impossible," said Neil. "In 1915, it would have taken almost a week to get from New England to the Napa Valley."

"That's right," nodded Billy Ritchie. "And yet both

of these photographs are authenticated, and their dates are plumb correct."

Neil peered closer at the calm, amused face of the Wampanaug medicine man. Even though the pictures were almost seventy years old, they had a curious freshness about them, as if they had been taken only a few weeks ago. He said, "That's strange, that's really strange."

"Not strange at all when you know who that is," said Billy Ritchie. "That's the best-known of all the Indian men, the most powerful Indian sorcerer who ever lived. That's Misquamacus."

"Misquamacus?"

"That was what they called him, among a whole lot of other names. But the reason I spent some time finding those photographs is because of what that trapper told me, up in the Modoc Forest. He said that when the day of the dark stars came around, this man Misquamacus would be the fellow to bring all the twenty-two wonder-workers together. This man Misquamacus, he said, was obsessed with taking his revenge on the white folks, and that his whole aim in life was to see white people die in the cruelest way possible."

Billy Ritchie began to stroke his cat again. "I'd say that the cruelest way possible would be to call down Nashuna and Pa-la-kai and Ossadagowah, and let them loose. Now, that *would* be cruel."

FOUR

They talked until midafternoon. Billy Ritchie, as the Old Crow loosened his tongue, began to ramble about his childhood, and the old days in Calistoga and the hot springs country, and the girls he'd known and chased. Neil began to feel claustrophobic in the small, airless house, but he stayed because he wanted to know more about Bloody Fenner, and about the day of the dark stars.

He said to Billy Ritchie, "Do you think that Bloody Fenner could have done anything to irritate the Wappos, or any of the tribes? Something they might have wanted revenge for?"

Billy Ritchie shook his head. "I don't know, sir. I never heard tell of him falling out with the Indians. The way I heard it, they was always the best of friends, and that's what made him so treacherous to whites."

"But you don't know for sure?"

"Who does? All that happened one hundred and forty years ago, and there wasn't more than a dozen men in the whole of the Napa Valley who could read or

91

write, so they didn't keep no diaries. They were dark days, for sure. Mighty dark days."

Neil took out his handkerchief and wiped sweat from the back of his neck. "Well, tell me this," he said. "If Bloody Fenner had done something to upset the Indians, way back in the 1830s, how would an Indian medicine man go about taking his revenge?"

"You mean today? Here and now?"

"That's right."

Billy Ritchie puffed out his cheeks. "I can only tell you what I know from stories, and from what that trapper told me. A lot of those real mystical Indian rituals, well, they're so secret that half the Indians don't know them. But what you have to understand is that a medicine man's spirit—what the Indians call his manitou—that never dies. It's reborn, lifetime after lifetime, for seven lifetimes in all, until the medicine man has performed enough magic on earth to earn himself a place up in the stars, alongside of the great spirits.

"The point is, the manitou can only take on flesh if it finds itself a suitable human being to lodge itself in. It can take on plenty of other shapes, sure. The Narragansets, for instance, used to have stories about medicine men who came back to life by using rocks for flesh, or water, or even wood. There's some pretty hair-rising stories about the stone men of the Narragansets who used to walk at night. But a man made of rock or wood is just as vulnerable as rock or wood, and so the medicine man wouldn't take on that kind of flesh unless he had nothing else."

Neil, even though he was trying hard to control it, was shaking. He saw, as vividly as he had the night before, the wooden arm reaching out from the wardrobe, the fierce face glaring from the polished walnut. He said, hoarsely, "Go on."

Billy Ritchie shrugged. "I don't know much more about it. It's not the kind of stuff a white man gets to hear about easily."

Neil opened another can of Coors. His throat was dry, and he felt as if he'd been hung up all afternoon in a tobacco-curing barn. He swallowed lukewarm beer, and then he said, "What would happen on the day of the dark stars? Would the medicine men need to find human beings to lodge themselves in? Would they need to use ordinary people's bodies to get themselves reborn?"

"Sure they would," nodded Billy Ritchie. "They'd pick themselves a bunch of folks, probably the kind of folks who wouldn't put up too much of a mental fight, if you get what I mean, and they'd use their living bodies, their flesh and their blood and all, to come back to life."

Neil whispered, "The children. My God, *the children.*"

Billy Ritchie said, "What did you say? You'll have to speak up. I bust an eardrum when I fell off of that horse."

Neil stood up. If what Billy Ritchie said about Indian medicine men was even half-true, it was the most terrifying thing he'd ever heard in his life. Everything fitted the random and scary events of the past few days, and made sense out of them. The day of the dark stars was going to happen soon, just the way Toby had said. Toby couldn't have possibly known about it unless he was really being possessed for real. And the wooden man from the wardrobe convinced him.

It seemed insane, but nothing else explained what

93

was going on. *The children of Mrs. Novato's class were being gradually infiltrated, mind and body, by the most powerful gathering of Indian medicine men that had ever taken place, at any time in America's history. Toby, his own son, was among them.*

Toby, when he thought about it, may even have been the catalyst for the whole horrifying possession. Toby was a Fenner, a descendant of Bloody Fenner, and if Bloody Fenner had helped the Indians in the past against the white man, then maybe he was doing it again. The ghost or the spirit of Toby's forefather was back in Sonoma County, after a hundred and forty years, and preparing for another massacre.

Neil thought about the man in the long white duster. The man who kept begging for help. Maybe he was a ghost, too—a kind of sad warning stirred up from the past. From what he said, he may have been one of the twenty settlers who died up at Conn Creek. One of the innocent folks who had died at the hands of the Wappos while Bloody Fenner pretended to ride off for help.

Neil took Billy Ritchie's hand and squeezed it.

"You've been a lot of help," he said softly.

"What did you say?" demanded Billy.

"I said, you've been a lot of help. I'm beginning to understand things that didn't make any sense before."

Billy Ritchie set down his bourbon glass. He stared up at Neil with a sharp, canny look in his eye.

"You're worried, aren't you?" he said.

"A little," admitted Neil.

"You think it's coming—the day of the dark stars?"

"I've seen some signs."

"What kind of signs?"

"I've seen a wooden man. Least, I think I have. And

I've heard voices from the people who were killed up at Las Posadas."

Billy Ritchie rubbed his chin. "It doesn't sound too good, does it?" he said. "It doesn't sound too good at all."

"I don't know what to *do*," said Neil. "If it's really medicine men, then they've chosen the kids at my son's school."

"They would, if you're a Fenner. They'd look for a spirit guide, you see. Someone to help them reincarnate themselves. Out there, out in what the Indians used to call the 'outside,' the spirits of those medicine men would look for the ghost of someone who once helped them when they were human. Bloody Fenner would be just their man."

"But what can I do?" asked Neil. "Is there anything I can do about it? I mean, how can I stop it?"

Billy Ritchie brushed cat hairs off his fingers. "I wouldn't like to say," he confessed. "That old trapper never got as far as telling me what to do if the day of the dark stars ever actually arrived."

"But what about all those children? What about my son?"

"It's going to be worse than that," said Billy Ritchie. "Well—I know there isn't nothing worse than your own son being hurt. But the day of the dark stars is when the Indians take an eye for an eye, and you just think about the thousands and thousands of Indians who died because of what the white man did to them. If these medicine men really do turn up, and if they really call down their demons, then we're going to see death and horror like you can't even imagine."

Neil was silent for a few seconds, and then he squeezed Billy Ritchie's hand again. "I'm going to start fighting back," he said determinedly. "I'm going straight to the cops, to begin with, and we're going to have those children protected."

"Well," said Billy Ritchie, "I just hope you can. Maybe it takes a Fenner to wipe out a Fenner's wrong deeds. Don't think it's going to be easy, though. And keep on your guard. If your ancestor's around, then you've got yourself some stiff competition. Allen Fenner wasn't called Bloody for nothing."

"*Allen* Fenner? That was his name?"

"It sure was. Didn't you know that?"

Neil shook his head. "Nobody ever told me before. Everybody just called him Bloody."

Billy Ritchie tickled his black cat's ears. "Bloody's good enough," he said simply. "Bloody's good enough."

Sergeant Murray sat behind his desk with the same patient expression he used for people who complained about dogs fouling their front lawns, or kids throwing stones at their windows. Outside, a breeze had sprung up from the ocean, and dust blew in gritty clouds across the police station parking lot. It was nearly five o'clock, and Sergeant Murray was due to go home at five. He was a big, chubby man, with a face as large as a pig's, and he was feeling hungry.

Beside him, his air-conditioning unit rattled and burbled and whined. From time to time, as Neil talked to him, he took a paper clip out of the small plastic tray on his desk, unbent it, and dropped it into his wastebasket with an audible *ping*.

Neil told him about Toby's nightmares, about the paintings at the school, about the wooden demon, and about Billy Ritchie. Sergeant Murray listened, asking no questions, and when Neil was finished he wedged his fat fingers together and had a deep, silent think.

Eventually, he lifted his head and said, "Neil—we've known each other a good few years."

"What does that have to do with it?"

Sergeant Murray pulled a face. "Everything, when it comes down to it, Neil. A cop who didn't know you too well might book you for wasting police time. As it is—"

"*Wasting police time?*" said Neil, astounded. "You think I've spent a whole day over at Calistoga, and driven all the way back here, just to *waste your time?*"

"Neil," said Sergeant Murray, raising one porky hand to restrain him, "I don't mean that you've done it with bad intent. I don't mean that you've done it *deliberately*."

"Well, what the hell *do* you mean? I know this is weird stuff, George. I know it sounds crazy. But I've told you the facts as they are, and you can't sit there and tell me that something pretty threatening isn't going on here. You can't ignore it."

Sergeant Murray glanced at the clock and sighed. "Neil," he said, with immense patience, "I'd like to believe that what you've been telling me is true. I'd really like to believe it. But the fact of it is, you've only got the word of some cranky old-timer to go by, and a couple of bad dreams that Toby's been having, and that's all you know."

"What about the photograph? The picture of Misquamacus? George, there were three days between those pictures, and yet they were taken on opposite sides of the continent!"

There was a pause, and then Sergeant Murray continued, "Neil, I'm sorry. I haven't seen those pictures. But they don't constitute no proof. Anyone could have

97

written any kind of date on the back of those prints, and you don't even know if they were taken where the old-timer said they were."

Neil sat back. "Then what are you trying to tell me?" he asked. "Are you trying to tell me you won't help?"

Sergeant Murray looked a little abashed, but he said, as reasonably as he could manage, "I'll help when there's good cause to, Neil. You know that as well as I do. But if I put a guard on those schoolchildren, that means that a whole lot of taxpayers' money is going to be tied up for a long time, and a whole lot of people are going to be asking me why. Now, what am I going to say? That I've put a patrolman on school guard because Neil Fenner believes the children are being taken over by Red Indian ghosts? That I've risked the security on a whole score of homes, and I've had to halve the beach patrols, just because we're being threatened by medicine men from a hundred years ago? Come on, Neil, you have to see my point of view."

"You're laughing at me," said Neil.

Sergeant Murray slowly shook his head. "I'm not laughing at you, Neil. Sometimes, circumstantial evidence appears to be pretty convincing. It's easy to make yourself believe that something's true, just because it appears to fit the facts as you know them. But what you have to ask yourself is, do you *know* all the facts? Or enough of them to make a sound judgment?

"George, I'm only asking because of the children. They're at risk, and I believe it's up to us to protect them."

Sergeant Murray stood up and hitched up his gun belt. Outside in the police station yard, Officer Turnbull was arriving to relieve him. He gave Neil an awkward, embarrassed smile.

"Listen, Neil," he said, "I'll give you this much. If you can *prove* to me that something funny is probably going to happen here—if you can give me one piece of real evidence—then I'll do what I can to help. But as it is, the way things stand, I have to tell you that I'm powerless."

Neil looked unhappy. But he nodded and said, "Okay, George. I guess you're right. It sounds crazy, and maybe it *is* crazy."

Sergeant Murray fitted his cap onto his sweaty pink head. "They said that Thomas Alva Edison was crazy, didn't they? Just think about that."

Neil said quietly, "There's a difference between being a genius inventor and a frightened father, George."

He went back home. Susan and Toby were sitting at the kitchen table. Susan was finishing her supper, corned beef hash and home fries, and Toby was drawing. As Neil came in the back door, Susan looked up and said, "Well?"

He came over and kissed her, and ruffled Toby's hair. "What do you think? He said he was sorry, but he couldn't spare the manpower. The taxpayers wouldn't stand for it."

"Even though the taxpayers' children might get hurt?"

"Susan, he didn't believe me. Not one word."

"Did he *try* to believe you?"

Neil shrugged. "I guess he made a token effort. But it's pretty farfetched stuff. I sat there and I listened to myself trying to convince him, and the more I told him the stupider it all sounded."

She put down her fork and went to the stove. She dolloped hash onto a plate for him, and set out a dish of crackers and cheese. They didn't eat too fancy these days, because of the way Neil's business was going, but they managed. Weekends, they sometimes ate steak, especially if he had a new order to refit a yacht, but there wasn't much demand for a one-man craftsman around Bodega Bay.

Neil washed his hands at the kitchen faucet and sat down. He asked, "How are you doing, Toby?"

"I'm okay," said Toby, without looking up.

"What are you drawing there? It looks like some kind of a spaceship."

Toby crooked his arm around his picture so that Neil couldn't see. "It's a secret," he said.

Neil started to eat. Susan sat next to him and watched him with concern and a little pain. She touched his hand as it rested on the table, and gently stroked his suntanned knuckles.

She said, "Did you really believe that old man yourself? You don't think he was pulling your leg?"

"Why should he?"

"For the sake of a drink, and a joke with his friends after you'd gone. I mean, you know what Doughty's like with his stories. Why should Billy Ritchie be any better?"

Neil set down his fork. "I don't know. I just believe him, that's all. I can't think of any other reason for what's been happening, except that I'm losing my marbles."

Susan rubbed her forehead tiredly and thoughtfully. "The trouble is," she said, "the man in the white coat is one thing, and the nightmares are one thing, but all this business about twenty-two medicine men coming back to life to get their revenge on the white man . . ."

"I know," he said, in a soft, hollow voice. "But you

100

were here when Toby talked about the day of the dark stars, and the gateway, and all that stuff. You heard him as clear as I did."

"Maybe Billy Ritchie simply *pretended* he knew what they were. Think about it. He's alone in that house all day, with nobody to talk to. He's quite likely to say *anything*, just to keep you interested."

Neil didn't answer. He finished his hash in silence, and then he pushed his plate away from him and sat with his elbows on the table and his chin in his hands.

Susan said, "Honey, you mustn't let it get you down. I know what you're feeling, but something's bound to happen soon, and you'll forget all about it."

Neil looked across at her. "The only *something* that's going to happen, as far as I can make out, is a damned great massacre."

She averted her eyes. "You shouldn't speak that way," she said quietly.

"What way? Is it the 'damned' you don't like, or the 'massacre'?"

"I don't like any of it," she retorted. "I don't like these nightmares and I don't like all this maddening talk of ghosts and manitous and men in long white coats who vanish as soon as you look at them. If you want to know what I really feel, I'll tell you. I don't believe a single word of it. I think you're probably tired and over-worked, and maybe you're worried about money, and you're letting this whole ridiculous business run away with you."

She had tears in her eyes as she spoke, and she was twisting her apron in her hands. She looked up at him and said, "You're not behaving like Neil anymore. You used to be so solid, so down-to-earth. It's not like you to think about devils and demons. I don't know what's happened to you."

Neil bit his lip while she spoke. Then, with as much control as he could manage, he told her, "I can tell you what's happened. For the first time in the whole of my life, I've seen a ghost for real. For the first time in my whole life, I've come across something spooky and supernatural that I've *had* to believe in because it's there in front of my eyes. Worse than that, it's threatening Toby and it's threatening the rest of his class. I've seen it, Susan, and I can't stand by and let things get worse just because nobody else happens to believe me."

He got up from the table and pushed in his chair. "Right now I'm going to go upstairs and smash that wardrobe, and then I'm going to burn it. I don't care if Mrs. Novato thinks I'm crazy, and I don't care if George Murray thinks I'm crazy, and I'm sorry to say it, but I don't care if *you* think I'm crazy, either. I'm going to protect Toby the best way I know how, and that's by making sure those spirits don't get hold of him."

Toby had stopped drawing and was staring at him. Neil, pocketing a box of matches from the hutch, said, "How about a bonfire, Toby? We'll break up that horrible old wardrobe, and then we'll take it out in the yard, and—"

Toby opened his mouth and roared.

It wasn't a child's roar. It wasn't even a human roar. It came out of his wide-open mouth like an avalanche of sound, like a terrifying locomotive blasting through a black tunnel. It was the kind of sound that drowned everything, that opened up visions of endless spaces and impossible distances. Susan screamed, and Neil found himself clutching for the pine hutch for support. The cups and plates rattled with the rumbling vibration, and a vase dropped on to the quarry-tiled floor and shattered.

Toby's mouth closed. He sat at the table, the same small mop-headed boy, but somehow hideously changed. His eyes were bloodshot and congested, and they stared at Neil with a terrible, knowing strength. His hand clutched at his wax crayon and slowly crushed it, shedding fragments of red wax across his drawing.

Neil took a step toward him. "It's *you* again, isn't it?" he whispered. "It's *you*."

Toby watched him silently and emotionlessly, but as Neil moved around the room, his eyes followed him all the way.

"I want to know who you are," said Neil. "I want you to give me some kind of sign."

Toby smiled, without humor or human compassion. He said, in a hoarse, echoing voice, "There will be no signs. You will not interfere. You will leave the gateway intact."

Neil replied, "No signs, huh? Well, in that case, I'm afraid the gateway goes. You can't just use my son that way and expect me to cooperate. I'm going to go upstairs right this minute and turn your so-called gateway into cheap firewood."

Toby growled, "I shall kill you."

Susan, across the other side of the kitchen, whimpered. She could see now how malevolent and red Toby's eyes were, and how his hands clenched and unclenched with impatient strength. She said, "Toby, for pity's sake."

Toby ignored her. He kept his eyes on Neil. At that moment, Neil was in no doubt at all that whatever was using Toby to speak this way, could and *would* destroy him. He could already feel the temperature dropping in the kitchen, and he could see the red line of the thermometer by the stove gradually sliding downward.

"I'm going up there," said Neil. "If you want to stop me, then you're going to have to fight me."

He turned and opened the wooden door that led up to the stairs. In Toby's room, across the landing, he could already hear shuffling and bumping sounds, as if a heavy piece of furniture were being shifted around. He turned and took a last look at Toby, but Toby didn't move. The boy simply sat at the table, his face calm and smooth with intensely self-possessed hatred. Neil didn't like to leave Susan, but he guessed that Toby probably wouldn't harm her—Toby or whatever demonic thing was using Toby to speak to him.

"You are very unwise," said Toby dispassionately.

Neil climbed the stairs as far as the landing. The bedroom door was closed, but now the bumping noises were louder and more frantic. It sounded like chairs and tables and beds being hurled from one side of the room to the other. He heard a lamp smash, and then a window break.

"*Allen,*" begged the voice, a persistent whisper beneath the clattering and thumping. "*Please, Allen . . . help . . .*"

His heart was beating in slow, painful pulses as he approached the room. From underneath the door, strange, cold lights were flickering, like a blue neon sign that was short-circuiting. There was an odor, too, a chilly smell of burned electricity, mingled with an indescribable sourness. His throat was dry, and he felt so frightened that his legs hardly responded when he tried to go nearer.

"Fenner," said a coarse voice, and he turned abruptly around. It was Toby, standing halfway up the stairs, his reddened eyes fixed on him in undisguised anger. "I'm warning you, Fenner. Leave that wardrobe alone."

"You just keep away," said Neil. "I'm going to do what I have to do, and nobody's going to stop me."

"You're a fool, Fenner," grated Toby. From behind him, framed in the light from the kitchen, Susan pleaded uncomprehendingly, "Toby! Toby, what's the matter? Toby!"

"*Allen . . .*" said the haunted whisper. "*Allen, for God's sake . . .*"

There was a bursting, explosive sound from within Toby's bedroom. Neil crossed the landing, took hold of the doorknob, and forced the door open. Immediately, there was another explosion, and he was sucked by a rush of freezing air into the darkness of the room itself. He fell against the opposite wall, jarring his back, and he lay with his hands protecting his head while the air screamed and howled all around him with a hideous cacophony of sound. Behind him the door slammed shut.

He opened his eyes. The room was quieter now, but still dark. The sounds died away to whispers. He strained to see what was happening, but it seemed as if the moon had died, as if the stars had gone out.

Then, gradually, he became aware of a faint white phosphorescence on the other side of the room. He couldn't make out what it was at first, but as his eyes grew more accustomed to the darkness, he could make out the shape of a human head and human shoulders.

He said, in a voice that was much more off-key than he had hoped, "Is there somebody there? Who is that?"

There was silence for a long time. He listened, but he couldn't hear anyone breathing. There wasn't any doubt, though, that what he could see was a human figure. It was sitting on the chair beside Toby's wardrobe, and he could even see the glimmer of its eyes. It only occurred to Neil after several tense, hushed minutes that the wardrobe had been returned to its usual resting-place.

He said, "Is there someone there? I want to know who you are."

The figure appeared to move, and as it moved, it *creaked*. It was a sound that terrified Neil beyond anything. It was the sound of wood, under stress. It was the sound of a man whose limbs were made out of varnished timber. It was the sound of a demon come to life in the form of a human, but in the substance of the forests.

"You are interfering in the schemes of the gods," said the figure. "You are meddling with the past and with the future."

Neil swallowed, although there was nothing in his throat to swallow except the dryness of his fear.

The faint phosphorescence wavered, and Neil saw the shine of a cheekbone of gleaming walnut. The flicker of eyes that were wood, and yet saw. He glanced toward the door of the room, but he knew that even if he tried to make a run for it, the wooden man could get there first.

"Who are you?" he said.

There was silence, and then that horrendous creaking sound as the figure rose to its feet. It slowly stepped toward him, its wooden heels clattering on the floor, and then it stood over him, tall and dark and menacing.

"You want to know who I am?" it replied. Its voice sounded peculiarly distant, as if it was speaking from centuries away. "I am the wooden form of the greatest of those outside. I am not here, in this wood. I am not in your son, although your son speaks to you in my voice. I am beyond the barrier, in the hunting grounds to which all manitous are consigned after their lives in the physical world have ended."

"Why are you here?" asked Neil, in a shaky voice. "What do you want from us? Is Billy Ritchie right? Is it the day of the dark stars? Have you come to kill people?"

The wooden figure turned stiffly away. "It is not for you to know."

Neil, scared, climbed slowly onto his feet. Even when he was standing up, the wooden figure loomed a good four or five inches over him. Neil stepped back across the room, reaching out behind him with his hands, trying to orient himself in the deep, cold darkness.

"You are a Fenner," said the wooden man. "You will be spared because your ancestor helped my brothers. But only if you accept what is happening, and do not try to resist us. If you resist, I shall feed you as scraps of meat to the demons of the north wind."

Neil answered breathlessly, "I have a right to know. I'm Toby's father. You're going to use Toby and I'm going to stop you."

The wooden figure didn't move. But it said, in its eerie, distant voice, "Before you talk about your rights, white man, before you talk about stopping me, remember the thousands of Indian families you slew, and of all those red men who died without rights. Not just fathers and sons, but mothers and daughters. Think of the women you raped and mutilated, of the braves you scalped. Then tell me that you have a right to know — anything."

Carefully stepping backward, sweating and trembling, Neil found the edge of Toby's bed. He reached behind him and fumbled under the comforter for the sheet. He heard the wooden man creak and those heels knock against the bedroom floor, and he froze. But then the wooden man stayed where he was, and Neil softly tugged the sheet out, and rolled it up into an untidy ball behind his back.

The wooden man said: "I am the greatest of those outside, the unquestioned master of the wonder-workers of ancient times. I am the chosen of Sadogowah, the instrument of Nashuna. I have scores to settle from times deeper than you can imagine, white man. I have a score with the Dutchmen, for the diseases they brought to Manhattan. I have a score with the pilgrims, for the ways they taught the Wampanoags and the Nansets. I have a score with the settlers and the farmers and the railroad men, for the Cheyenne who died, and the Sioux who died, and the Apaches and Paiute. We were at one with the lands, white man, and all the forces and the influences of the lands, and all the gods and the spirits for whom trees grow and stones are thrust up from the earth. We were the greatest of the nations of the earth, and you slew us with rifles and diseases and empty promises. We shall have our revenge, white man, in the way that is prophesied on the great stone redwood, and you shall all taste blood."

Neil slid his hand in his pocket and felt for the box of matches. He could almost hear old Billy Ritchie now. *"A man of rock or wood is just as vulnerable as rock or wood."*

The figure said, "The white man, Fenner, helped my Wappo brothers in years gone by. He helped them because he understood their struggle, and because he had Wappo blood in his own veins. That is why your son is chosen, white man. That is why we were led at last to

108

bring down the spirits of the great Nashuna and Ossa-dagowah in this place, at this time."

Neil managed to fumble a match from the box. He scratched it against the side and he smelled burnt phosphorus, but it didn't catch. He was sweating, in spite of the bitter cold, and his teeth were clenched in tension. As it spoke, the wooden figure came closer and closer, until it was standing only two or three feet away, its dark wooden head towering over him.

"I have a personal score to settle, too," the wooden man said, in that uncanny voice that was far away, and yet so close that Neil seemed to be hearing it inside his head.

"A personal score?" asked Neil. He scratched again at the side of the matchbox.

"I have visited your time before, in the body of a young woman. I was reborn to wreak vengeance on those who had laid waste to the islands you now call New York. I was born as a human, in my own flesh, but I was destroyed in that form by a white charlatan and a treacherous red man from the plains. That is the personal score I have to settle. I will find the white man called Erskine, and the red man called Singing Rock, and I will destroy them both."

The figure's body creaked again and it raised one of its arms.

"I am the Guardian of the Ring which holds back those demons which are in no human shape. I am the Messenger of the Great Old One, the Chosen of Sado-gowah. I am the Keeper of the Elder Seal, and the worker of wonders unknown in future times. My name is Quamis, known to the Wampanoag as Misquamacus. I have arrived for the day of the dark stars."

The wooden man raised both arms and stretched out

for Neil's throat. Neil, with a high-pitched whine of fear, ducked sideways, and simultaneously struck at his match. It flared up, and caught at the crumpled sheet.

In the sudden leaping light of orange flames, Neil glimpsed a wooden face that was contorted with anger. Fierce eyes glistened above a hooked Indian nose and a mouth drawn back on wooden teeth. It was Misquamacus, the same face he had seen in Billy Ritchie's photographs, only this time it was vengeful and twisted with rage.

The sheet flared up even more violently, burning Neil's hand. With a sweep of his arm, he threw the fiery cloth over the wooden man's head, so that the figure was enveloped in flames. Then he pushed his way toward the door, and struggled to open it.

"Susan!" he yelled. "Susan! Open this door! It's jammed! Susan!"

He frantically looked behind him. The wooden figure of Misquamacus was standing beside Toby's bed, and already its head and shoulders were starting to blaze. There was a rank odor of burned cotton and wood.

"Susan!" he shouted, rattling the door knob. "Susan, for God's sake!"

He thought for a terrible moment that Toby might have done something to Susan, might even have killed her, but then he heard her calling, "I'm here! I called the police!"

"Push the door!" called Neil. "I can't get out of here! Push the door!"

He turned around again, and to his terror, the fiery figure of Misquamacus was walking slowly toward him, arms outstretched to seize him. There were flames rippling up from the wonder-worker's chest, and his head

110

was a mass of fire, but he kept coming, and Neil could feel the heat from his burning body.

"You are as weak as the grass against me," said the blazing lips. "I shall devour you if you try to cross me, and I shall offer you up to the most terrible of my gods."

"*Susan!*" Neil screamed. He shook and tugged at the door, but it still wouldn't budge.

"The door is fastened by my will alone," said Misquamacus. "You will never open it in a hundred moons."

The room was filling with blinding, choking smoke. Through its billows, impossibly tall and shuddering with flame, the wooden figure stalked nearer, until Neil had to abandon the door and scramble toward the window. He glanced quickly out through the broken pane. It was a long drop onto hard ground, and even if he didn't break his neck, he'd probably wind up with a couple of fractured legs.

He turned back toward the medicine man. The breeze from the window was feeding the flames, and the wooden body burned with a soft, sinister, roaring sound.

"I have you now, white man," whispered the charring mouth. "I have you now." Beside him, the linen cover of Toby's bedroom chair began to smolder and burn, and one of the drapes caught afire.

Neil raised his arm to protect his face from the heat. The fiery fingers clawed closer, and one of them seized his sleeve, viciously strong and searingly hot. He kicked out against the wooden figure, but it slammed him against the window frame, and he heard his back crack. All he seemed to be able to see was fire, and the grotesque outline of a face wrought in blazing charcoal.

111

Suddenly, the flames burst out higher. The bedroom door was open, and even more oxygen was nourishing the wooden figure's fire. Neil wrenched his arm free and dropped to his knees, scorched and agonized.

The next thing he knew there was a strange series of sounds. They were slow and ghostly, and they sounded like the surf on the ocean shelf, like something being played in slow motion. Above him, the wooden figure faltered, turned, and then abruptly began to burst into thousands of shattering, whirling fragments of blazing ashes.

The fire exploded over Neil as he lay crouched on the floor, raining all around him. His neck and his hands were prickled with cinders. But then there was nothing but burned-out chunks of blackened walnut, and a fine dusting of gray ash. Neil blinked, and slowly raised his head.

For a fraction of a second, he thought he saw the outline of a man's feet, and the hem of a pale-colored coat. He thought he saw a hand move, the way a hand moves when a gun goes back to its holster. But then there was nothing but the landing, and Susan, pale-faced and frightened, under the harsh light from the lamp on the ceiling.

She came into the room and helped him up. He brushed ash and burned wood from his shirt and coughed. His hands and his forearm were blistered, and his hair was singed, but apart from that he was unhurt.

"Neil," Susan wept. "Oh, Neil."

He held her close. He was trembling, and he felt shocked, but he had the feeling that he had been saved by some kind of spiritual intervention, that a ghostly force had recognized his danger and come to save him. It gave him, for the first time since Toby had started having nightmares, a feeling of strength and confidence. He gently stroked Susan's hair and said, "Don't cry. I think we're going to make it. I think we're going to be all right."

She looked up at him, her face smudged with tears.

"But what did you *do* in here?" she asked him. "Why is everything burned?"

He stared at her. It occurred to him, with a feeling of awful coldness, that she still didn't believe what was going on. She hadn't seen the wooden figure, after all. She had heard nothing but noises. Now, he was standing amid cinders and ashes, with no way to prove what he had seen or heard.

He said, slowly, "The wooden man was here. That's all that's left of him."

"The wooden man?" she frowned. "Neil, I—"

He pointed savagely toward the wardrobe. "The wooden man was here and he talked to me. He told me who he was, and he told me what was happening, and everything that old-timer told me up in Calistoga was right. The Indian medicine men are being reborn, in the bodies of our children, and they're going to kill as many white men as they possibly can."

"Neil, stop it! Neil, *please*, it's just your imagination!"

"What about the way Toby spoke downstairs? You think that's imagination?"

Susan held him tight. "Toby's just unsettled, that's all. He sees you behaving like this, and it scares him. He says things because he's sensitive, because he doesn't understand what's happening."

"He says things because he's possessed by a Red Indian magician!" shouted Neil. "He says things because Misquamacus makes him!"

"Oh, yes?" said a voice. "And who's Misquamacus?"

Neil looked up. On the landing, in his neatly laundered police uniform, stood Officer Turnbull. He was a lean, punctilious cop with a blue chin and a sharply pointed nose, and Neil had never particularly liked him. He stepped into the room and surveyed the ashes and the burned furnishings with professional detachment.

Neil let Susan go, and stood watching Officer Turnbull poke around without speaking. After a while, Officer Turnbull gave him a dry smile, and said, "You didn't answer my question yet."

"I was speaking metaphorically," mumbled Neil. "It wasn't intended to be taken as the literal truth."

Officer Turnbull eyed him for a few seconds. Then he said, "I see. And what's the literal truth of what happened here? You decide to have a cookin instead of a cookout?"

Neil wiped soot from his face. "I was just breaking up that old wardrobe," he said. "I guess I had an accident with the matches."

Officer Turnbull sniffed. "Pretty disastrous accident, I'd say. You sure you weren't bent on burning the place down?"

"Why the hell would I do that? I had an accident. I told you."

"Well," said Officer Turnbull, "some folks who find themselves short of cash think they can make a little extra from torching their houses. It's the insurance money, you understand?"

Neil looked at him, disgusted. "Get out of here," he said sharply.

"I'll go when I know what happened," Officer Turnbull told him. "What was that you just said about Misky-something?"

114

"It's a pet name," said Neil. "It's something we call Toby. Now, will you please get out of here and give me the chance to clean the place up?"

Officer Turnbull took out his pen and studiously wrote in his police notebook. Then he cast his eyes around the room again, and said, "Let's make this the last fire we have in here, huh? Bodega's a nice little community, and the last thing we want is to have it looking like the South Bronx."

"Is there anything else?" asked Neil, with thinly disguised impatience.

"I reckon that's all. But I'll have to file a report."

"You can do what you like. Thanks for dropping round. It's nice to know that you can count on the cops, as long as you've done something they can understand."

Officer Turnbull tucked away his notebook, shrugged, and went downstairs. They heard the kitchen door close, and the sound of his patrol car leaving the yard. Neil sighed, and stepped over the ash and debris to the landing.

Susan said, "You didn't have to speak to him like that. He was only doing his job. You should be grateful he came."

"Yes," said Neil dully. "I suppose I should. Where's Toby?"

"He's downstairs in the kitchen. I think he's all right now. After you went into his bedroom—well, he seemed to relax. He became his normal self again."

"That was because Misquamacus left him, and took on the shape of a wooden man."

Susan didn't answer that. She said, "Let's go downstairs. Maybe I should bathe those blisters. Those hands are going to be sore in the morning."

Neil leaned against the wall. He felt suddenly exhausted, and his eyes hurt. It seemed almost too much to fight this frightening thing on his own. If only Susan believed him. If only one person believed him, apart from old Billy Ritchie.

He said, "I'm okay. I guess my arm could use a little ointment, but everything else is all right. Could you make me some coffee?"

She kissed his cheek solicitously. "Sure. Whatever you want. You just rest up tonight, and in the morning you'll feel fine."

He took her hand. "Susan," he said, looking at her steadily. "Susan, I'm not going nuts. I saw that wooden man up there as close as I'm standing here now."

She gave him a quick, noncommittal smile. "Yes, honey. I know. There was a wooden man."

They went downstairs. Toby was back at the table, finishing his drawing, and when Neil came down he looked up at him with deep, serious eyes. Neil regarded his son for a long, silent moment, trying to see the spirit of the wonder-worker who might be lurking someplace inside him, but there didn't seem to be any sign at all.

He came up close and hunkered down beside Toby's chair. The boy gave him a cautious grin, and said, "What's the matter, Daddy? Is everything okay?"

"Sure," nodded Neil. "We just had a little accident with matches, that's all. You should learn something from it. Don't play with fire."

"Yes, sir," said Toby, politely.

For some reason, Toby's manner seemed to discourage any further conversation, and Neil couldn't think what else to say. He glanced at Toby's drawing, and asked, "How's it going? You finished it yet?"

"Sure."

"Can I see it?"

116

Toby nodded. "If you want."

The boy took his crooked arm away from the paper, and Neil took it off the table and examined it. It was almost an abstract, colored mainly in blues and grays and dull greens. There seemed to be clouds, with twisting tentacles writhing in between them, and a suggestion of a face that wasn't truly a face at all. It was crude, and drawn with Toby's usual heavy-handedness, but there was something strangely subtle and disturbing about it as well.

"What is it?" asked Neil.

Toby gave a quick shrug. "I don't know, sir. It isn't a person."

Neil ran his fingers lightly over the waxed surface of the drawing. In the back of his mind, he heard that strange, distant voice again, the voice of the wooden man. "*I am the Guardian of the Ring which holds back those demons which are in no human shape.*"

He ruffled Toby's hair, and laid the drawing back on the table. From across the kitchen, Susan was eyeing him closely.

"It's a nice picture," said Neil, for want of anything else to say. "It looks like some kind of octopus."

Susan said, "Your coffee's almost ready."

Late that night, when Susan and Toby had gone to bed, Neil went silently downstairs and into the den. He sat at his desk in the darkness, and moved the telephone toward him. He looked at the dial for a while, as if he were thinking, and then he picked up the receiver and called information.

It took him a half-hour to locate the number he wanted. It was a Manhattan number, from an address

117

on Tenth Avenue. He checked his watch. It was almost three o'clock in the morning in New York, but he knew that he wouldn't be able to wait any longer. He had to know now, before another day dawned, before the spirits gained even more time and even more strength.

The phone rang and rang for almost ten minutes. When there was no reply, he put down the receiver, dialed the number again, and let it ring some more.

Eventually, he heard the phone at the other end being picked up. A nasal, sleep-worn voice said, "Yes? Who the hell's this?"

Neil coughed. I'm sorry to wake you. I wouldn't have called at all, but it's desperately urgent."

"What's happening? Is the world coming to an imminent end?"

"Something almost as bad," said Neil.

"Don't tell me. They're banning hot dogs because they give you bowlegs."

"Mr. Erskine," said Neil, and he felt himself unexpectedly close to tears, "I'm calling you because there's nobody else."

"Well," answered the voice, "if it's *that* critical, you'd better tell me what you want."

"This isn't a joke, Mr. Erskine. I'm calling because of Misquamacus."

There was silence. To begin with, Neil wondered if Mr. Erskine had put the phone down. But he could still hear the singing noise of the transcontinental telephone cables. The silence lasted almost half a minute. Then Mr. Erskine queried softly, "*Misquamacus*? What about Misquamacus? Where did you ever hear about Misquamacus?"

"Mr. Erskine, I have *met* Misquamacus. Or a form

118

that Misquamacus took. He came this evening, and it was only luck that I wasn't killed."

Again, there was silence.

"Are you there?" asked Neil.

"Sure I'm here," said Mr. Erskine. "I'm just thinking, that's all. I'm thinking that I'm hoping that you're not telling me the truth, only I know that you are because nobody knows about Misquamacus except for the people who helped me get rid of him."

"Then it's true?" said Neil. "What Misquamacus said about you was actually true?"

"You say you've seen him," Mr. Erskine retorted. "What do you think?"

Almost swamped with relief, Neil said, "It's true. It must be true. My God, the whole damned thing is true."

"That's what makes it so frightening," Mr. Erskine pointed out. "Did you say you saw him?"

"Only a form that he took. The form of a wooden man. And he's been speaking through my son, Toby, who's eight. He says that he's coming back to take revenge on the white men. His spirit—his manitou—is going to take possession of Toby and get reborn."

"Almost the same as it happened before," said Mr. Erskine soberly. "Listen—will you hold on to the phone while I fix myself a seltzer?"

"Sure," said Neil, and waited. After a few moments, the phone was picked up again, and Mr. Erskine said, "Do you know what he's trying to do? Has he given you any kind of idea?"

Neil answered, "Not very clearly. It's something to do with the day of the dark stars, which is a day when twenty-two of the most powerful medicine men from all ages in history and all different tribes are supposed to

119

get themselves reborn and call down some of the Indian gods. It's the day when they're supposed to kill one white man for every Indian who ever died at white hands."

"That sounds about Misquamacus's style," put in Mr. Erskine. "Did you say two of the most powerful medicine men?"

"No, no—*twenty*-two."

"Twenty-two? You've got to be kidding."

"That's the legend. And that's what Misquamacus told me."

There was more silence. Then Mr. Erskine said, "Listen, fellow, I've got to talk to someone about this. Why don't you leave me your number, and your name, and I'll call you back."

"Sure," said Neil. "My name's Neil Fenner, and I live in Bodega out in northern California. Not far from Sonoma, you know? My number's 3467."

"I got that," Mr. Erskine told him. "Give me a couple of hours, and I promise I'll come back to you."

"Mr. Erskine—"

"Call me Harry, will you? We haven't met yet, and we don't know who the hell each other is, but if you're talking seriously about Misquamacus, then I think we'd better get ourselves on first-name terms."

"Okay, Harry, that's fine. But what I wanted to say was that Misquamacus told me he had some kind of personal score to settle."

"A personal score?"

"That's right. With you, and with some Indian called Singing Rock. He said that you'd destroyed him when he tried to get himself reborn some time before, and that he was going to fix you for it."

Harry Erskine sounded uncomfortable. "I see," he

said quietly. "Well, I guess that figures. Misquamacus is the revenge of a whole nation, all wrapped up into one. If he says he's going to kill us all, then by God, Neil, he means it."

FIVE

At school that day, Mrs. Novato noticed that her class was curiously quiet and diffident. They went through their morning's lessons without any fidgeting or misbehaving, and filed out for their lunch break in an orderly way. She sat at her desk, watching them through the window, wondering what it was about them that disturbed her so much.

It was only when she saw them gathered at the far end of the school yard, talking solemnly among themselves, that she realized what it was. None of them had laughed all day. None of them had smiled.

She got up from her seat and walked to the window, eating an apple. She hoped they weren't catching anything. It was the class outing to Lake Berryessa on Monday, and she didn't want to have it spoiled by colds or flu.

She was curious to see what the children were doing. Normally, they ran around the yard, playing tag or ball. But today they were standing in a circle, all by themselves, and they had linked arms. They were circling around and around, their feet shuffling as if they were dancing. She had never seen children do anything like that before, and she found it strangely upsetting.

A gray cloud crossed the sun, and the school yard went dull. But the children continued to shuffle and sway, and she was sure she could hear them singing.

At that moment, Mr. Saperstein, the visiting music teacher, came in through the school porch and waved a hand to Mrs. Novato in greeting. He was wearing his frayed Panama hat and his frayed linen suit, and he had a camera slung over one shoulder and a flute case over the other.

"Hello, Mrs. Novato. How are you getting along? Doesn't the weather get worse every year? It's the Russians and their magnetic fields. We should tell them to stop or pay the price."

Mrs. Novato was frowning as she stared at the children, and she didn't answer. Out in the hall, Mr. Saperstein paused, and then came into her classroom and said, "What's so fascinating? I could have walked in naked."

Mrs. Novato looked at him quickly and smiled. "Oh, I'm sorry. I was just fascinated by what my class is doing."

Mr. Saperstein raised his spectacles and squinted out into the dull sunlight.

"They're dancing, aren't they?" he said. "What's so strange about that?"

"It might not have been strange in the days of square dances and folk festivals," said Mrs. Novato, "but these children have never danced like that before in their whole lives. They don't know how."

Mr. Saperstein shrugged. "They obviously do, or they wouldn't be doing it. It's interesting, though. It

124

looks like a Greek folk dance. The way they're all holding on to each other's shoulders and jogging around like that."

He took his camera off his shoulder, made some fussy adjustments for the distance and the light, and then took three pictures of the children as they hopped and danced around.

"I have some reference books on folk dancing at home," he said. "When I have these developed, I'll see if that dance looks anything like one of the old-time Greek or Mexican dances. Maybe the children inherited some kind of folk memory. You never know."

Mrs. Novato nodded absentmindedly. "Thank you, Mr. Saperstein. I'd be interested to find out."

The dance broke up almost as quickly as it had begun, and for a while, the children wandered around the school yard, talking quietly or playing games. Today, they kept apart from children from other classes, and if a teacher appeared in the yard, they seemed to turn away and shun her.

Over by the wall of the kindergarten annex, under the shade of a maple, Toby was talking to his best friend, Linus Hopland, while Andy Beaver and Ben Nichelini were squatting beside them drawing patterns in the dust with pointed sticks.

"My daddy almost burned the house down last night," said Toby. "He was trying to break up this old wardrobe in my room, and he burned it right on the rug. You should have seen my room."

"Is your old man crazy?" asked Linus, scratching his bright red hair.

"My pa says he is," put in Andy. "My pa says your pa's gone bananas. He says your pa was up at police headquarters yesterday, trying to talk George Murray into chasing after ghosts."

"I don't think my daddy's crazy," said Toby, simply. He spoke with unusual seriousness, and his eyes seemed glazed, as if he were thinking about something else altogether. "I think he's kind of nosy, that's all. He should learn to keep out of things that don't concern him."

"All parents are like that," said Debbie Spurr, coming across the yard with her yo-yo. "My mom said that if I had any more dreams, she was going to take me to see a psychiatrist. So all I do now is tell her I don't dream anymore. Parents are real dumb when you think about it."

"I think the dreams are good," said Ben Nichelini. "I had a dream about this man cutting up these women, cutting them into pieces. He cut them right open, tummies and everything, and they were still alive."

Debbie sat down beside Toby and laid her hand on his shoulder. She was pale today, and distracted, and she looked waiflike in her thin blue gingham dress. "The dreams are important," she said. "If we didn't have the dreams, we wouldn't know how important we are. We're important."

"It's the blood I like," said Andy. "Sometimes there's nothing but blood, and you know it's their blood, and not yours, and you can practically feel it, it's all sticky and warm. We were strong on the day that happened. We felt how strong we were. We knew we could kill them if we tried. I can't wait for it to happen again."

Toby said, "We mustn't speak of it. The time is close. We must join ourselves by the spell of the tree demons before we can act together. Where are the lizards?"

"Daniel and John are bringing them," said Andy.

"They were out last night collecting them, too. They've got a whole boxful."

Toby looked up at the school clock. "They must hurry. We don't have much time. I had the dream last night of the final days. I had a dream of revenge against all those who hurt me. This is long, long overdue."

Linus said, "I dreamed we fell out of the trees on their backs, and we pulled them down so that they were trampled by their horses. I dreamed we dragged a man across seven miles of bush and forest and stony ground, until his body was raw meat and he was screaming to die. The elder ones can do better, though."

Andy put in, "What did you think of Mrs. Novato this morning? he looked pretty upset to me."

"She sure did," agreed Debbie. "Anybody would have thought we weren't behaving ourselves or something. And she's been staring out of that window for the whole recess."

"She's okay," said Ben. "At least she told Toby's dad where to get off."

"She didn't so," argued Toby. "She said we were okay, that's all. She said the dreams didn't mean anything."

Through the stirred-up dust of playtime, Daniel Soscol and John Coretta came across the yard, carefully carrying a large brown cardboard box. They looked from right to left to make sure they weren't being watched by the teacher in charge, and then they came up to the annex and laid the box down beside the trunk of the maple.

"How many did you get?" asked Toby. His voice was serious again. His childishness seemed to ebb and flow, like someone trying to shout a message across a windy strait. He stood up and watched Daniel take the lid off the box. Inside, clawing and climbing all over each other, were lizards from the roadside and the rocks.

"I got the ten, like you wanted," said Daniel.

Toby poked the lizards with his finger. "Good. You'd better get everybody together."

Daniel and John walked off, and went around the playground assembling all the children from Mrs. Novato's class. They gradually gathered in the corner by the annex, out of sight of the main schoolhouse, and Toby stood up on a root of the maple tree so that he could talk to them.

The children stood quite silent, as if they were dazed. They ignored the stares of children from other classes, and the noise of cops and robbers and tag.

Toby said, "This is the ritual of joining ourselves by the spirits of the tree demons, as it was ordained by the gods of the desert lands and the plains. It joins together the brothers from the hills and the forests and the brothers from the waste places. It binds them so that they can work their wonders together, so that their powers are one. We have little time, so let us begin it now."

The children stood in two parallel lines, eleven children on each line. Daniel Soscol brought the cardboard box, and Toby took out the first lizard. He held it up by its tail, writhing and jerking, while the first four children drew closer together.

Toby whispered, "Ossadagowah, son of Sadogowah, we bow ourselves before you. We call upon your powers, feared of elder times, in the days before the white man touched the sacred lands, and we call upon you Nashuna, and you Pa-la-kai, and upon the demons of the lakes and the forests and the crawling beasts upon the earth. We call upon those from beyond the darkest

128

stars, those who have no human shape, and we beg their aid."

Each of the first four children, Toby and Daniel and Debbie and Petra, took a wriggling leg of the lizard between their lips. Then, at a slight nod from Toby, they each bit into their leg, and the lizard's limbless body dropped to the dust.

Then Debbie and Petra turned around to the next two children, Andy and John. Toby brought another lizard out of the box and held it dangling between them while he spoke the words of the incantation again. Again, the four children brought their faces together and took one of the reptile's legs in their mouths. Again, they bit, with a slight crunching sound, and the lizard's body dropped to the yard.

Andy and John, in their turn, faced the two children behind them, and Toby produced yet another lizard. The ritual was repeated ten times, all the way down the line, until the school yard was littered with the writhing bloody bodies of ten lizards. Daniel Soscol, his face serious, collected them, and put them back in the cardboard box.

Toby continued, "We are joined by the strength of the demons of the trees, and nothing can set us apart. The day is almost here. Let us be heard by the gods of elder times, from beyond the rings which guard the entrances of time and distance. Let us seek their power in taking our revenge."

From the classroom window, Mrs. Novato could see the children gathered around Toby, listening to what he was saying with intent faces. She watched them for a while, and then she went across the porch into the next classroom, where Miss Martinez was chalking up the names of trees in preparation for her next lesson.

129

Mrs. Novato said, "Joan—look out of the window for a moment. Over there, by the annex."

Miss Martinez put down her chalk and walked to the window. She said, "What am I supposed to be looking at?"

"My children. Look at them. What do you think they could be doing?"

"I don't know," shrugged Miss Martinez. "Playing, perhaps?"

"Yes, but playing what? They all look so serious. And you never find the whole class playing together like that, not usually."

Miss Martinez looked for a few moments more, and then went back to her blackboard. "Don't ask me," she told Mrs. Novato. "Children are always plotting something or other."

That afternoon, out on the wharf at Bodega Bay, while Neil was putting the finishing touches to the brasswork on the *White Dove*, Dave Conway came out from the fish market and called him.

"Neil—there's a long-distance call. Sounds like someone called aspirin."

"Thanks," said Neil, and climbed onto the jetty. He walked quickly under a sky that was hazy but cloudless, and he wiped the sweat from his face with the back of his hand.

Inside the fish market, there was a sweet, salty smell of crabs and flounders and bass, and the telephone was sticky with scales. He picked it up and said, "Yes?"

"Neil Fenner? This is Harry Erskine. Listen, I have some news for you."

"News? What kind of news?"

"Bad news, mainly. I talked this morning to John

130

Singing Rock out in South Dakota. He's a medicine man, you know? But a modern one. I mean, he knows all the old spells but he tries to apply them in an up-to-date way."

"What did he say?"

"He said that he'd heard of the day of the dark stars, and he was sure that what you told me was genuine."

Neil switched the receiver from one ear to the other. "Is that all? He's sure I'm genuine? Listen, I wouldn't have *called* you if I hadn't been genuine. I wouldn't have known your name, even. There was no way I practically got myself killed because of an overworked imagination."

"You sure didn't," said Harry. He sounded as if he were sucking cough drops. "The day of the dark stars is supposed to be mentioned in stories that were handed down by tribes from all over America. Most Indians have heard of it, apparently—either from their parents or their grandparents, but there aren't many Indians to-day who can remember what it's all supposed to signify. They've gotten themselves too integrated, you know? Even Singing Rock sells insurance on the side."

"Did he say what I could do about it? The trouble I have here is that nobody believes me, not even my wife. Nobody else saw the wooden man but me, and they're putting the children's nightmares down to hysteria, or indigestion. Everybody thinks I'm going crazy."

"You're not. Singing Rock says that the Hopi have stories about the day of the dark stars, and so do the Oglala Sioux and the Modoc and the Cheyenne and the Wyandotte. The Paiute used to call it *the day when the mouth would come out of the sky and devour the white devils*, but they always were kind of wordy."

"So what can I do?" asked Neil. "Can I exorcise these manitous, or what?"

"Not with a bell and a book and a candle. I learned from the last time I met Misquamacus that you can't dismiss Red Indian demons with white man's religion."

"But how did you destroy Misquamacus before?"

"It's pretty hard to explain. But Singing Rock says we just don't have the same kind of situation here at all, and he doesn't think we could manage a repeat performance. Last time, Misquamacus was weak and confused and on his own. This time, it sounds as if he's strong, and on his own territory."

"You don't sound very optimistic, Harry."

"I'm supposed to sound optimistic? You call me up and tell me twenty-two Indian spirits are after my blood, and I'm supposed to sound optimistic?"

"I'm sorry," Neil put in hastily. "What I meant was, it sounds like we don't have an easy way out of this."

"Listen," said Harry, "I'm going to fly out to San Francisco on Sunday morning, which is the earliest I can get away. Singing Rock is coming out from South Dakota, and he says he should get to California by Monday morning at the latest."

"You're actually coming out to help? Well, that's terrific."

"Neil," said Harry, "we're coming out because we faced Misquamacus before. If we hadn't, we would have put you down as a crank, just like everyone else has. But the last time we faced him we came about as close to the happy hunting grounds as I ever want to get, and I don't want that to happen again. This time, I want to face him forewarned and forearmed, and I want to make sure that he doesn't have a chance to conjure up any of those demons that jump out at you and bite your head off."

"Are you joking?"

"Do I sound as if I'm joking?"

Neil stepped aside to let a fishmonger pass with a barrow of fresh blue-green lobsters.

"No," he said. "You don't sound as though you're joking at all."

"Okay," replied Harry. "Now, this is what Singing Rock wants you to do. He wants you to keep a close watch on your son, and he wants you to make sure that he doesn't go off on his own this weekend. Do whatever you have to do—take him bowling, or swimming, or whatever it is you people do out at Bodega Bay. Just don't let him out of your sight. And one more thing. Make sure that he doesn't get together with any of his classmates from school. If you can go, get him out of school right now—so much the better. Singing Rock says that before the twenty-two wonder-workers can emerge, they have to go through some kind of performance with lizards or something, and they have to do it all together."

"Lizards?" frowned Neil.

"Don't ask me," said Harry. "I know as much about Indian magic as I do about dancing the Highland fling. Apparently, the medicine men do something repulsive with lizards."

"Okay," said Neil. "I'll do what I can."

"There's something else," Harry put in. "If you think that Misquamacus is really starting to get a grip on your son—if your son starts talking like Misquamacus and looking as though his face is changing—then call me right away. If it gets really bad, then get the hell out of there."

133

"But what about Toby? If it does get bad, what's going to happen to him?"

"It's pretty hard to say. He might have a chance of survival. But if you and your wife stay around too long, you're going to find yourselves in much worse danger than he."

"What kind of danger? What are you talking about? What do I have to look for?"

"You don't have to look for anything," said Harry dryly. "Whatever it is, it's going to come looking for you."

He met Doughty on the jetty. The old man was sitting on the front bumper of Neil's pickup, smoking his pipe. Neil said hi.

Doughty stood up. He questioned, "Did you hear the news?"

Neil shook his head. "What news?"

"Billy Ritchie died this morning. I thought you might have heard."

Neil felt cold with shock. "He *died*? How did it happen? He looked fit enough to me, apart from his legs."

"His house was burned out," said Doughty. "His neighbor said it was a freak stroke of lightning, sent the whole place up like a bonfire."

"Lightning? We haven't had an electric storm for weeks."

"I know. But that's what the neighbor said. The whole place was sent up like a bonfire. Poor old Billy, not having the use of his legs, was trapped in his living room. Burned to death, black cat and all."

Neil swallowed, and his throat was as dry as a nylon rug. The day seemed suddenly hot and oppressive, and the clank and clatter of boats' rigging was like the tolling of toneless, funereal handbells.

Neil admitted, "I saw him only yesterday. I was talking to him, as close as we're standing now."

Doughty looked away, and puffed a couple of times at his pipe.

Neil said, "Did you find out anything else about it? Or was that all?"

Doughty turned around, and eyed him up and down. "All? What more do you want? You know what they've always said in Napa County. Where there's a Fenner, there's a bad wind blowing."

"What kind of a saying is that?"

Doughty shrugged. "I'm not sure I know. But I guess it's one of those sayings that's based on experience."

Neil stared at the blue-gray Pacific for a while, at the wavelets which lapped at the fishing boats and pleasure cruisers tied up at the jetty. Then he said, "Billy Ritchie talked about the old days, about the times when Bloody Fenner was still alive, and about the Indian massacres. He told me all about Ossadagowah, and some of the other Indian demons."

Doughty took the stem of his pipe out of his mouth and spat a distance of ten feet into the water. "So what are you saying?" he asked. "You think he talked too much, and some of them Indian demons set ablaze to his house?"

Neil looked at him sharply. "It's nothing to joke about, Doughty. Those demons are dangerous, just as much today as they were in the old days."

"Neil," growled Doughty, in his old sea-dog voice, "you're letting yourself get out of hand."

"You think so? What if I tell you I saw a ghost with my own eyes right out there on the bay? What if I tell you that one of the most powerful Red Indian medicine men who ever lived came alive in my house last night?"

Doughty thought about it, and then reached out and held Neil's arm. "I know what you must be feeling, Neil. I know you've been working hard. Maybe you're feeling even worse now, because of poor Billy going up in smoke. But you're not going to make anything better if you keep on letting these ghoulies and ghosties scare you so much."

Neil frowned. "Have you been talking to Susan?"

Doughty kept his eyes steady for a moment, then looked away.

"When did she come down here?" asked Neil.

Doughty shrugged. "Yesterday afternoon, while you was up in Calistoga."

"And what did she say? That I was crazy?"

"Not at all," insisted Doughty. "She said she was worried about you, that's all, and she asked if you'd been working too hard on them boats. I told her no, you seemed fine to me. But she was still worried about some of the things you'd been saying, and some of the things you'd been thinking. She said you were acting like a man with something on his mind. She's been thinking of getting you down to a shrink, I can tell you."

Neil rubbed his face with the flat of his hand. "Do *you* think she's right?" he asked Doughty. "Do *you* think I need analysis, too? Do *you* think I'm a head case?"

Doughty didn't answer.

Neil said, "Well? Am I sane or insane? Am I dreaming or am I awake? Why don't you tell me the way you feel?"

Doughty said uncomfortably, "It's not for me to say, Neil."

"But what the hell do you think's going on here? Toby starts seeing ghosts in long white duster coats, the kids in his class start having nightmares about Indian massacres, and now Billy Ritchie gets himself killed in a freak fire, the day after he told me about redskin demons. None of this is normal, Doughty, but it's happening for real, and it's no use this town pretending it doesn't exist."

"Neil—" began Doughty. Then he changed his mind and shook his head.

"What were you going to say?"

"Oh, dammit, Neil, you've got to realize you're fighting yourself an uphill battle. Everybody's thinking you've lost your marbles. Don't you think you'd be better off forgetting the whole business?"

Neil turned away in exasperation. But then, in a low, intent voice, he told Doughty, "Listen—if I was like you, if I tried to pretend that nothing was happening, then this town would suffer the worst tragedy it's ever known. It's coming, Doughty, I warn you. It's coming soon. I didn't want to believe it myself, and even now I wish I'd never gotten myself mixed up in it. But it's happening because of Bloody Fenner, my ancestor, and I don't have any choice. If I don't fight back, then you and me and Susan and Toby and thousands of people are going to die, and that's all I know."

"Neil—"

"That's it, Doughty. No more advice. No more nothing. From now on, anybody who doesn't believe me is against me, and that's the way it has to be."

He left Doughty sitting on the pickup's bumper, and

went down to the *White Dove* to collect his metal polish and cleaning rags.

In the middle of the night, with bluish moonlight irradiating the room, he woke up suddenly and lay silent, listening to Susan breathing beside him and Toby softly snoring in the cot across by the door. He must have stayed like that, unmoving and watchful, for almost ten minutes, for the brilliant edge of the moon slowly appeared in the corner of the window, and the light grew brighter and brighter.

A voice whispered, *"Neil."*

He raised his head. There was nobody there. The moon glistened on the rails of the wide brass bed, and on the handles of the painted pine bureau, but even in the shadows behind the closet and in the alcove by the door, there were no apparitions, no ghosts in long white coats or clad in shiny wood.

The voice repeated, *"Neil."*

He looked all around the room, straining his eyes, his heart beating quickly and irregularly. It was as still and silent as when he had first awakened.

"Where are you?" he whispered.

There was a pause, and then the voice said, *"Beside you."*

He jerked his head around. Next to him, Susan was fast asleep, her blond hair spread on the pillow, her lips slightly parted.

"Where?" he asked. "I don't see you."

Susan's lips moved almost imperceptibly, and a man's voice spoke out of her throat. *"Here. Beside you. I can't show myself because of Quamis."*

"Is Quamis here?"

"You bet. He's inside your son. He's like a moth in-

side of a chrysalis, and it won't be long before he bursts out of there and spreads his wings."

Neil breathed, "Who are you? What's your name?"

"You've seen me before. The name's Dunbar. I was out of Sacramento in '31. I thought you was Allen at first, you looked so similar. The spitting image of Allen."

"It was you in the beard and the long white duster?"

"That's right. In those days, there was me and nineteen others, and our wives, and all of our children. The Wappos took us by surprise up by Las Posadas, and killed us all. Allen was the scout on that trip, and went for help."

Neil stared at Susan. She seemed to be more than asleep. Her breathing was slow and shallow, as if she was in a coma. The voice continued, *"Allen went for help, but he didn't get back in time. He said he was going to go for the Mexican camp down in the valley, make his way back up the creek. But he never came back. They cut us all down, the Wappos, women and children too, and I saw my dear little Margie with an arrow clean through her face."*

"Why are you here?" asked Neil. "What do you want from me?"

The voice sighed. *"I'm here because I'm here. It's not for any reason. It's dark out here on the outside, Neil, and time doesn't mean what it does to you. All times are the same time. It's '31 still, Neil, and the Wappos are still cutting us down, and always will. We're still waiting for Allen to help us. We're still dying, Neil."*

The voice began to falter, and grow faint. Neil said, "Dunbar—don't go. Dunbar!"

"I'm here, Neil."

"Dunbar, what do you know of Quamis?"

139

There was a longer pause. Then Susan breathed, "*Quamis is everywhere. Always has been and always will be. The Indians told us he never died and never would. Maybe that was part story, but then maybe it was part truth, too. You could hear about Quamis from the woods of Massachusetts clear across to Denver, Colorado, and even beyond that. They said he lived in the wind that blew through the Georgia pines, and in the grass of the plains east of the Platte River. A great wonder-worker, they used to say, and still do.*"

Dumbar's last words were so faint in Susan's mouth that Neil could hardly hear them. He had to bend his ear close to her lips so that he might distinguish any syllables at all amid the hoarse breathing that came from her somnolent larynx, and he was sure that there was more, but it was inaudible. He thought he heard the word *assistance*, but he couldn't be sure. It may have been nothing more than a sibilant whisper.

He sat up. The moon was now fully visible, and the light in the bedroom was almost unnaturally bright. He felt strangely calmed by Dunbar's visitation, as if he had been reassured that he wasn't alone in his fight against Misquamacus. Perhaps it was Dunbar who had destroyed the blazing wooden image last night. After all, he remembered seeing the faintest hint of a white coat, and a hand holstering a gun.

He reached down the bed and adjusted the patchwork quilt so that it covered Susan's bare feet. Then he glanced across at Toby to make sure that he was still asleep. Toby was less restless since they had moved him into their own bedroom, but he still mumbled as he slept, and had bouts of fierce tossing and turning.

Neil stiffened. Toby was sitting up in bed and was staring at him. His small face was white, white as the silvered light from the moon, and his eyes were intense and glittering. He wasn't smiling. He wasn't frowning. His expression was calm and controlled, and because of that, it was even more frightening. Eight-year-old boys grin, or cry, or show some feeling, thought Neil. Why is Toby just staring at me like that?

"Toby," he said in a hesitant whisper.

Toby continued to stare.

"Toby, are you okay?"

Toby's eyes sparkled with malevolence. His features seemed to shift and change in the moonlight, one layer of features superimposing another, until he looked liked someone else altogether. Someone older, someone infinitely older, and someone infinitely more evil.

"Toby," insisted Neil.

Toby rose slowly from the bed, and seemed to glide toward him. He stood only a few feet away, and then he spoke in the voice of Misquamacus, in that hollow distant voice that sounded as if it was inside Neil's own head, and yet which echoed with countless miles and eons of ancient time.

"You have spoken to the white magician Erskine," said Misquamacus.

Neil edged one foot out of bed, and then swung his leg to the floor. His muscles were tensed, and he was ready to make a dive for Toby and bring him down. He didn't have any idea what Misquamacus might try to do, or even how powerful he was, but he wanted to be ready for a fight.

Misquamacus said, "It is good that you have spoken. He will come, along with my treacherous blood brother, Singing Rock, and I shall show them that my manitou is indestructible, and that my vengeance spans fifty thousand moons."

Neil said steadily, "You must let Toby go. I want you to get out of my son."

Toby smiled, a slow, laconic smile. "You are power-less to prevent me from lodging here. I shall remain un-til I am ready. I am here at the direction of my white spirit guide, your ancestor, and because I am here by consent, no magic in the world can move me."

"I'm going to take Toby away from here," said Neil. "I'm going to take him to Europe. Anywhere. Just so long as he's out of your reach."

Toby shook his head, still smiling. "You cannot take the boy. If you attempt to interfere in the day of the dark stars, you will surely die more painfully than any other white man."

Neil climbed out of bed, and stood over his son, feel-ing cold and frightened, but deeply determined. If Harry Erskine and John Singing Rock had destroyed Misquamacus once, then somehow they must be able to do it again. He said, "I'm warning you, get out of my son. If you don't leave him now, I promise you I'll tear you to pieces."

Toby half-turned his head toward the bed where Su-san lay sleeping. He regarded her for a while, and then he raised one arm and pointed to her. Very softly, he incanted, "Spirit of snake, spirit of storm, spirit of cloud, obey me."

Abruptly, with a deafening crash, the bedroom win-dows imploded, spraying stars of glass all over the room. A shrieking wind blew into the room, a wind as bitterly cold as dry ice, and Neil was knocked sideways, so that he stumbled against his bedside table and jarred his shoulder on the edge of his wardrobe.

Toby remained still, unmoved by the gale, and pointed again at the bed. In front of Neil's horrified

142

eyes, the bed sheet rose and twisted like a rope, and entwined itself around Susan's body. Over the storm, he heard her scream, and then shriek "Neil! Neil!" and he could see her struggling against the bedclothes. But the dreadful wind seemed to have drained away all of his energy, and the distance from the wall to the bed had become miles instead of feet.

Raising his arm to protect his eyes, Neil saw Toby's face fixed in a grotesque, wolfish grin, with his lips drawn back across his teeth. There was an ear-shattering flash of lightning, followed by a rumbling vibration which lifted the whole floor, and sent Neil staggering off balance again.

Susan screamed louder, a scream of pain and total fear. In the flickering, sizzling lightning, Neil saw her arched back on the bed, her eyes wide, her hands struggling and tearing at the sheets. Then the abrasive wind was tearing at her flowery cotton nightgown, ripping it in tatters which whirled around the bedroom.

"*Susan!*" yelled Neil, and tried to claw across to the bed. But the howling gale pressed him back, and sparkling shards of glass blew up from the floor and cut at his hands and his face.

The sheets had taken on a bulky shape that pressed on Susan's body, and twisted between her bare thighs in a thick, animate rope. She was hysterical now, screaming an endless scream which pierced the storm and the wind at an almost intolerable pitch. But the sheets bound her to the bed, forcing her shoulders back against the mattress, and her legs wide apart.

Neil howled to Toby, "Toby! That's your mother! That's your mother!"

But the boy simply turned and smiled at him, and lifted his arm again toward the bed.

"Toby!" roared Neil.

The bedclothes forced themselves onto Susan in a hideous, jerking motion, like the hindquarters of a rutting dog. Neil felt himself blacking out for a moment; then he opened his eyes again, and it was still happening, it was still real. His Susan, his wife, was being raped in front of his eyes by her own sheets.

Susan shrieked. He saw crimson blood staining the linen entwined between her legs. She began to twitch and tremble as if she was suffering an epileptic fit, but the bedclothes kept up their febrile shaking. There was another blinding burst of lightning, and the shattered window frames flew into the room. Then, suddenly, there was darkness, complete and seamless darkness, and the wind died away with a shuddering whistle.

Neil lifted himself from the floor. Gradually, through the broken window, the light of the moon began to shine again, soft and white at first, but then with the same strength and clarity as it had before. He stumbled over to the bed, where Susan lay with the crumpled sheets on top of her, moaning and whispering under her breath.

He clutched her close, stroking her hair, kissing her cold forehead. He mumbled, "Susan, oh God, I'm sorry. Susan, I'm sorry."

She opened her eyes and saw it was him, and then she began to sob uncontrollably. He held her close, trying to soothe her, and he turned toward Toby, who was still standing by the end of the bed, his eyes shining with hateful amusement.

"You bastard," Neil said, between his teeth.

Toby's expression remained unmoved. "It is no worse than what the white pony soldiers did to our daughters in times gone by," he said in his distant voice. "It is far

144

more forgiving than what they did to Tall Bull at Summit Springs."

"Damn you, Susan wasn't *there* at Summit Springs. She's never met an Indian in her life, apart from the few that come down here to help in the summer. You can't punish generation after generation for what was done in the past! It's over, it's too late!"

Toby slowly shook his head. "For those Indians whose territories were stolen and whose people were killed, it will never be over. They live on the reservations now with the memory of what was done, and they will never forget."

Neil held Susan tightly against him. "Some of them have forgotten already," he retorted. "Some of them can't even remember what the day of the dark stars is supposed to be."

"That doesn't matter," replied Misquamacus. "Their life as outcasts in their own land is enough to remind them. And none of them has ever forgotten Misquamacus. The name of Misquamacus is an Indian secret that has been held close to their hearts for more than a hundred years. Now, it will be revealed to the white man, and the white man will never regret knowing an Indian secret so bitterly."

Toby's face seemed to change, and the hostile glitter in his eyes began to dwindle, like the burned-out wicks of kerosene lamps. He raised his small hands for a moment, and then he collapsed onto the floor. Neil quickly but gently laid Susan back on the bed, and crunched across the broken glass to pick him up. Toby's face was pallid, and he was breathing heavily, but Misquamacus didn't appear to have hurt him.

"Toby," whispered Neil. "Oh my God, you poor kid."

He laid the boy back in his bed, and drew the covers

up to his neck. Then he went back to Susan, who had stopped sobbing now, and was lying staring at him with a shocked, glassy look in her eyes.

"What happened?" she asked, in a haunted voice. "I don't understand what happened."

Neil looked down at the bloodstained sheets, and in a fit of rage and frustration he dragged them off the bed, and tried to rip them with his bare hands. He didn't do very well. They were pure cotton, with double hems. Finally, panting, he tossed them across the room into a corner.

Susan said shakily, "There was a man, Neil. A tall man with necklaces and feathers. He didn't have any clothes on."

Neil sat down beside her and held her. "It was nothing. It was just a nightmare."

"But he seemed so real. I could even smell him. He was covered in some kind of oil. He got on top of me, Neil. I tried to stop him. *He got on top of me.*"

"Susan," he hushed her, "nothing happened. It was nothing more than a nightmare, that's all."

Frowning, still stunned, she reached her hand down between her thighs, and then raised her fingers to her face. They were dark and sticky with blood. She looked at Neil in total horror and desperation, her eyes pleading with him to explain it, to make it safe, to say that whatever had happened was a freakish dream, and to prove it, too.

"I'm hurt," she breathed. "I'm hurt inside."

He pressed his hand to his eyes in exhaustion. "I'll get Doctor Crowder," he told her. "Just relax, honey. Stay where you are. It can't be anything too bad."

He crossed the room, glancing only briefly at Toby.

146

His son was fast asleep, breathing evenly and quietly, and the color was back in his cheeks. Neil closed the bedroom door behind him, and went downstairs as quietly as he could. He picked up the phone and dialed Doctor Crowder's number.

At the kitchen door Doctor Crowder belted up his overcoat and put on his hat. Neil handed him his worn leather bag, as old and faithful as a pet spaniel, and gave him a brief, tired smile.

"I want to thank you for coming out," Neil said. "I guess we've been keeping you awake lately."

Doctor Crowder pulled a weary, resigned face.

"Is it very serious?" asked Neil. "I mean, it's not going to spoil Susan's chances of having any more children, is it?"

Doctor Crowder shook his head. "The vaginal tissues are lacerated, that's all. It's an injury we usually associate with cases of violent rape."

"Did Susan tell you what happened?"

Doctor Crowder looked away. "She didn't seem too clear about it. She seemed to think you must have had some kind of argument."

Neil went cold. "Argument? What are you talking about? We didn't have any argument! What does she mean, argument?"

"Well, it's not for me to put words in her mouth," said Doctor Crowder, "but you must admit that the room was kind of busted up."

Neil stared at him. "Do you want to know what did that? Lightning. That's what did it."

The old doctor wouldn't meet his eyes. "I see," he said heavily.

Neil seized his shoulder. "Doctor—you don't believe me, do you?"

Doctor Crowder wouldn't answer.

Neil said, "You think I'm crazy. You think I set fire to my house last night, and tonight you think I raped my own wife. That's it, isn't it? You think I'm a head case!"

Doctor Crowder tried to pull away, but Neil took hold of both his arms and turned him around to face him.

"You think I'm going out of my mind, don't you? You see my bedroom all busted up and immediately assume I had a fight with Susan. You see blood on the sheets and you think I've assaulted her. You don't stop to think that I might actually be telling the truth, do you?"

"The truth?" asked Doctor Crowder, shakily. "What truth?"

"The truth that Toby is possessed by the greatest Red Indian medicine man who ever lived. The truth that he called down lightning to smash up the room, and a wind that you couldn't even stand up in. The truth that he had Susan's own sheets and bedclothes rape her in revenge for the way the white men used to rape Indian women."

Doctor Crowder could only stare at him. There was a long, awkward silence. The pine railroad clock on the kitchen wall ticked away the hour of three and chimed.

Eventually, the old doctor opened the kitchen door, and said, "Look out there, Neil. What do you see?"

Neil wouldn't look at first, but then he glanced sideways and saw the dark, quiet night.

"I see my own backyard," he said huskily.

148

"That's right," nodded Doctor Crowder. "And is it raining out there?"

Neil shook his head.

"Is it snowing out there? Is there thunder? Is there lightning? Is there any wind at all?"

Neil said, "It's a warm night."

"That's right," Doctor Crowder told him. "It's a warm, still night. No lightning, no wind. Not even a breeze. And you're trying to tell me that your bedroom was wrecked by an electric storm?"

"*It was magic!*" yelled Neil. "*It was done by magic!*"

Doctor Crowder looked embarrassed. But he took Neil's hand and shook it, and said, "I'll come around in the morning to see how Susan's getting along. She's sleeping now. A mild sedative. I think it might be wise if you got yourself some sleep, too. I mean that, Neil. You could have been working too hard."

Neil was about to burst out again, but then he checked himself and nodded, and said, "Okay, doctor. I'll try. I'll see you in the morning."

He closed the kitchen door after Doctor Crowder had left, and drew up one of the kitchen chairs. He sat at the table for almost ten minutes, with every nightmarish incident of the whole night whirling around in his mind. Again and again, with eerie vividness, he saw the jerking, sexual movements of Susan's sheets, and the expression of malevolent triumph on Toby's face.

After a while, he got up to make himself a cup of coffee. He saw his face reflected in the dark window, and he thought how tired and washed-out he looked. He filled the electric hot pot, and went to the cupboard to find the instant coffee.

The clock chimed the half-hour. He walked across to

the sink to set his cup on the drainboard, and then, to his horror, he realized that somebody or something was staring at him. He turned, shocked, and saw a pallid face pressed against the glass of the kitchen window.

SIX

"I hope I didn't scare you too much," Harry Erskine said.

Neil, still fidgeting, gave him an uncertain grin. "I was just feeling edgy, that's all. And I didn't expect you till the morning."

Harry stirred his coffee, and set the spoon down in the saucer. "I was through for the day, and my date came down with the chicken pox, so I took the first plane going. There was me and fifty-five rabbis, so I figured the flight just had to arrive safe."

"You rented a car at the airport?"

"It's in back of your yard. A yellow Pinto with a slipping transmission. Still, what can you expect for four dollars a day?"

Harry was a round-shouldered thirty-five-year-old with an obvious penchant for permanent-press suits and shirts that could drip dry over the tub. He could have looked quite distinguished, except that his facial features didn't seem comfortable with each other. His nose was a little too large, his eyes a little too deepset, his chin reasonably determined but too fleshy. His mouse-brown hair was thinning, and his cheeks had the permanent pallor of Tenth Avenue.

Neil said, "Do you want something to eat? I could fix some eggs."

"Unh-hunh. Leave it till the morning. You've done enough tonight without short-order cooking."

Neil sat down at the table. "You say you're a mystic?" he asked Harry. "I didn't think anyone could make a living at being a mystic."

"I don't," Harry told him. "I do free-lance work for my old advertising agency to make ends meet. But I prefer to be my own boss, you know, and I'm good at mysticism. I read old ladies' fortunes with the tarot cards, and I hold young ladies' hands and tell them what their palms foretell. Usually, they foretell a cheap Italian dinner with me, followed by a nightcap at my apartment."

"You don't seem to take it too seriously."

Harry looked at him. "I take Misquamacus seriously. What I do for a living, that's just fooling about. But Misquamacus, and the spirits that Misquamacus can raise up, now that's a whole different ball game."

Neil poured himself a cup of coffee and sipped it. "What I don't understand is, if you've already destroyed Misquamacus once, how he can possibly come back again."

"You'll have to ask John Singing Rock about the finer details of that," said Harry. "But the way I understand it, a manitou is indestructible, like a spirit. It lives forever, and not even the greatest of the gods can destroy it. All you can hope to do when you're fighting a reincarnated manitou like Misquamacus is break the spells that bind it to its physical form. When we first faced Misquamacus, he was reborn in the body of a girl I knew. Actually reborn, like a fetus. But we were able to use the electrical power of a computer to destroy him. Least, that's the easiest way I can explain it."

"What about now?" asked Neil. "What's he going to do to Toby?"

Harry shook his head. "I just don't know. I talked to Singing Rock about it, and he was going to consult some of the elder medicine men of his tribe. You see, whatever Misquamacus *is* doing, he seems to have learned some lessons from the last time. Last time, he was reborn from the seventeenth century, and it must have been his first leap through time. He was alone, and he was caught off-balance, and once we worked out a way to get rid of him, then the struggle wasn't too unequal. But this time—well, God only knows. He seems to have found himself a whole bunch of friends, and a way to reincarnate himself without having to grow like a fetus."

Neil said, "He's growing inside Toby's mind. I can see it. I can look at Toby, and Toby isn't Toby at all."

"Misquamacus is a pretty powerful guy," said Harry. "He's also mean, and vengeful, and if I didn't know he was going to come and find me anyway, I would have stayed as far away from what's going on here as humanly possible. Nothing personal, of course."

Neil finished his coffee, and went to stack their cups in the sink. He said, "I want to thank you for taking the trouble to fly out here, anyway. I know a lot of people who wouldn't have bothered. Half this damn town, to begin with."

"They've been giving you a hard time?"

"They think I'm crazy. And tonight, after that sheet business, they even believe I assaulted Susan. If I don't

153

do something soon, they're going to commit me, or run me out. Even Susan doesn't believe me."

Harry took a pack of mint-flavored dental floss out of his coat pocket and broke off a piece.

"You want some?" he asked.

"No, thanks."

"I think it helps to stop me smoking," said Harry, sawing away at his teeth. "It's also supposed to do wonders for the dental bills."

"Do you want to see Toby?" asked Neil.

"Sure. He's upstairs now?"

"He's sleeping. I guess Misquamacus is conserving his strength right now."

"How about your wife?"

"The doctor gave her a sedative. She won't wake up."

Harry put away his floss and stood up. "Well," he said, with a pale grin. "I feel a little like Saint George about to size up the dragon for a rematch."

Neil opened the door to the stairs and led the way up to the landing. It was dark and still up there, and the ticking of the grandfather clock was the only sound they could hear.

Harry whispered, "Will you show me the wardrobe first? The one the wooden man came out of?"

"Sure," said Neil, crossing the landing. "It's in here."

He opened the door to Toby's room. He had nailed a sheet of hardboard over the window, so it was gloomy, and still smelled of ash and smoke. Harry took a cautious peek around, and then stepped across to the walnut wardrobe.

"Is this it?"

Neil nodded.

Harry oepned it and looked inside.

154

"We had something like this before, only not nearly so dramatic. Misquamacus manifested his head out of a solid cherrywood table, right in front of us. It was real frightening."

He closed the wardrobe door. "He's an Indian of the woods, you see, from Manhattan originally, and in other lives the Miskatonic River and some of the back forests of Massachusetts. He was an Algonquian, and a Wampanoag, and maybe a dozen other nationalities. Singing Rock knows more about him than I do. After we sent him back outside, Singing Rock made quite a study of Misquamacus."

Neil ran his hand through his hair. "I don't know what the hell I would have done if I hadn't found you," he said.

"Don't count chickens," warned Harry. "From what I saw of Misquamacus the last time, hell could be a much more comfortable alternative."

They left Toby's room, and walked quietly along the landing until they came to the main bedroom. Neil raised his finger to his lips and then slowly opened the door, beckoning Harry to follow him.

Toby and Susan were both fast asleep. The moon had passed by now, and the room was thick with shadows. The luminous dial of the bedside clock, which chattered softly in the corner, said three-thirty.

"This is your boy?" said Harry, quietly hunkering himself down beside Toby's bed. He touched the flushed, sleeping cheek, and stroked the untidy hair. Toby stirred slightly, and his small hand opened a little, but his breathing remained calm and even.

"The trouble is, this is a war," Harry whispered. "It's not just one evil character trying to get his own back.

It's the red nation fighting to get their revenge on the white nation. A real war."

He stood up, still looking down at Toby. "And the sad thing is that, in wars, it's always the innocent people who get hurt the worst."

Neil watched Harry tiredly.

"Do you want to get some sleep?" Neil asked. "There's a big couch in the front room, and I can find you some blankets."

Harry said, "Yes, for sure. Have you ever tried sleeping on a plane with fifty-five rabbis? They spent the whole flight chattering about how they were going to go see Carole Doda. I'm sometimes glad my mother was a Catholic."

Stepping around the end of the bed, Neil went to make sure that Susan was warm and comfortable. He bent over her and listened to her steady breathing for a while, but he didn't kiss her or touch her. He felt as if he had somehow failed her, as if he hadn't protected her as a husband should. There didn't seem to be any way to make up for what had happened except to destroy Misquamacus, and to free his house and his family from the terrible curse that seemed to have descended on them.

Harry was waiting for him by the door, darkly silhouetted by the light from the landing. He said, "Are you okay? You look as if you could use some sleep yourself."

Neil took a last look at the bedroom and nodded. "I feel bushed, to tell you the truth."

He was about to close the door when he heard Toby stirring in his bed. The boy whimpered and moaned, and seemed to struggle for a while with his sheets. Harry turned and raised a questioning eyebrow, but

Neil said, "I think he's all right. He's been pretty restless ever since the dreams started."

Harry gave a small, nervous grunt, and made sure that he kept his eye on Toby's sleeping body until Neil had closed the door. It was only when they were halfway down the landing that both of them felt a strange cold surge in the air, as if an ocean wave had suddenly rippled under the rug. The grandfather clock at the end of the landing abruptly stopped ticking, and there was a sharp odor in the air, like burnt electricity.

Harry said, in a hollow voice, "He knows I'm here."

"How can he?" asked Neil.

"He knows, that's all. It's what he's been waiting for."

Neil looked at Harry with a face lined with exhaustion and anxiety. "I just hope we've got the strength to fight this thing," he said, hoarsely. "I just hope to God we've got the strength."

On Sunday afternoon, a dry windy afternoon of duststorms and tumbling newspapers, Harry and Neil and Toby drove around Bodega to visit Toby's classmates at home. Toby had been quiet and pale all morning, but he hadn't objected when Neil ushered him into the battered Pinto, and asked him to direct Harry to each of his friends' houses. He was Toby today, with no sign of the malevolent personality of Misquamacus, although he was unusually listless and distracted. If Neil hadn't known what was wrong with him, he might have guessed that he was coming down with flu.

"Singing Rock said it was very important to take a look at the opposition," remarked Harry, smoking a Camel Light down to halfway and tossing the butt out of the window. "He said we need to know names, or

157

signs, or anything which might tell us who these twenty-two medicine men are. Some medicine men, even the most famous, had weak spots we could use to break them up."

"You think Toby's classmates are really going to tell us that stuff?"

Harry shook his head. "Of course not. But we have to do our best. If we could find out just one name, that'd be something."

Toby said flatly, "Here. This is Andy Beaver's house, right here."

They pulled up outside a small weatherboard house with an overgrown veranda and a yard full of rye grass and strutting chickens. Henry Beaver, in denims and suspenders, was sitting on the veranda reading the *San Francisco_ Sunday_ Examiner*. Andy was jumping through the grass with a toy pistol, playing explorer.

Harry got out of the car and leaned against the roof.

"How do you do," he called to Mr. Beaver.

Henry Beaver folded his paper, dropped it beside him, and then crossed his arms over his huge belly. "How do you do yourself," he replied.

Neil climbed out of the car, too, more cautiously. "Hi, Henry," he said, with an awkward smile.

Henry Beaver didn't smile back. "Still chasing ghosts, Neil Fenner?" he asked. "Caught one yet?"

Harry closed the door of the Pinto and walked across to Mr. Beaver's veranda railing. He leaned his arms on it, and then rested his chin on his arms, and regarded Mr. Beaver very seriously. Mr. Beaver, uncertain and unsettled, glanced at Neil for some kind of explanation. Neil remained expressionless.

"Mr. Beaver," said Harry benignly, "I flew in from

New York City last night because I heard of the trouble that Mr. Fenner had been having here in Bodega."

Henry Beaver looked him up and down. "You're not FBI, are you?" he wanted to know.

Harry shook his head. "I'm a special investigator of matters pertaining to specters and apparitions. I'm an occultist, if you know what I mean."

"Not exactly," replied Henry Beaver suspiciously. "Is it something to do with eye tests, or what?"

"You're thinking of an oculist, Mr. Beaver," said Harry, in a smooth, salesmanlike tone. "But you're almost right. I investigate strange things that people have seen, and I try to determine the truth of them. You got me?"

"You mean ghosts, things like that?"

"Well, yes, if that's the way you want to put it."

Henry Beaver slowly shook his head and picked up his newspaper again. "I'm sorry, mister, but nobody ain't seen no ghosts around here, except for Neil Fenner there." He nodded toward Neil with an emotionless face. "The truth is, we don't believe that kind of garbage around these parts, and that's the long and short of it."

Harry wasn't at all put off. He climbed the veranda steps and sat down on the end of Mr. Beaver's lawn chair.

"Mr. Beaver," he said, "I don't want you to be too hasty. You see, the truth of the matter is that some very reliable apparitions have been appearing to school-age children all over California, particularly in these parts, and my people have been very interested in hearing some firsthand reports."

"Your people?" asked Henry Beaver. He still looked massively unconvinced.

159

"The people I work for. The Occultist Investigation League of America."

Henry Beaver sniffed. "Well, so?"

"Well, it's possible that your son Andy might have seen something and not told you about it," said Harry. "He could have easily glimpsed a ghost or some kind of a specter, and not thought to tell you. Maybe he thought you'd laugh at him. Maybe he just forgot to mention it."

"Andy?" squinted Mr. Beaver. He was rapidly growing confused.

"That's right, Andy," said Harry. "And the nice thing about the whole investigation is that we pay a hundred dollars for every authenticated spectral sighting."

He took out his worn leather wallet, and produced a ten-dollar bill, which he waved in front of Mr. Beaver's face. It looked to Neil as if that was the only money he had left.

"See this sawbuck?" smiled Harry. "You can have this and nine more like it if Andy comes up with a ghost sighting that we can substantiate."

Henry Beaver's eyes followed the bill backward and forward. Then, without taking his eyes off it, he called out of the corner of his mouth, "Andy! Come on up here, boy!"

Andy Beaver, gingery and disheveled from play, appeared round the corner with his toy pistol. He frowned at Harry, and then at his father, but Henry Beaver waved him forward and said, "This gentleman here wants to ask you some questions, boy. You just go ahead and answer the best way you can."

Andy peered over at the Pinto. "Hi, Mr. Fenner," he called, and he gave a quick wave to Toby. Harry watched him keenly for any indication of a special wave or a hand signal, but it didn't look like anything more than one schoolboy saying hi to another.

Harry put his arm around Andy's shoulders and led him along the veranda to a quiet corner. He perched on the rail, and Andy stood looking at him, his hands in his jeans pockets, his eyes screwed up against the sun.

"Toby tells me you've been having some nightmares," said Harry. "Something about blood, and killing."

Andy looked away, without answering.

"He says you've been having nightmares about Allen, and the day the Wappos caught Dunbar and the rest of the settlers up at Conn Creek."

Andy turned back toward him again, but still said nothing.

Harry said, "Toby tells me that you're one of the twenty-two."

Andy's eyes fixed themselves on Harry with a strangely luminous stare. They were pale blue, but as he stared they seemed to widen and darken. It was hard to image that these were the eyes of an eight- or nine-year-old boy. They seemed to be infinitely wise, and knowing, and deeply self-contained in their malevolence.

"You are Harry Erskine," said Andy. "We have been waiting a long time for you."

"You and Misquamacus?" asked Harry, trying to appear unruffled. A chicken stalked up onto the veranda, lifted its head questioningly, and then stalked away again.

"You will discover nothing," Andy growled. "I know why you have come, but you will discover nothing. The day is fixed, and you cannot prevent it."

"The day of the dark stars?"

161

"The day when the mouth comes from the sky."

Harry took out a cigarette, and lit it with the engraved Dunhill lighter that John Singing Rock had sent him at Thanksgiving. He blew smoke out of the side of his mouth and watched Andy closely, trying to size up what kind of Red Indian personality was concealing itself inside this small boy's brain. It certainly wasn't as dazzling as the mind of Misquamacus, judging from his first encounters with the greatest of all the wonderworkers. But it was dignified and powerful and proud, and he was quite sure that it would be quite enough on its own to wipe out all of them—him and Neil Fenner and Singing Rock and half of Bodega.

Harry said, "You're going to call down Ossadagowah?"

Andy didn't reply, but continued to stare at him fixedly.

"From what I've heard, that would be kind of dangerous to everyone around, including Indians," Harry remarked. "Isn't Ossadagowah the great demon that nobody can send back to the stars? The demon that only returns outside of its own free will?"

Andy said huskily, "You believe you know much, white man, but your knowledge is like one grain of sand in the deserts. It will not help you, neither will your traitorous friend Singing Rock."

Harry shrugged. "Who knows? We licked Misquamacus before."

"You achieved nothing. What you did served only to give him more strength than ever. This time he will return whole and with his powers intact, and you shall understand before you die the true meaning of strong medicine."

Harry smoked for while in silence. Then he said,

"Okay. I get your warning. The day of the dark stars is coming and you're going to knock us all around the ball park. At least, you think you are."

Andy gave a small, unpleasant smile. Then he turned his head slightly, so that he was looking toward Harry's rented Pinto, and he crossed his arms over his chest. He repeated three times, "An-hut-ko, an-hut-ko, an-hut-ko."

Harry turned around. Smoke was beginning to rise from under the Pinto's hood, and from out of the rear-wheel arches. He yelled at the top of his voice, "*Neil! Get Toby out of that car!*"

Neil, shocked and surprised, immediately pushed forward the folding front seat and lifted Toby out of the back.

"*Now run!*" shouted Harry.

Henry Beaver had hefted himself off his lawn chair and was looking at Harry in blank amazement. But then there was a sharp crackling of fire, and flames started to lick out of the Pinto's radiator and air vents.

"Your goddamn car's on fire!" said Mr. Beaver, in disbelief. "You can't burn your goddamn car in front of my house!"

There was a soft, billowing explosion. Chunks of car tumbled lazily into the air, trailing fire and smoke. Harry, standing on the veranda, was struck on the arm by a flying upholstery spring, and a long piece of fender sailed across the yard and landed on Mr. Beaver's roof.

The five of them stood there watching the remains of the car burn themselves out. A couple of neighbors came from across the street and watched, too, and after a while a man came with a garden hose and doused the last few flickers.

Neil, tightly holding Toby's hand, came along the

veranda wide-eyed and shaken. Toby himself seemed almost indifferent, and even when he came close to Andy he showed no sign of boyish excitement or any urge to talk about the explosion. Neil said, "What happened? What the hell was all that about?"

Harry rubbed his eyes and then looked sardonically at Andy.

"Nothing," he said, with a wry grin. "It was just one of those little bugs that Ford haven't quite sorted out yet."

"But the whole damn car—"

"Neil," said Harry earnestly. "Let's just forget it, shall we? I think we need to go talk about this someplace private."

Andy, looking slightly dazed, said, "Did that car just blow up? Boy—did that car just blow up?"

Harry patted Andy's gingery hair. "Yes, kid," he said. "It just blew up. It was only a little trick I do to attract people's attention."

Henry Beaver, scratching his undershirt, came up and said, "You ain't going to leave that wreck there, I hope? And what about my hundred?"

Harry sighed. "I'm sorry, Mr. Beaver. What your son saw was very far from being an authentic mystical vision. In fact, I'd go so far as to say that he almost owes *me* money, it was so far from being authentic."

"He owes *you* money?" said Mr. Beaver, uncertainly.

"Sure. But we can get around that without any argument. Supposing you just have that wreck cleared away for me, and we'll forget the whole thing."

They stood, a tense, silent group, and nobody was laughing. Andy raised his eyes and looked at Harry, and behind his childish expression were depths upon depths of ancient and arcane mysteries. Toby lifted his eyes, too, and they were even fiercer. The eyes of Misquama-cus, he who could call down the demons who were in no human shape.

Harry said, "Neil, I think we'd better get out of here."

When they arrived back, by taxi, at Neil's house on the Pacific hills, there was a note waiting on the kitchen table, propped between the salt and pepper shakers. Neil read it quickly, and then crumpled it up and tossed it into the trash can.

"She's left you for mother?" asked Harry gently, taking a cookie out of the pottery jar on the sideboard and biting into it.

"Something like that. She's staying with Doctor Crowder and his busybody wife."

"After she cooked us such a nice lunch, too," remarked Harry.

Neil snapped, "Aren't you ever serious? My boy's going crazy with some Red Indian spirit inside him, and my wife's walked out on me, and all you can do is crack half-assed jokes."

Harry pulled an apologetic face. "Just tell me what else you can do when you're faced with almost certain extinction."

"What's that supposed to mean?"

Harry took out another cookie, and started to munch it. "It means that we don't stand a chance. Did you see that car blow up? Do you know what did that?"

"I don't know. Was it Toby?"

"Unh-hunh. It was Andy. He just folded his arms and said a few words and that whole damn car went up like a torch."

Neil said, "I don't understand it. He might have

hurt Toby, and if Toby has Misquamacus inside of him . . ."

"I don't suppose it would have mattered if you'd left Toby sitting right where he was. Misquamacus has as much control over fire as he does over wood and water. I didn't want to take any risks, that was all."

Neil let out a long, dispirited sigh. "Maybe I should call Susan," he suggested.

Harry shook his head. "She's probably safer where she is right now. It's you and me and Singing Rock who are going to have to face up to the brunt of this thing. As I said, I don't think we stand much of a chance. Misquamacus is determined to get us this time, and a few hundred thousand more white folks, and he's not going to fail."

There was a long, silent pause. Then Neil said quietly, "Harry."

"What is it?"

"Well, it's something that occurred to me last night, when those sheets were attacking Susan."

Harry deliberately didn't look at him, but finished his cookies and then took out his pack of Camel Lights.

Neil continued, "I figured that one of the reasons why Misquamacus chose Toby and all the rest of those children was because he wanted to make his reappearance inside people that the community normally goes out of its way to protect. I mean, if he'd chosen twenty-two convicts at Folsom, it might have been an easier choice for us to get rid of them."

There was another pause, and then Neil said, "Last night, I seriously considered going for my shotgun and blowing Toby's head off."

Harry lit a cigarette and eyed Neil narrowly through the rising smoke.

"Sure you considered it," he said.

"You're not shocked?"

"Why should I be? Plenty of fathers have sent their sons off to die to protect their countries. Why should you be any different?"

"He's my only son, Harry."

Harry stood up and went to the open kitchen door. The wind had dropped a little now, and the sun was shining from a high, hazy sky. Four or five birds were taking a dust bath just outside the cellar doors.

"As it turns out," said Harry, "the best thing you did was feel too sentimental to go get your gun. Any artefact, whether it's a stone pot or a knife or a bow and arrow or a twelve-gauge shotgun, has some kind of spirit inside it, some kind of manitou. This table has a manitou, this door has a manitou, although they're obviously very lowly spirits, nothing to get scared about. But the problems start when you try to turn a weapon onto a powerful wonder-worker like Misquamacus. He can actually control the manitou inside of your gun, maybe even the manitou inside of the bullet you fire, and turn your own gun against you."

"You're kidding," said Neil. "You mean we can't use guns against these medicine men?"

"No way. Not unless we want to massacre ourselves in ten seconds flat with no break for commercials."

"Jesus," breathed Neil. "That never occurred to me."

Harry turned away from the door. "It's this way," he said. "We're basically a European culture, with European ideas of religion and spirituality. That makes us outsiders in this country, without any real understanding of the spirits that live in the soil and the rocks and the water. The Indians spent thousands of years getting to know them, getting to understand them. They know

167

the ways of conjuring them up, and the ways of controlling them. We're just floundering about here, Neil, with no spiritual help to call on, and with about every odd you can think of stacked against us. They're going to—"

Just then Toby came into the kitchen with his catcher's mitt and his baseball. Harry changed the subject in mid-sentence, and said glibly, "—bring me a new rental car up in the morning, as soon as their office opens."

Toby ignored him and said to his father, "Can I go out to play in the yard, sir?"

"Sure, as long as you don't go any further than that."

"Is mommy coming back today?"

Neil shrugged. "Maybe. When we've sorted out all our problems."

"Daddy—" began Toby.

Neil raised his eyes. For one fleeting moment, he had heard Toby as he used to be. Toby the child. Even Harry turned around, and then glanced back at Neil and lifted one questioning eyebrow.

"What is it, Toby?" asked Neil, softly.

Toby blinked, as if he'd started to think of something, and then forgotten it. His eyes clouded again.

"Nothing, sir."

He went out into the yard to play with his ball, and Harry sat with Neil at the table for a while, finishing his cigarette.

The day slowly began to darken.

The next morning, Harry invited himself along on Neil's regular drive up to the school to drop off Toby. They sat side by side in the front of the pickup truck in silence. The weather was heavy and threatening again, with a sky the color of bruised fruit. Harry smoked too much, while Neil looked pale and tired, and drove badly.

Only Toby was composed, sitting with his hands held together in his lap, unsmiling and quiet.

The pickup truck circled the school yard in a cloud of lingering dust and stopped. Harry climbed down and helped Toby jump after him.

The yellow school bus was already parked by the fence, waiting to take the children up to Lake Berryessa for the day. Neil had awakened early to make Toby some peanut-butter sandwiches, and they had stopped at the store on the way to school to buy him a Milky Way and a package of Fritos.

"Have a nice day," said Harry. "Don't fall in the lake."

Toby looked at him gravely. Then he turned and walked across to the corner of the yard, where the rest of his classmates were beginning to assemble. Harry recognized the carroty hair of Andy Beaver, and a couple of the other children that Toby had pointed out on their trip around Bodega the previous day. Harry gave Andy a cute little wave, but the boy simply turned and ignored him.

Mrs. Novato came out of the schoolhouse and started to count heads. Harry was about to climb back up into the pickup, but then he changed his mind and said to Neil, "Wait here a minute, will you?" and he walked across the yard to where Mrs. Novato was standing.

"Good morning," he said, in a friendly way.

"Good morning," said Mrs. Novato distractedly.

Harry coughed. "I was wondering," he said.

"Oh, yes?" said Mrs. Novato. "Daniel—keep still, will you? I've already counted you five times."

"My name's Harry Erskine and I'm a friend of Neil Fenner."

"I see."

Harry cleared his throat again. "What I was wondering was, ma'am, if you could do me a favor if anything weird starts happening in your classroom."

Mrs. Novato stopped counting, her finger poised in midair. She turned to Harry and said in an offended tone, "Something *weird*? What on earth are you trying to suggest?"

Harry gave her a defensive smile. "I'm really not trying to suggest anything. But Mr. Fenner has been kind of worried about some of the nightmares your kids have been having, as well as some of the peculiar events that have been happening in his home, and, well . . ."

Mrs. Novato took a patient, schoolmarmly breath. "Mr. Erskine," she said, "I have already given Mr. Fenner far more leeway to investigate his suspicions than I should. Several of the children's parents complained to the principal about that business of setting their nightmares down on paper, and as a result I came very close to losing my position. Apart from that, it does seem from what I hear that Mr. Fenner is suffering from—well, overwork."

Mr. Saperstein walked past, and Mrs. Novato said, "Good morning, Mr. Saperstein."

"Okay," said Harry, "I can guess how you feel. But you can still do me that favor."

"Mr. Erskine, let me assure you that nothing weird has ever happened in this class or is ever likely to. Now, please. I have enough on my hands conducting the correct number of children off to Lake Berryessa and back again, without troubling myself with weirdness."

"Sure, I've got you," said Harry. "But I'm staying

with Mr. Fenner if you do want to call me."

"I *don't* want to call you."

"But you might."

Mrs. Novato closed her eyes and sought strength and fortitude under her lids. Then she said, "Very well, Mr. Erskine. Should I ever wish to call you, which will be never, I will know where not to do so."

"That's fine," smiled Harry. "Now have a good trip, okay?"

Harry walked back to the pickup truck and climbed in, slamming the door behind him.

"Well?" said Neil.

"I just asked her to let us know if there was any trouble," Harry told him. "Not that she's likely to. She's hidebound by educational bureaucracy, and apart from that she's married."

"What's that got to do with it?"

"Nothing much," admitted Harry. "It's just that I find it hard to work my charms on married women of Mrs. Novato's age. They're too old to be oversexed and too young to have husbands who can't raise it."

Neil started the motor. Before he released the brake, though, he took a last look at Toby through the dust-filmed windshield. His son was standing clutching his lunchbox, his blond hair as untidy as ever, in a blue windbreaker and denim shorts. The other children were gathered around him, and he was obviously talking to them about something lengthy and serious.

"I've got a feeling about today," said Neil.

"You think today is the day?" asked Harry.

"I don't know. But there's a tenseness around. Don't you feel it? Like there's a storm brewing."

Harry shrugged. "It's hard to tell. But in any case,

171

there isn't much we can do until Singing Rock arrives. He said he'd be here by lunchtime."

"It's just those kids going off alone, with all those spirits inside them, all of those manitous. That really scares me. What do you think I felt like this morning, giving Toby his lunch and wondering if he wasn't even my son at all, but some kind of ghost out of the past? I'm just standing there doing something really normal, like making sandwiches, and for all I know he might go off on that trip and never come back."

Harry laid a hand on his shoulder. "Stop feeling so guilty, will you? It's not your fault this has happened, even if it *was* your ancestor who led Misquamacus here. I mean—what control could you have possibly had over that? There's nothing we can do until the medicine men show themselves. We can't kill the children; we can't even take them away from here. Apart from the fact that Misquamacus would prevent us, the police would probably arrest us for kidnapping, and we wouldn't do anybody any good sitting in the Sonoma County pokey."

Neil released the brake, and drove the pickup out of the Bodega school yard without saying another word. He didn't even look back in his rearview mirror to see Toby and his classmates being ushered by Mrs. Novato onto the bus. Harry turned around in his seat, and saw how solemn and unsmiling the children were, and a sensation of sick tension began to rise in his stomach. He knew just what Neil meant about a storm brewing. It could have been the unusual humidity, or the soft but uncomfortable wind. But it could have been the beginning of the day of the dark stars, too.

* * *

They met John Singing Rock at the bus station. He was fifty years old, his face creased with the soft crisscross wrinkles of a South Dakota Indian, but his eyes were sharp and bright, and he walked across the concrete parking lot to greet them with the tensile step of a man twenty years younger. The last time Harry had seen him, his hair had been short and swept back with brilliantine, and he had worn a creaseless mohair suit. But modern trends had obviously blown with the winds across the plains of mid-America, because his hair was longer now and kept in place with Gillette Dry Look, and he wore a camel-colored sport coat and bright red slacks.

He set down his suitcase on the concrete and held out his arms. Harry embraced him, saying nothing, and for a moment they stood there close, while the other bus passengers looked at them with curiosity.

Harry stood back, still holding Singing Rock's hand. "You look like you've been shopping at Gucci," he grinned. "And what's this with the hair?"

Singing Rock touched his graying sidepieces. "I had to give up that greasy kid's stuff," he said. "It kept leaving marks on my tepee."

Harry laughed, and gripped Singing Rock's arm affectionately. "It's good to see you," he said. "If I ever went past South Dakota, I'd drop by more damned often."

Singing Rock said, "Is this Mr. Fenner?"

Harry nodded and introduced them. Neil shook hands a little hesitantly, but Singing Rock reached out and placed his hand on top of Neil's, and said warmly, "You're wondering why I don't have bones through my nose and feathers in my cap?"

Neil was embarrassed. "I guess I never met a medi-

173

cine man before. I didn't really know what to expect."

Harry picked up Singing Rock's suitcase and the three of them walked across to Neil's pickup.

Singing Rock said, "I'd prefer to wear traditional costume. What's the point of being a medicine man if you don't look like one? But the costumes are pretty rare these days. They take years to complete, and when they're finished they're works of art. These days, you can't really walk around in a work of art. You might spill catsup on it."

Harry helped Singing Rock into the pickup, and then they drove off toward Neil's house. The sky was still oddly dark, and there was a feeling that rain clouds were building up.

Harry said, "Neil has a hunch that the day of the dark stars might be today. Or soon, anyway."

"Any particular reason?" asked Singing Rock.

"I don't know," Neil told him. "It's a feeling like someone's trying to warn me."

"Like when Dunbar warned you of Misquamacus?"

"Harry told you about that?"

"Harry told me about everything. The slightest detail could be vital."

Neil brought the pickup to a stop at a road junction, waited for a carload of women to pass, and then turned left.

He said, "It's not exactly the same feeling. When Dunbar first showed up, I could hear his voice, appealing for help. Toby heard it, too. Both of us saw him, or his ghost. A tall man with a light-colored beard and a long white duster coat. But today, the feeling's just a feeling. I haven't heard Dunbar's voice since last night. This is much more general."

Singing Rock said, "You're very unusual for a white man, Mr. Fenner, if you don't mind my saying so."

"What do you mean?" asked Neil.

"You were prepared to believe in the supernatural before you started trying to think of rational explanations for what you saw. Most white men think of the rational explanations first, and only believe the supernatural when they have no other choice. Even then, they frequently don't believe it."

"How could I ignore it?" said Neil. "I spoke to Dunbar. I was only ten or twelve feet away from his ghost, and there isn't anybody alive who can tell me I was dreaming."

"And you saw Misquamacus, too, as a wooden man?"

"That's right."

Singing Rock glanced at Harry, and from his expression, Harry could see that he was deeply disturbed about what he was hearing.

Singing Rock continued, "I don't want to alarm you too much, Mr. Fenner, but there's something I believe you ought to know."

"Call me Neil, please."

"All right, Neil. What you have to know is that every manitou, according to Indian belief, is reincarnated seven times, and that each time it lives and dies and lives again, it gains strength and wisdom. After its seventh life on earth, it's wise enough to join the gods outside, in what the Micmac used to call Wajok, the abode of the great ones."

"I see," said Neil, turning right and driving up the dusty roadway that wound over the hills toward his house. "So what does that have to do with Misquamacus?"

175

"Just about everything. The last time Harry and I encountered Misquamacus, he was into his fourth, or more likely his fifth, reincarnation. I could judge that because of the vast distance of time he had covered in one leap—from 1650 to the present day. It takes a powerful medicine man to do that. Now, from what you've told us about the things you found out in Calistoga, Misquamacus lived again in the 1830s, and that would have been his sixth reincarnation."

Neil wiped dust from his mouth with the back of his hand. The house was in sight now, and he was driving more slowly.

"You're trying to tell me this is his last reincarnation?"

"I believe so," nodded Singing Rock. "He's almost ready to take his place in Wajok, and that means he's immensely powerful, immensely strong, and almost unbeatable by any other medicine man. He had to go through a physical rebirth the last time we met him, like a human fetus, but now he's growing himself inside of your son's mind. Don't ask me how he does it. It's beyond my medicine. But he's doing it and, even before he's finished doing it, he's demonstrated some magic that no present-day wonder-worker could even touch. Creating that wooden man, Neil, takes occult powers that could make earthquakes. And that's *before* he's emerged from your son's mind, *before* he's ready to zap us with everything he's got. There isn't any doubt at all that he's going to call down Ossadagowah, and when he does that, we're really up against it."

Neil stopped the pickup outside his backyard and took out the keys.

"Are we going to die?" he asked Singing Rock quietly.

Singing Rock sighed. "That is one prediction I don't care to make," he replied. "But remember this is Misquamacus's seventh *and last* reincarnation. After this, he won't have any further opportunities to take his revenge on the white people, except if this manitou is summoned to earth by other medicine men. And when you consider the general condition of Indian magic in America today, I'd say that's pretty unlikely."

They pulled up outside Neil's weatherbeaten house and climbed out. Neil led the way across the yard and into the kitchen, and he showed Singing Rock to the bathroom to freshen up. Harry carried his suitcase into the parlor.

"Does Singing Rock drink?" asked Neil, taking a six-pack of Coors out of the icebox.

"I don't think so. But he might appreciate a cup of coffee."

Singing Rock returned, hung his sport coat on the back of his chair, and rolled up his shirt sleeves. His arms were muscular and sinewy, and decorated with elaborate patterns of tattoos and scars. As he sat down at the pine table, Neil had the feeling that he had some experienced, professional help at last.

"I want to see everything," said Singing Rock. "The children's paintings, the wardrobe upstairs, the sheets that attacked your wife. I want you to tell me everything, too, all over again, in as much detail as you can remember it. If we're going to win out against these medicine men at all, we have to know as much about them as possible."

Neil reached up to one of the top cupboards and brought down the sheaf of paintings from Toby's classmates. Singing Rock went through them all meticulously, peering at every figure, and comparing one nightmare picture closely with another.

As he examined the pictures, he asked Neil to tell him about the first appearance of the visitation they knew as "Dunbar," and everything that Billy Ritchie had told him about Bloody Fenner and that grisly day up at Conn Creek.

Neil was nervous at first, but as he drank and talked, he found he was able to confide in Singing Rock, and tell him everything about his days of fear and horror. Singing Rock glanced at him from time to time, and the Indian's eyes were understanding and wise in a way that Neil had never seen before in anyone. Harry, who had heard it all before, sat at the end of the table smoking and drinking his beer out of the can.

Eventually, when Neil had finished, Singing Rock laid out the paintings on the kitchen table, twenty-two garish illustrations of the same terrible incident.

"I think it's pretty clear what's happened," he told them. "The medicine men needed to draw on the strength of an Indian victory to help them in their reincarnation. It's difficult to explain it exactly, but they've used the massacre at Las Posadas as a focal point for their rebirth, like a politician trying to make a comeback by reminding people of his past achievements. The massacre was what Misquamacus meant when he was referring to the gateway. He didn't want you to disturb the historic vibrations that he had been setting up with Allen Fenner's guidance. You—because you're a Fenner yourself—would have been more likely to upset things than anyone."

Neil asked, "But why did Dunbar appear? Misquamacus wouldn't have wanted him around, surely?"

Singing Rock slowly shook his head. "I'm not entirely certain. The most likely explanation is that all this spirit activity connected with the incident in which Dunbar died was enough to disturb his manitou, and he began to make ghostly appearances. You have to remember that this is the single most powerful psychic incident that has ever occurred in modern America, and it involves more upheaval of the ethos than you can possibly imagine. Why do you think you can feel all this tension? The spiritual planes are in chaos and crisis. No wonder a few shades from the past are turning over in their graves."

Harry said, "What we really need are the ghosts of the entire Seventh Cavalry. Do you think you could manage to raise them up?"

Singing Rock smiled. "You'd be sorry if I did. The Seventh Cavalry was a great deal more vicious than the Indians most of the time."

Neil looked over Singing Rock's shoulder at the school paintings. "Do these words mean anything to you?" he asked. "I couldn't make them out at all."

Singing Rock picked up one or two of the paintings. "They're in different dialects," he said, "but they all seem to refer to the day of the dark stars in one way or another. *Ta-La-Ha-Lu-Si* was the name the Patwin Indians used for Napa Valley. It simply means 'beautiful land.' *Kaimus* was the Wappo name for the town of Yountville, which is halfway up the valley, as you obviously know. These words here, though, *sokwet* and *oweaoo* and *pados* are all Algonquian."

"What's a 'sokwet' when it's at home?" asked Harry. "It sounds like the first requirement for double pneumonia."

"*Sokwet* is the Alqonquian word for 'eclipse.' It seems to be tied in here with the word *wata*, which means

179

'star.' So I think we can safely assume that one of these children was talking about the day of the dark stars itself. The word *oweaoo* means 'circle,' and *pados* means 'boat,' but since they're written here in isolation, they're not particularly helpful. I suspect we'll discover what they mean, though."

"Sure," said Harry. "The hard way."

Singing Rock said, "These paintings themselves are very interesting. When you first look at them, you'd think they were painted by children."

"Of course you would," said Neil. "They *were* painted by children."

Singing Rock shook his head. "This style is primitive in some respects, but it isn't childish. Look at this one. You can find carvings and drawings in this style among the Wabanaki and the Etchemis. This one shows the Indians dressed in the costumes of Arapahos. And this one here looks distinctly Iroquois."

Neil shuffled through the paintings with a frown. "You mean the medicine men inside the children created these paintings? Not the children themselves?"

"Not fully," said Singing Rock. "These were done a few days ago, at a time when the medicine men wouldn't have taken hold of the children's minds completely. But their tribal characterstics have certainly shown through. I can identify Sioux, Micmac, Hopi, Apache, Shoshoni, and Modoc, as well as the ones you've got in your hand."

"Does that help?" asked Neil.

"It helps a great deal. It means that I can tell who some of the medicine men are. Each tribe has its own mythical medicine heroes. The Wabanaki, for instance, had Neem, the bringer of thunder. The Apaches used to revere a medicine man called No Name, who was said to wear a live rattlesnake as a headdress. Misquamacus will almost certainly have called on the best medicine man from each tribe, and so it won't be too difficult to make a list of the team we're going to be up against."

"Singing Rock sees the eternal struggle between red men and white men as a kind of occult football game," remarked Harry.

Neil sat down. "What I don't quite understand is, what are these demons like, these things they're going to call down to destroy us? I mean, what are they actually *like*?"

At that moment, as if prompted by fate, the telephone in the front room began to ring. Neil said, "Excuse me," and went to answer it.

Singing Rock and Harry waited while Neil talked. Harry crushed out his cigarette and swilled down the last of his beer. Then Neil came back into the room, and his face was flushed with anxiety.

"What's wrong?" asked Harry. "You look as though you've seen a ghost."

"It was Mr. Saperstein, from the school," said Neil. "He heard you talking to Mrs. Novato in the school yard, and he guessed you'd want to know."

"Know? Know what?"

Neil looked at him, and Harry could see that he was very close to collapse. Singing Rock advised, "You'd better sit down."

Neil shook his head. "Mr. Saperstein wants us to come down there right away. He took some photographs of Toby and the rest of the class last week, when they were dancing in the playground. He's just had the pictures developed, and he says that something's shown up on them that's almost driven him mad."

SEVEN

Mr. Saperstein met them in his office overlooking the back of the school. It was a cramped, converted storeroom, and it was heaped with music scores and books on composers and cellos with broken strings. Harry and Neil and Singing Rock could hardly crowd themselves inside, and Mr. Saperstein had to move a battered trumpet case and a bust of Beethoven with a chipped nose before Harry could sit down.

"I'm sorry I eavesdropped on your conversation with Mrs. Novato," Mr. Saperstein said apologetically. "It was just that I was passing, and I really couldn't help myself. I'm afraid I've always been a bit of a busybody."

"Good thing you were," said Singing Rock flatly. "This is a desperate time."

Mr. Saperstein unlocked his desk drawer and took out a paper folder.

"I should explain that I'm pretty keen on photography," he said. "I take my camera around most of the time. It was quite natural for me to shoot a picture of the children in the school yard. I had a little exhibition of school photographs at Sonoma last year, and it was really quite successful."

Harry put in impatiently, "Do you think we could just take a look at the shots?"

Mr. Saperstein raised one hand. "What you have to realize is that I came into Mrs. Novato's classroom, and she said she could see her children dancing in a strange way. I looked out of the window, too, and she was right. They were kind of shuffling around in a circle, with their arms on each other's shoulders. I thought it could have been a Greek dance, you know, like in *Zorba the Greek*?"

Harry sighed. "The pictures, Mr. Saperstein?"

"Of course," said the music teacher, opening the folder. "But before you look at them you must realize that all I saw in that school yard was children. Nothing else at all."

One by one, Mr. Saperstein passed around the large black-and-white prints. There were five of them, each showing the school yard from Mrs. Novato's classroom window, and the children shuffling around in a circle. In the first picture, Neil could pick out Toby and Andy and Daniel Soscol and Debbie Spurr. But there was something else besides. Out of the center of the circle of children, mostly obscured by their bodies, a sort of whitish haze seemed to be forming, like a twisting column of smoke.

In the next picture, the haze was widening, and rising even higher above the children's heads. It was beginning to form into tentacular coils, which in the third picture were writhing almost up to the lower branches of the maple tree at the edge of the school yard.

The fourth and the fifth photographs were the most

184

alarming. They showed a towering beast, draped with scores of curling arms, like a kind of gaseous squid, high above the children. Although it was faceless and formless, it possessed a terrible and evil aspect, as if it was formed out of the essence of ancient malevolence. It seemed verminous and unhealthy, and riddled with diseases of the mind and the spirit.

"What *is* that thing?" asked Neil. "Is that some kind of photographic illusion?"

Mr. Saperstein replied, "No trick, Mr. Fenner. They were developed for me by Charlie Keynes down at the newspaper office. He does all my prints. He swears blind that this is the way they came out."

"Maybe the light got into the film, you know, and fogged it," suggested Neil.

Mr. Saperstein shook his head. "That's not fogging, Mr. Fenner. Any amateur could tell you that."

"You're right, Mr. Saperstein," concurred Singing Rock, quietly. "These pictures are not fake."

"But how can you tell?" asked Neil. "It must be easy to take an airbrush or something and—"

Singing Rock smiled, and benignly silenced him. "No amount of airbrushing could ever portray what's on this photograph, Neil, because no artist knows what this creature looks like or what it is. This creature is one of the shapeless ones who guard the threshold between this world and outside. They are messengers of the ethos in which the great old ones have dwelled for more centuries than I could count.

"This thing is a herald, if you can call it that, for Pa-la-kai the demon of blood, and Nashuna the demon of darkness, and for Quul the demon of insanity. Those three, in their turn, are servants of Rhenauz the demon of evil, and Coyote the demon of corruption. Above all these, though, and guarded by a pack of creatures called the Eye Killers, is Ossadagowah, the son of Sadogowah, the demon who can be conjured up but can never be returned, except of his own free will."

"Then what's this thing?" asked Harry. "Just a minor-league stooge?"

"In comparison, yes," said Singing Rock. "Its name is Sak, which simply means 'the past.' It is a beast that has existed on this planet for countless millions of years, or so the Algonquian say. Its chosen duty has always been to encourage humans to summon the elder gods, so that the elder gods may devour them as sacrificial gifts, and reward Sak with whatever a beast like that might want as a reward."

"A gold ball-point pen?" asked Harry. "Who knows what demons want?"

Neil couldn't even find it in himself to laugh. He kept looking at the pictures of Toby, and the face of Misquamacus was sharply clear in every one of them.

Singing Rock stood up. "Sak will want more than that and, unfortunately for us, he's going to get it pretty soon. When I talked to the elders of my tribe about this matter, they said that before the day of the dark stars could dawn, several essential rituals had to be completed. The *penultimate* ritual was the summoning of Sak, who would make the way ready for Ossadagowah. After that, all the twenty-two medicine men have to do is join their strength together in the name of whatever spirits they choose—tree spirits or water spirits or rock spirits. Knowing what little we do about Misquamacus, I'd say they probably chose tree spirits."

Harry said, "You think they're already done that?"

Singing Rock nodded. "Almost certainly. If you want me to hazard a guess, I'd say they probably did it on

Friday, before they all had to go home for the weekend. When they went out on that school trip this morning, they were ready for the day to begin. The day of the dark stars, or the day when the mouth comes down from the sky."

"You mean it could be today?" asked Neil, frightened.

Singing Rock checked his watch. "It's almost noon. The day of the dark stars begins at noon and lasts through until the following noon. It's supposed to be twenty-four hours of chaos and butchery and torture, the day when the Indian people have their revenge for hundreds of years of treachery and slaughter and rape, all in one huge massacre."

Mr. Saperstein took his photographs back and looked at them in bewilderment. Then he said to Singing Rock, "Is this true, what you're saying? Or is it simply fantasy?"

Singing Rock pointed to the misty, wriggling shape of Sak. "Is *that* true?" he asked. "Or is *that* simply fantasy?"

Mr. Saperstein took off his glasses. "It's incredible. I don't know why I didn't even see it at the time. It's enormous."

"That's one thing we've learned, Mr. Saperstein," said Harry. "Demons and spirits can be seen through some photographic lenses, even when they're almost invisible to the naked eye. It's happened before."

"I thought I was going crazy," said Mr. Saperstein. "I took those pictures out and looked at them, and I was sure I was going crazy."

"That's what I thought," said Neil softly. He held out his hand to Mr. Saperstein. "Join the club."

Singing Rock said, "We have much less time than I

187

thought. If the day of the dark stars begins at noon today, that means Ossadagowah and the rest of the demons will be summoned when Nepauz-had, the moon goddess, appears."

Mr. Saperstein opened another of his desk drawers, shuffled through it like a rat looking for eggs in a hayloft, and at last produced a battered maroon diary. He licked his thumb and turned the pages until he came to the one he wanted.

"Moonrise tonight is 10:02," he announced. "I presume that's what you mean."

"Thank you, Mr. Saperstein, it is," said Singing Rock. "And that means we have less than ten hours to prepare ourselves. Quite apart from that, we don't even know where the children are."

"They went to Lake Berryessa," said the music teacher. "It was their school outing."

"They were *supposed* to go to Lake Berryessa," said Singing Rock. "But remember the legend speaks of twenty-two medicine men."

"So? What does that have to do with it?" asked Harry.

"It could have everything to do with it," said Singing Rock. "There are only twenty-one children in the class, and therefore the twenty-second medicine man must be emerging inside one of the adults aboard that bus."

"There's only Mrs. Novato and the driver," said Mr. Saperstein, aghast. "You don't think that Mrs. Novato—?"

Harry said, "I wouldn't have thought so myself. She didn't look like the type. Too homely, even for your average medicine man from 1830."

"Who's the school bus driver?" asked Singing Rock.

"Well, it's usually Jack Billets, from Valley Ford,"

said Mr. Saperstein. "But I think he's been off sick lately. I don't know who they used today. I didn't see him."

Neil picked up Mr. Saperstein's telephone and dialed the operator. When he was through, he said, "Amy? Is that you? Listen, this is very urgent. Do you have Jack Billets's number, down at Valley Ford? Sure. Could you put me through?"

He waited a little while, and then they heard a faint voice at the other end of the telephone.

"Jack?" asked Neil. "This Neil Fenner. Yes. Hi. Listen, I heard you were sick. That's right. Well, I hope it improves. But listen, Jack, do you know who's taking the bus up to Lake Berryessa today? It's pretty important, you know?"

The faint voice replied, and then Neil said, "Thanks, Jack. I'll buy you a drink for that. Okay, fine. Thanks a whole lot."

He set the phone down, and then looked at Harry and Singing Rock and let out a long, controlled breath. "The driver is an old retired sailor who sits around the dock at Bodega Bay. A guy named Doughty. I met him on Friday, and he did everything he could to persuade me not to go on with all the fuss I was making about the children. He said Susan had told him to talk to me. Now I know it was a damn sight more than Susan. It was Misquamacus."

Neil tapped his finger against his head, and snapped, "It was Misquamacus, inside of *here*!"

Neil went to the window and looked out over the back of the school, at the green, rounded hills beyond the fence, at the distant grayness of ocean mist. He said softly, "It all makes a lot more sense now. It was Doughty who suggested I go visit Billy Ritchie, and that

189

was how I found out about Misquamacus in the first place. If I hadn't have known about Misquamacus—if I hadn't have believed in the day of the dark stars—then I wouldn't have called you or Singing Rock to help me."

Singing Rock, from his chair in the corner of the office, smiled and nodded.

"You're beginning to understand the deviousness of Misquamacus, aren't you? He wanted both of us here in California, Harry and me, so that he could take his revenge on us before any other white man or mercenary Indian. It would have used too much energy, too much magic, to bring us by any mystical means. So he simply had Doughty put you on to Billy Ritchie, who was the only person around who could tell you the truth."

Neil tiredly rested his head against the window. "And when it was all over, he made sure that Billy Ritchie was killed."

"Harry told me about that," said Singing Rock. "It was a favorite method of quick death, the lightning-that-sees. It strikes like an occult guided missile. Misquamacus once used it against two of Harry's closest friends."

"All this accounts for something else, too," said Neil. "The appearance of Dunbar's ghost in the bay. He was there because Doughty was there. He was warning me, just like he kept trying to warn me everyplace else."

Singing Rock looked at his watch again. "The first thing we have to do is find out where that school bus is. Then, before it gets dark, we have to get those children together somehow, so that I can arrange a medicine circle around them. One of the elders has given me a spell that was supposed to have kept Coyote away from the daughters of Roman Nose, and that should keep their activities confined for a little while. It's not ideal, but it's better than taking their first attack in the chest."

Mr. Saperstein said, "Is there anything I can do? I'd like to help. I don't quite understand what's going on, but if you don't mind that, you're welcome to whatever I can do."

Harry suggested, "Why don't you call the Highway Patrol? Tell them that some of your kids went off on a day trip to Lake Berryessa, and that a mother just telephoned to say that her son took her Librium pills in his lunch box, thinking they were candies."

Singing Rock stood up. "That should do fine. If you want us, Mr. Saperstein, we'll be over at Neil Fenner's house. And thank you."

The teacher gave a nervous, self-deprecating grin. "It's been a pleasure, I guess. It's such a relief to find out you're not going out of your mind."

"Mr. Saperstein," said Singing Rock, resting a gnarled hand on the music teacher's arm, "there may be times in the next twenty-four hours when you wish that you were."

Singing Rock worked over the kitchen table until midafternoon, the blinds drawn to keep the light from distracting him, and an angular desk lamp over his papers and magical artefacts. While Harry and Neil paced the veranda waiting for Mr. Saperstein to call with news from the Highway Patrol, the South Dakota medicine man laboriously prepared lists of the enemies they were about to face, and gathered together as many spells as he could to hinder and obstruct those enemies. Out of his suitcase came bones, hanks of hair, and earthenware jars of powder.

Just after three o'clock, when the sky was low and

heavy with metallic gray clouds, he came out of the kitchen door and stretched.

Harry asked him, "Are you finished in there?"

Singing Rock shrugged. "As finished as I'll ever be."

"I never knew Indians were such pessimists," retorted Harry. "No wonder you lost the West."

"We were pessimists because we'd already lost the East," Singing Rock reminded him.

Harry lit another cigarette and coughed. "I sometimes wonder whether you're fighting on the right side. With an attitude like yours, you and Misquamacus would make a fine pair."

Singing Rock raised his head a little, and looked across at Harry with eyes that were bright and penetrating.

"One day, in one of my lives, I hope to be far greater than Misquamacus," he said.

Harry raised an eyebrow. "You're trying to tell me that *you've* lived before, too?"

Singing Rock smiled. "It always used to amuse the Indians, before they began to understand how callous the white men actually were, how much the white men knew about living, and how little they understood about life."

"You're in a very philosophical mood."

Singing Rock pulled across a weather-bleached chair and sat down, resting one booted foot on the veranda railing. "Maybe I am," he said quietly. "But I believe we'll be facing Misquamacus again tonight, and this time he'll be ready for us."

Harry walked to the edge of the veranda and rested his hands on the railing. He felt unpleasantly sticky and hot, and the afternoon seemed completely airless. Even out here, it was like being shut in a cupboard. The smoke from the cigarette drifted lazily away in blue puffs.

"Well," he said, "I suppose it's a great honor to be first on the zapping list of the greatest Indian medicine man who ever lived. Just think, I may never have to eat at the Chock full o' Nuts again."

Neil said, "Have you worked out who most of the medicine men are?"

"Yes," said Singing Rock. "They come from the times before the white men arrived on our shores, in those ancient days when Indian magic was at its height. In those days, the gods themselves were supposed to have walked America, and these medicine men worked out their apprenticeships as shamans and wonder-workers with the gods themselves to guide them. Their power is inestimable. Together, under the direction of Misquamacus, they will be devastating."

"Do you have a plan?" asked Neil.

"Sure," put in Harry. "We promise them beads and firewater, just like we used to do in the old days. Then, when they're trying on their beads and drinking their firewater, we steal their sacred medicine circle and build a downtown shopping mall on it."

Singing Rock took out a pack of chewing tobacco and grinned. "I'm sorry, Harry. It won't work a second time."

Neil bit his lip. "Listen," he said, "that's my son out there. My son and all my son's friends. What's going to happen to them?"

With a measured bite, Singing Rock took a mouthful of tobacco and chewed it steadily for a moment. Then he spat out onto the dust.

"That's something I've been meaning to talk to you about," he said, in his deep, serious voice. "You have to understand that if Misquamacus successfully emerges out of Toby's mind and takes on physical shape, then the drain on energy which Toby suffers will almost certainly be fatal."

Neil felt as if someone had hit him from behind. *"What?"* he said weakly.

Singing Rock lifted both his hands. "I am telling you that because you must be prepared for the very worst. There is very little chance that once the medicine men have used those children to reincarnate themselves, they will allow them to live."

"Then what's the use?" asked Neil. His face was very white. "What's the use of trying to save them at all?"

"It's not just the children," said Harry. "We're trying to prevent this whole state from being torn apart. But there's something else, too, isn't there, Singing Rock?"

Singing Rock hesitated, then nodded. "I guess you have a right to know the best as well as the worst. If by any slim chance we *do* manage to defeat these medicine men, and send them back to the outside, then the children will be restored unharmed. It is hard to explain to a white man why this should happen, but there is an eternal natural principle in Red Indian magic of balance and redress. A sort of occult Newton's Law."

Neil turned away and walked to the end of the veranda. Harry glanced at Singing Rock with an expression that suggested he might go after him and try to reassure him, but Singing Rock shook his head.

"Leave him. If he's going to help us, he has to face up to the truth."

Neil heard Singing Rock's words, but he didn't turn around. He looked out over the small yard that, until last week, had been his plain but happy home. With a feeling that brought tears to his eyes, he noticed that

Toby had left his Tonka bulldozer out by the woodshed. He would have been annoyed normally, in case it rained and the bulldozer got rusty. But now it didn't matter. Toby was never going to play with it again. It might as well stay there.

Inside the house, the telephone was ringing. He guessed it was probably Mr. Saperstein, but somehow he couldn't summon the energy to move from where he was. He heard Harry go inside and bang the kitchen door. His senses seemed to be dulled, and all he wanted to do was find a bed someplace and go to sleep.

Out of the corner of his eye, though, he was sure he could see something wavering in the grass beyond the fence. He peered more intently, and shaded his face against the dull, coarse light that filtered through the heavy clouds. There was something out there that was shifting and flapping like a pale transparent flag. Then it began to grow clearer, an instant photograph developing on plain paper. It was the figure of Dunbar, in his wide-brimmed hat and his coat, and with his gun belt slung low around his hips.

"Singing Rock!" said Neil, breathlessly.

Singing Rock raised his eyes, and then quickly looked to the place where Neil was pointing.

"It's Dunbar!" said Neil. "That's him—the man in the long white duster coat!"

The Indian medicine man rose to his feet. As he did so, Dunbar lifted his hat from his head and waved once. Then, gradually, like the morning mist from the ocean, he faded away again.

"Did you see him?" asked Neil, almost frantic. "Did you see him out there?"

Singing Rock said, "Yes, I saw him."

"Thank God. Thank God for that. I was beginning to think I was imagining him."

"I don't know that his warnings can do anything to help us," said Singing Rock. "It looks to me as though he's just some disturbed spirit, vaguely manifesting himself around the fringe of all this astral activity."

Neil didn't take his eyes away from the grassy slope where Dunbar had vanished. "I'm not so sure," he said softly. "I believe he helped me when the wooden man was after me, and I believe he's going to try to help me now. Whenever he appears, I have this feeling of reassurance."

Singing Rock looked briefly over at the hills beyond the fence. "Don't rely too much on spirits," he said. "Some of them are very treacherous. We have stories in South Dakota of demons who would take the shape of friendly dogs, and lead hunters into rivers and over the edge of cliffs."

"Dunbar isn't like that," Neil said.

The kitchen door opened and Harry came out, holding a torn piece of brown envelope in his hand.

"Have they found them?" asked Neil. "Have they told you if Toby's all right?"

Harry squinted at his scribbled notes. "They've found them. The bus is up at Lake Berryessa, where it was supposed to be. A Highway Patrol car spotted it parked on the bridge over Pope Creek."

"Parked on the bridge? What was it doing there?" asked Neil. "Did they say where the children were?"

Harry nodded. "The children are inside the bus. When the Highway Patrol officers tried to drive up close to see what was wrong, their patrol car caught fire and exploded. One of the officers is suffering from serious burns."

"Oh God," said Neil. "It's started."

"You're damn right it's started," said Harry. "That must have been Master Andy Beaver at work. The automotive arsonist."

Singing Rock said, "The boy called Andy Beaver is harboring the Paiute medicine man Broken Fire. I think so, anyway. He was the only child who referred to the day of the dark stars as the day of the mouth coming from the sky, which is an expression that only the Paiutes ever used. And, of course, he has Broken Fire's talent for setting things ablaze at a distance."

"Broken Fire?" asked Harry. "Was he strong?"

Singing Rock laid a hand on his shoulder. "One of the strongest, I'm afraid. The only possible weaknesses he had were an inability to appease the demons of cholera and disease, and no talent for saving the souls of his people who had been sent to the great outside by drinking too much whiskey, or by falling under iron horses. In other words, he was a master of every occult event except those which stemmed from things the white men had done—like spreading diseases, and building railroads, and distilling alcohol."

Neil said, "For Christ's sake don't let's stand here discussing the situation. Let's get *out* there."

"Neil's right," put in Harry. "If the Highway Patrol starts getting upset, they're going to bring their guns out, and that's going to be no fun for anyone. Especially them."

"Very well," nodded Singing Rock. "Can you bring my suitcase, Harry? And Neil—if you have any beer or soft drinks, and any cookies or cold cuts, then bring them along. It's going to be the hardest night you ever went through."

"Let's just hope it isn't the hardest and the *last*," said Harry, pushing open the kitchen door.

Inland, as they drove in Neil's pickup through the Valley of the Moon, the afternoon was densely hazy and hot. They negotiated the curved, cultivated hills that rose between Sonoma and Napa counties, past hillside farms of tan-colored cattle and furrowed fields, and then they were sloping down into the broad flats of the southern Napa Valley. Ahead of them, blue and forested against dim sky, was the rugged outline of the Vaca Mountains. It was up there, beyond those peaks, that Lake Berryessa lay. A long rectangular sheet of ruffled water, twelve miles long and two miles across.

Singing Rock, steadily chewing tobacco, said, "In certain parts of New England, the Indians called rounded mountains *uncanoonucks*, which simply translated means 'women's breasts.'"

Harry, joggling up and down comfortably in his seat as Neil sped the pickup along the blacktop, commented, "What name do they have for medicine men who try to keep you amused by telling you trivial oddities of Indian lore?"

His elbow resting casually on the pickup's window ledge, Singing Rock turned to Harry and smiled. "The same name they have for irritable paleface mystics."

Neil leaned over and turned on the pickup's radio. He twiddled the dial through blurts of country-and-western music, snatches of evangelism, burbles of laughing. He said, "Maybe there's some news about the school bus. The story should have gotten out by now."

Singing Rock asked, "How long is it going to take us to get up to the lake from here?"

"Maybe another twenty minutes at most," Neil told

him. They were speeding along the freeway through Napa now, and he was switching lanes to leave the main road and head east through the city and up to the mountains.

He added, "I hope to God we're not too late. If anything happened to Toby now, I tell you——"

Harry said reassuringly, "You heard what Singing Rock said. Nothing's going to break until the moon goddess appears. It's—what—four o'clock now. We've got six hours to go."

They drove through the outskirts of Napa, along Lincoln Avenue. The traffic was heavy and flowing at a slow, sedate twenty miles an hour. There was nothing that Neil could do except hold his speed down and wait until they were clear of the city. At each red traffic signal, he sat biting his lip and drumming his fingers on the steering wheel.

"Come on, come on, you bastard," he muttered under his breath, as they finally crossed the city limit behind a rusting Matador. He put his foot down, and they pulled ahead, roaring along the eucalyptus-shaded avenue that led to the mountains.

A couple of miles east of Napa, the road began to rise sharply, and twist and turn itself between scrub and rocks. The pickup's tires howled and whinnied as Neil kept his foot flat on the floor and spun them around one tight curve after another. They passed by fields of dry grasses, fences, and dusty roadside pull-offs. They crossed bridges and culverts. And up above them, the sky grew heavier and darker, thick with inky clouds. A branch of lightning flickered momentarily in the distance, and dried leaves rushed across the road in the draft of the oncoming storm.

Harry said, "The goddamn *sky's* threatening enough, let alone the situation."

Singing Rock raised a hand to hush him. "We're getting close now. Very close. I'm going to need all my concentration."

They drove around a curving downward grade, and the lake at last appeared. Its waters were almost black, even darker than the lowering clouds up above it. A surface wind lifted the waves in plumes of white spray, like the scattered feathers of a fallen bird. They looked sinister and unsettled, impenetrable depths that were waiting for the dead and the drowned.

"The Pope Creek bridge is around here," said Neil, driving them along the rocky shoreline. Hardin and Maxwell and Burton creeks all run in together with Pope and they make quite an inlet."

They rounded the corner toward the bridge, and they were confronted by a roadblock: half-a-dozen Highway Patrol cars, with their red lights flashing, a contingent of police from Napa, and a barricade of red-and-white sawhorses.

A cop in aviator sunglasses waved Neil to the side of the road.

"I'm sorry, fellow. You're going to have to turn around and go back. The road's going to be closed here for quite a while."

Neil said, "My boy's on that bus. I'm Neil Fenner. His name is Toby Fenner."

The cop said, "You got some proof of that?"

Neil handed over his driver's license. The cop scrutinized it, nodded, and gave it back. Then he pointed to the rough pull-off just before the bridge itself. "Park your vehicle there, please, off the highway. Then cross to the other side of the road and make yourself known to that officer with the bullhorn."

Neil said, "Are they okay so far? The kids?"

The cop tugged at the peak of his cap. "As far as we know, sir. But nobody's been able to get within fifty feet of the bus, and we can't raise any answers with the bullhorn. A couple of officers got themselves hurt real bad."

"I heard," Neil told him.

Turning off the road, Neil parked the pickup where the cop had directed him. Then he and Harry and Singing Rock climbed out, and surveyed the place that Misquamacus had chosen for his battleground.

The creek was deep and wide here, and the bridge spanned almost three hundred feet. It was a straightforward, two-lane bridge, with a crisscross steel balustrade running along each side. A sign warned that it was forbidden to dive from the bridge into the creek, but Neil could remember seeing kids jumping off the railing into the water below just for the hell of it. It was a fifty-foot drop, but if the creek was flowing well, it was safe enough.

On the other side of the bridge was a wide dusty area which visiting tourists used as a motor-home park. The Highway Patrol had cleared it now and fenced it off. A police helicopter had landed there, and Neil could see a very senior police officer climbing out.

Halfway across the bridge stood the yellow school bus. It was parked diagonally across the highway, so that only a motocyclist could have passed by on either side of it. It was still and silent, and its doors were closed. What was strangest of all, though, was that its windows were all blank white, and it was impossible to see what was going on inside it.

Neil said, "What's that stuff on the windows? I can't see a damn thing."

Singing Rock shaded his eyes, and then nodded. "As I thought. It's ice."

"*Ice?* In this heat?"

"Almost certainly. Within that bus, they have opened a gateway to the outside, and the outside is colder than anything you could possibly imagine."

"If it's colder than my apartment on a February night, then it's cold," said Harry.

Neil shaded his eyes, too, and examined the bus more carefully. Apart from the whorls of frost and ice on the windows, the ventilators on the roof were encrusted with ice, and even the highway itself sparkled with frozen crystals for ten or fifteen feet around.

"They must be dead," he whispered. "No human being could survive in that kind of temperature."

"No, they're not dead," Singing Rock told him. "They're in a trance, of a kind, because they're preparing the gateway for the arrival of their gods and demons. If you could look inside that bus now, you'd probably see them sitting quite still in their seats, and the whole place would be totally dark and cold. You'd think they were dead, but they're not. This is what they have to do before Nepauz-had appears, in order to make it possible for Nashuna and Pa-la-kai and Ossa-dagowah to manifest themselves."

Neil said, "Hadn't we better go talk to that officer in charge? Tell him what we know?"

Harry lit a cigarette and shrugged. "I don't suppose he'll believe us for one minute. I vote we do what we have to do without telling anybody."

"But how can we? They may be planning to use weapons, and then what's going to happen?"

Singing Rock rested his hand on Harry's shoulder. "Neil's right," he said. "There could be terrible consequences if the police decide to use their weapons. At the moment, they don't know what they've got on their hands. A mysterious busload of children with frozen windows, and a police car that's blown up. They're going to tread wary. But when the medicine men start bringing down the first of the demons, then it's going to be all hell around here, and we could just as easily get ourselves killed as anybody else. Bullets, as a New York taxi driver once told me, ain't got eyes."

Harry blew out smoke. It seemed to hang where he had exhaled it, a motionless cloud in the still, humid air. Across the lake, it was now so dark that it was impossible to distinguish the hills on the opposite shore, and the water itself seemed to be heaving and foaming in unhealthy excitement.

"Okay," he agreed. "But if you can convince the Highway Patrol that there are twenty-two medicine men in there, you're a better man than I am, Singing Rock."

The three of them walked across the road to where a group of seven or eight policemen were watching the bus and talking among themselves. One of them had a map spread out on the roof of a patrol car, and he seemed to be discussing the possibility of bringing sky-hook helicopters in across the lake to lift the bus bodily off the bridge.

"The trouble is, we have a cold factor which is unknown," he was saying, "and we also have no idea what's going on in that vehicle. The last thing we can afford is to injure children unnecessarily."

Neil introduced himself. The police captain was an officer of the old school, with a uniform that looked as if it had only just come back from the dry cleaner, and shoes polished to the brilliance of fresh-poured tar. His face was ruddy and blemished with liver spots, but his eyes were small and intense, like a polecat's, and his mustache was neat and prickly.

"I'm Captain Myers, Highway Patrol," he said, extending his hand. "Are these two gentlemen parents, too?"

Harry said, "I wish I was, but you know how it is. My date got the chicken pox."

The captain frowned. "We're trying to keep unauthorized people away from this area. We have a serious and delicate problem here, with a great many young lives at stake, and we really don't need civilian interference."

In his quietest, most dignified voice, Singing Rock said, "Captain Myers, we believe we know what's happening here, and we believe we may be able to prevent a disaster, if you let us try."

"Who are you?" demanded Captain Myers.

"They call me John Singing Rock. I am a medicine man from the Pine Ridge Reservation in South Dakota. A Sioux."

"You're an Indian medicine man?" asked Captain Myers, in disbelief.

"That's correct."

"Well," said the captain, with a barely suppressed smile, "I've had some offers of help from all kinds of people. Firemen, wrestlers, circus people, you name it. But you're the first Indian medicine man."

"Captain Myers," said Harry, "he's serious. What's going on here is directly concerned with Red Indian magic. If you're going to get those children out of there alive, then you're going to have to listen to what he's got to say."

"Who are you, his caddy?" asked Captain Myers.

"No, sir. I just happen to be one of the only living people who's ever seen what the hell it is you've got in that bus there."

"You're one of the only living people who's ever seen children? What are you trying to tell me?"

"Not children," put in Singing Rock. "Not children at all. But the reincarnated bodies of twenty-two ancient Indian medicine men."

Captain Myers paused for a moment, looking from Neil to Harry to Singing Rock and back again.

"Sergeant," he said coldly, "I want these men escorted away from here. I want them to get the hell out. I also want you to take their names and their addresses, so that I can bust all three of them for obstructing the police at a critical and dangerous time."

He looked back at Singing Rock. "I don't know who you people are, or what kind of a stunt this is, but I warn you I'm going to find out, and then I'm going to put your ass in a sling. Twenty-two ancient Indian medicine men! They don't even talk that crazy in the nuthouse."

Singing Rock said earnestly, "I know how you feel, captain. It does sound crazy when you first hear it. But it's the absolute truth. It's happened before in New York, and it's happening again here. The spirits, the manitous of all those ancient wonder-workers have infiltrated the minds of the children. Right now, they're preparing to summon down one of the greatest of their ancient gods."

Captain Myers fixed his eyes on Singing Rock for a long moment. Then, without a word, he turned his back and continued to check over his map.

Harry shouted, "Are you pigheaded or are you just pigheaded? Didn't you hear what the man told you?"

"Yes!" snapped Captain Myers, jerking his head around. "And it makes me heave! Every time there's a murder, or a kidnapping, or an officer hurt in the course of his duty, the goddamned sewers open and people like you come crawling out! People who try to capitalize on human suffering and sensational crime! Now, get out of here before I have you arrested and locked up! You're wasting my time!"

Harry looked at Singing Rock and gave a shrug that meant, well, we did try. Then the sergeant came forward, a big man with furry red forearms and a belly as big as a baby hippopotamus, and said, "Come on, you guys. Back in that truck and get moving."

Under escort, they walked back across the roadway to Neil's pickup. It had grown so dark now that Captain Myers was calling for spots and floods. From out of the west, another police helicopter came fluttering, its lights flashing against the oppressive clouds. There was a heavy metallic odor in the air, and lightning was walking across the far peaks of the Vaca Mountains. Every now and then, they felt a deep, rumbling vibration through the ground, as if an earthquake was threatened.

Suddenly, they heard a voice shout out: "Sir! Captain Myers, sir! *Look at the bus!*"

They had almost reached the pickup, but they turned, and then they ran back to the crown of the road. Beyond the police barriers, one hundred and fifty feet away in the middle of the bridge, the bus was faintly shimmering with a green fluorescence. It had the same kind of ghoulish glow as a painted skull on a ghost-train ride, dim and pulsing. The wheels, the bodywork, the windows, were all outlined in light.

206

There was a noise, too, a rising noise. It was so high-pitched that they could scarcely hear it, but it had a whining, grating edge to it which set their teeth on edge and made them feel as if their very bones were vibrating.

The noise grew louder and louder and harsher and harsher until Neil and Harry both clamped their hands over their ears. Only Singing Rock remained unmoved, staring at the glowing bus with a stoic, concentrated expression. The police took cover behind their cars and drew their guns, and Captain Myers called over his bullhorn for a rifle marksman.

Soon, the noise was an unending, tortured, screaming sound, all at the same high pitch, and it seemed to blot out any sensible thought. Harry could vaguely hear shouting and the running of feet, but even his vision seemed to be blurred by the noise.

Another policeman called, "Look! The door's opening!" and a spotlight was immediately whipped across to light up the bus's front entrance. With a hissing noise, barely audible over the endless screeching, the doors jolted apart and slid back. The policemen raised their guns, and trained them carefully on the darkened exit.

One officer called, "Hold your fire!" and then they saw who was there. Down the steps of the bus, white-faced in the spotlights, stumbled Mrs. Novato.

Captain Myers stood up with his bullhorn and shouted: "Mrs. Novato? Mrs. Novato? Walk this way, please, Mrs. Novato. Keep walking and don't look back. When you reach the barrier, you'll find officers there to protect you."

He didn't know whether she'd heard him over the screaming noise, so he repeated the message slowly and carefully. Mrs. Novato, in her white pleated skirt and

207

her green blouse and her sensible shoes, stood there swaying and didn't acknowledge him at all.

"Walk this way, Mrs. Novato!" called Captain Myers. "Please, walk this way!"

When she remained where she was, he turned and called: "I want two volunteers to go out there and get her. On the double!"

Two officers scuttled across from behind the protection of their parked cars, and Captain Myers rapidly briefed them. But as he was talking, he suddenly paused and lifted his head. Mrs. Novato had taken an unsteady step toward them. Then she took another. Then another. Then she pitched forward and fell on her face.

"Get out there!" ordered Captain Myers, and the two officers, guns drawn, skirted around the police cars and sprinted out toward the bus. They weaved from side to side as they ran, and kept their heads low. When they reached the teacher, they took an arm each and ran back, trailing the heels of her sensible shoes along the road surface. They made it back to the protection of the barriers without any sign of interest or hostility from the cold, radiant bus.

They laid Mrs. Novato down on a plaid rug. The police medic knelt down beside her and took her pulse and blood pressure, and checked her eyes for response to light. It was only a few moments more before he stood up and said quite simply, "She's dead."

"How did she die?" asked Captain Myers. "Any quick ideas?"

The medic, a pale young officer with a six o'clock shadow and a pointed nose, said, "Feel her for yourself. The abdomen."

Captain Myers squatted down beside the body and gently touched the stomach with the flat of his hand.

"It feels pretty cold," he said. "But that's natural if that whole damn bus is frozen up."

"Feel harder," said the medic flatly. Captain Myers looked at him with a slightly aggrieved frown. He didn't like people who acted funny.

He tried to squeeze the flesh of the stomach in his fingers, but he couldn't. He looked up at the medic again, and said, "She's solid, like rock. She feels like a piece of frozen beef."

The medic bent forward and stripped back Mrs. Novato's white pleated skirt. From the knees upward, her thighs were pale blue, and they were as rigid and hard as marble. Her pubic hair was frosted white, and her lower stomach was solid but, worst of all, her vagina had been frozen so that it gaped obscenely wide, revealing blue-ribbed flesh inside.

Mrs. Novato's body, from the thighs to the breasts, had been subjected to such intense cold that it was totally solidified.

Captain Myers, horrified, couldn't resist touching her again, to feel how flesh that should have been soft and yielding had turned into something as cold and smooth as a stone pillar.

He stood up, and then he said in a dry, shaken voice, "We're going to treat this as homicide. I want you to get this body down to the autopsy people and I want you to tell them that they have to find out how this was done if it takes them all night and all day and all the next night. You got that?"

"Yes, sir."

A little distance away, ignored by the sergeant who was supposed to be escorting them back to their pickup, Harry and Neil and Singing Rock watched the revelation of what had happened to Mrs. Novato in silence.

Then Neil turned away, and whispered, "My God. Oh, my God."

Harry said softly, "How did that happen, Singing Rock?"

Singing Rock watched another medic arrive with a stretcher, and cover Mrs. Novato's body with a red blanket.

"They gave her to Sak," he said. "The ancient keeper of the gateway. That smoky demon you saw in Mr. Saperstein's photographs. I suppose a human woman was one of the rewards he wanted. He raped her, as you probably saw. The only difference between that and any other rape was that she would have suffered incredible mental horrors while it was happening, and the gaseous form of Sak is probably three thousand degrees below freezing."

EIGHT

Gradually, the police officers and medics returned to their posts, and the sergeant, although he was looking colorless and shaken, turned around to usher Harry and Singing Rock and Neil back to their pickup.

"What did you think of that, sergeant?" asked Harry. "Did you ever see anything like that before?"

The sergeant opened the door of the pickup for him and indicated that he should climb up.

"I've seen hundreds of stiffs in this job," he said harshly. "One more doesn't make no odds."

Singing Rock looked at him carefully. Then he said: "I know how easy it is to become blasé, sergeant, but let me give you one good word of caution. Tonight, just for once, don't be blasé. Look out for unexpected attacks. Take a lot of care."

The sergeant wiped sweat from his forehead with his furry arm. "You talk like you know what's going on here," he said.

"I do," said Singing Rock.

"Well, that *proves* you're nuts," replied the sergeant. "Anybody who thinks they know how a bus gets to shine like a dead mackerel, and how a woman gets herself frozen solid in the middle of Setember, they *have* to be going bananas."

Neil said angrily, "Why the hell don't you——"

"*Neil!*" interrupted Harry. Then, more quietly, "It won't do any good."

Neil took a look back at the bus, still standing on the bridge with its windows frosted up. He could hardly believe that Toby was inside there, taking part in some unspeakable and unimaginable ritual. He could hardly believe that Toby had summoned down the squidlike Sak, and had actually sacrificed Mrs. Novato to him. But he was here, on this gloomy and fearful night, sitting in his pickup at Lake Berryessa with an Indian and a sarcastic mystic from New York, and he knew that it had to be true.

He started the motor, and they drove off back down the highway.

Singing Rock fingered the amulets around his neck. "I think we're going to have to bide our time until it gets dark," he said. "Then we'll come back and see what we can do to lay down a medicine circle."

"How are you going to lay down a circle when the bus is on the bridge like that?"

"It's going to be very difficult. That's the reason Misquamacus chose to stop there. Nobody can come near without his knowing, and nobody can surround the bus with all the magical paraphernalia that you'd need to keep him permanently imprisoned there."

"So what's going to happen now?" asked Neil.

Singing Rock rubbed his eyes. "I'm not sure. I think we're going to have to play this the way it comes."

They drove in silence for a while along the darkening road. But after a few minutes, Harry said, "There's one small thing that's been bothering me. Something we never checked out. I thought about it last night, but then it slipped my mind again. I think if we've got ourselves a couple of hours to kill, we ought to go look for it."

"What's that?" asked Singing Rock.

"It's something that Toby mentioned to Neil real early on, when Misquamacus was first making himself known. He said something about *the prophecy that is still buried on the stone redwood.* Now, we never took the trouble to check out what that prophecy was, or where it was, or anything."

Neil reached the steep junction with Route 128, and turned right toward Chiles Valley. "It was my guess Misquamacus was talking about one of the trees up at the Petrified Forest in Calistoga," he remarked. "I never went there, but I heard there's a huge stone redwood that's still half-buried in the hillside."

Harry turned to Singing Rock. "You want to go take a look? I think we ought to. If there's something on that tree that we don't know about, and Misquamacus springs a nasty surprise on us, then we're going to regret it for the rest of our lives, which might be for five or ten minutes or so, if we're lucky."

"How are you doing for gas?" Singing Rock asked Neil.

"I'm fine. Let's head on up there. Even if we don't find anything, it's something to keep my mind off Toby."

The Petrified Forest was closed when they arrived. Although it was only a little after five, the sky was thunderously dark, and the rumblings and shakings of an approaching storm were growing steadily louder. They parked the pickup outside the gates, and then Harry walked around to the office and gift shop, where a single light was still burning. He rapped on the window, and mouthed, "Let—me—in."

A pretty brunette in a brown overall came to the door and unlocked it. She said, "I'm sorry, mister, we're all closed up. But we're open again tomorrow if you want to drop by. The place is really worth a visit."

"Look," said Harry, "is the manager in?"

The girl shook her head. "Not this evening, he isn't."

"Is there anybody here who knows something about this place, apart from you?"

She shook her head. "There's only Professor Thoren. But he's not really a tree professor. I should drop by in the morning if I were you."

"Who's Professor Thoren? What does he do?"

She frowned. "I'm not too sure. I'm only looking after the place while the manager's out. He's up at the Tunnel Tree right now."

"The Tunnel Tree? What's that?"

She smiled. "I don't know why you don't come see for yourself when we're open. It's real impressive. There's this stone redwood and it's more than three hundred feet long, lying on its side, if you understand me. It was buried deep in the rocks, and ever since about the turn of the century they've been tunneling alongside of it so that people can walk down the tunnel and take a look. It's real neat."

"And that's where Professor Thoren is right now?"

The girl nodded. "He's been here a year or so, trying to work out the Indian writing."

Harry stared at her. "I don't believe it. There's *Indian writing* on that tree? You mean that?"

"Sure there is. It was in all the local papers. They found it round about two years ago, when they were digging the tunnel along further. It's only scratches. What they call picture writing."

Harry said, "Of *course*. In Misquamacus's time, it must have been still hidden under the rocks."

"I beg your pardon?" asked the girl.

"It's granted," said Harry. He felt ridiculously excited. For the first time since he'd flown over to help Neil, he felt he was making some headway. It wasn't much, but it was something. It was an advance against Misquamacus, instead of another terrified retreat.

"I want to ask you a favor," he said. "I know you're closed, and everything, but I really need to speak to Professor Thoren."

The girl looked suspicious. "Do you know him personally? I mean, are you a friend of his, or something?"

"No, I'm not. But that picture writing he's looking at is something my friends and I have to see."

"Well, I'm sorry. You'll have to come back in the morning."

Harry gave the girl his deepest, most sincere expression, the expression he reserved for elderly lady clients who threatened to cross his palm with insufficient silver.

"You have to believe me," he said, "this is the most important thing in my whole life. I've been searching for ten years to see picture writing like this. Across Alaska. Down through Arizona. Everywhere. Ten years of hardship and struggle. And you're telling me to come back in the morning?"

The girl frowned at him, sympathetic but confused. "Well, I guess you could take a quick look," she told him. "But you'd have to pay the regular admission."

"I'll do it," said Harry. "And I'll pay for my friends, too."

215

"Friends?" she queried, but he was already peeling off six dollars.

Once the girl had reluctantly handed over three tickets, Harry walked quickly back to the pickup and rapped on the window. Neil and Singing Rock had been listening to the radio news, and they hushed him for a moment. Then, when the news was over, Singing Rock said, "They tried to get to the bus with half-a-dozen specially trained men. As far as they can tell, all six of them were struck down and killed. They're just lying in the road."

Neil said, "It sounds hopeless. How the hell can we fight against something as powerful as that?"

"I think I've got a clue," said Harry. "There's a Professor Thoren working up here, translating some Indian picture writing they found on a petrified tree about two years ago. Apparently it was all in the papers when they discovered it, but I don't remember reading it myself. Mind you—that was before I met Misquamacus. I wasn't much interested in Indians then."

"But Misquamacus said the writing was still hidden," said Neil.

"What did he know?" asked Harry. "I don't suppose they get the *San Francisco Examiner* in the great outside. And this petrified forest was only discovered around 1860, *after* his last reincarnation."

"How do you know that?" asked Singing Rock.

Harry turned and pointed. "It's painted on a sign right up on that tree over there. I thought Indians were supposed to have sharp eyes."

Singing Rock grunted in amusement. Then he climbed out of the pickup, and the three of them walked through the turnstile, under the shade of an ancient oak, into the park itself.

To reach the Tunnel Tree, they had to walk around a sloping path, up past a hilly meadow, and along the edge of a ridge. It was silent in the forest, except for the rustling of leaves and the scurrying of squirrels, and their footsteps sounded loud on the dry, leaf-strewn ground. Neil had brought along the flashlight from the pickup, but the woods were still dark and shadowy under the cloudy sky.

Halfway along the ridge, they came to an enormous fallen redwood, fenced off with chain link. Neil shined his torch on it, and the wood glistened and sparkled. Like all the petrified trees in the forest, it had been infiltrated with silicas from volcanic lava, which had turned it gradually into stone. The massive trunk, over four feet across and hundreds of feet long, disappeared into the rocky hillside, and beside it ran a narrow tunnel cut into the limestone and shored up with planks.

From within the tunnel, they could see lights.

"Okay," said Harry. "I think I'd better lead the way."

They entered the tunnel, heads bent, and walked along the boarded floor until they reached the end. There, sitting on a campstool in front of the petrified tree, with a battery of flashlights and cameras and drawing equipment, was a middle-aged man in jeans and a lumberjack shirt, peering closely at the bark through magnifying spectacles.

Harry stood beside him and waited. But the professor was so engrossed in what he was doing that he stayed where he was, his head bent, his heavy eyebrows drawn together like aggressive caterpillars, his hairy hand poised to draw a line of India ink on his drawing pad.

It was clammy and warm in the tunnel, and Harry tugged at his collar.

"Excuse me," he said. "Are you Professor Thoren?"

The professor's body flinched. Then, very slowly, he sat back on his campstool and turned toward them. His eyes were so grossly enlarged by his magnifying lenses that Harry felt a ridiculous momentary shock. But the professor took the glasses off, and replaced them with a pair of normal eyeglasses.

"Do you have any idea of the concentration it takes to make sense of these hieroglyphs?" he said, in a deep, New England accent.

Harry grinned and shrugged, and the professor sighed, "No, you obviously wouldn't. But your interruption, let me assure you, has cost me two hours' train of thought."

Singing Rock said, "We wouldn't have interrupted you at all, professor, but it's desperately urgent. Many lives are at stake."

"*Urgent?*" queried Professor Thoren. "How can anything to do with these hieroglyphs be *urgent*? They've been here for two thousand years, or even longer. This tree has lain here for six million years. In this sort of business, nothing is ever urgent. How can it be?"

Singing Rock said, "I can't explain, professor, and I think if I did you would find the situation too difficult to grasp. But I must assure you that we are serious, that we are perfectly sane, and that we must know urgently what it says in that prophecy."

Professor Thoren looked at Singing Rock carefully. "You're an Indian, aren't you? This is nothing to do with Indian rights, is it? Nothing to do with that Wounded Knee business?"

"I was there, at Wounded Knee, advising and helping," said Singing Rock. "But this particular problem has nothing to do with it whatever. This is a problem of Indian magic."

Professor Thoren got up off his campstool and folded it away. He was a tall, broad-faced man, and he had to stoop inside the confines of the tunnel. He said, "What makes you think these hieroglyphs are a prophecy? Do you know anything about them?"

"Nothing at all," said Singing Rock. "But they were mentioned in the context of an Indian legend."

"Well, you surprise me," Professor Thoren told him. "I thought I knew all the Indian legends there are to know. But nobody's ever mentioned to me that this could be a prophecy, and I'm only just beginning to come around to believeing it could be some kind of mystical prediction myself. Either you know something I don't know, or else you're way ahead of me."

"Let's just say we have inside information," said Harry uncomfortably. He didn't like tunnels much, they gave him claustrophobia, and he was praying that Professor Thoren would finish saying what he had to say and let them get out.

The professor looked at him quizzically. "Inside information? It sounds as if you heard it from Gitche Manitou himself."

"Not quite," said Harry. "But near enough. You know how these manitous gossip."

Neil said, "Professor Thoren, I have an eight-year-old son. He's in terrible danger right now, and these men are trying to save his life. If you could see your way clear to cooperating with them—well, I'd appreciate it."

Professor Thoren looked at their faces in the lamplight. Then he said, "I suppose I've heard of nuttier things. What do you want to know?"

Harry pointed to the hieroglyphs scratched on the rock-hard surface of the giant redwood. "Do you know, basically, what all of this means?" he asked the professor.

The professor ran his fingers over the lines of hieroglyphic script. There were triangles, curves, figures that looked like birds, circles, and dots. He said, "Basically, I suppose I do. I've translated it into literal English. The hieroglyphs are remarkably close to the inscriptions found on ancient stones in New England and middle America. I don't know who carved them, or why, or even how, because this petrified tree is as hard as anything you'll ever find. But it must have been an important message, because somebody took a lot of trouble to make sure it was preserved. It could have been here for two thousand years, or maybe a hell of a lot longer. It comes right out of the ancient past, right out of a time when this land was Indian country, all the way from the east coast to the west."

He glanced up at Singing Rock. "I don't particularly sympathize with Indians who want to change things back the way they were," he said. "But I know what you probably feel about America. If it had once been my country, I'd feel the same way."

Harry took out a handkerchief and mopped his face and neck. The tunnel seemed closer and hotter than ever, and quite apart from that, it was almost six-thirty, and there wasn't much time left before the moon rose.

"Professor Thoren?" he said. "The translation?"

"Well, I don't know how it's going to help you," shrugged the professor. "But here it is. The first hieroglyph here is a kind of opening announcement. You could almost say it means 'Now hear this.' But the rest of it reads: 'After the days when the greatest of the chiefs has passed beyond, and after the days when all the lands and the beasts that run on the land have been lost, then the magicians outside shall wait for nine hundred ninety-nine moons in darkness, until the day of the invisible stars, when they shall unite and call down Pala-kai and Nashuna and Coyote, the terrible ravager, and also call upon Ossadagowah, son of Sadogowah, and those outside who are in no human shape.' "

Professor Thoren paused, and looked up. "I don't suppose it makes any sense to you so far," he said. "But I can explain it if you want."

Harry, pale-faced and sweating, shook his head. "We know what it means, professor. Just get on with it."

Professor Thoren was about to say something, but then he assumed a resigned face and turned back to the petrified tree. "Okay. Right here, on the sixth line, it says: 'The wonder-workers shall take their due for the stealing of their lands and the beasts that run thereon. etcetera, and they shall also raise for this purpose *that which sleeps below the surface of the waters* and which has been waiting since elder times."

He looked up. "There is no corresponding word in the English language for *that which sleeps below the surface of the waters*, although it's represented here by just one glyph. It doesn't mean a fish, or a prehistoric monster, or anything like that. If you translated every nuance of this character, it actually means 'the great and feared god of ancient times who was banished below the waves and has been dreaming ever since of his return to the shores of earth.' "

Singing Rock's face was strained. He said, "Is there any more?"

Professor Thoren frowned. "You really take this seriously, don't you? You're not kidding around."

"Professor," insisted Singing Rock, "can you please tell me if there's any more?"

"There's one more line," said the professor. "It says something like: 'That which sleeps below the surface of the waters shall rise on that day on the bidding of Ossadagowah, and the massacre of the thousands shall begin.' The word they've used here for 'massacre' could mean 'butchery' or 'dismemberment.' It's a very ancient glyph which was often used to describe sacrificial rituals."

Singing Rock was silent for a while. He seemed to be searching deep down inside of himself for something he had heard years and years before, from the lips of the medicine men who had taught him when he was young. Professor Thoren glanced at Harry inquiringly, but all Harry could do was shrug.

At last, Singing Rock said, "Professor, I think we have to leave now. I'm very glad we found you here, and I want to apologize for sounding so abrupt and demanding. You've been most helpful."

"Hold up," said Professor Thoren. "You can't just waltz in here and take a whole year's work and then waltz out again without offering something in return."

"Oh, I'm sorry," said Singing Rock, and he reached into his coat pocket. "Would an ounce of chewing tobacco do?"

"Mister," said Professor Thoren impatiently, "what I'm talking about is a little cultural cross-pollination. I know what these hieroglyphs *say* but I don't know what they *mean*. I've never heard of anything like this. You can't simply walk out without telling me what you know about it."

"Professor," responded Singing Rock seriously, "the reason you don't know what they mean is because of all

222

Red Indian legends this is the most feared and the most secret. It is the legend of the greatest of the elder gods and it has been kept from the white man for centuries, because of what the white man might unwittingly raise up if he spoke the sacred spells."

"You believe this?" asked Professor Thoren. "You actually believe that if the spells were cast, you'd raise up some kind of ancient god?"

Singing Rock stared at him defiantly. Then, in a slow voice that was rich with dignity, he said, "Yes, professor, I believe it. I believe in the gods because they have often come to my aid when I was weak and uncertain. I believe in the gods because they still live and breathe and speak to me from the lands that once belonged to my people. I believe in the gods because they will care for my manitou when I pass to the great outside."

"Very well," said Professor Thoren, a little abashed. "Then what god is this, the one who sleeps below the waves?"

"There are many stories about him," said Singing Rock. "He was said to be cloudy and amorphous, and sometimes to be of such a size that he would tower over the earth. His face was a hellish confusion of serpents, and his jaws were like a chasm. So the stories say, anyway."

"He sounds pretty alarming. Who managed to banish him below the waves? It must have been someone with real magical talent."

"It was," agreed Singing Rock. "But in those days, almost every Indian wonder-worker was amazingly powerful. It was said that many of them could juggle with miniature suns, and cross the waters without a canoe. The wonder-worker who banished this particular god, though, was the greatest of all the wonder-workers.

223

It was Misquamacus, sometimes known as Quamis, or Quanquus. The stories say that Misquamacus dismissed him below the waters of the earth and placed a spell on the waters so that the god could never emerge again through the watery portal into the world of humans. He couldn't send the god back to the great outside, of course. Gods of that magnitude will only return of their own free will. But Misquamacus protected his people sufficiently well for them to flourish and grow, without being molested for human sacrifices or massacred as they slept."

"But it says here that the god is going to be raised again," Professor Thoren pointed out. "If he preyed on red men as well as white men, why would the wonder-workers want to do that?"

"A god who is released from a spell bears a debt of gratitude to those who let him out," said Singing Rock. "That is part of the exact balance of Indian magic."

"Even if whoever lets him out is the same person who put him under the spell in the first place?" asked Harry.

"It makes no difference," nodded Singing Rock. "You see, the god wouldn't have been put under the spell at all if he hadn't been savaging or frightening the wonder-worker's people, and so the balance would be maintained."

Professor Thoren said, "Does this elder god have a name? Something I might recognize?"

"Most of the elder gods have hundreds of names," said Singing Rock. "The Natick Indians of Boston used to call this god Paukunnawaw, the Great Bear, because he came at night like a bear and left their people hideously mauled. When Cotton Mather talked to the Naticks in the seventeeth century, he asked them what they

224

knew of the stars, and they pointed up to the sky and said *Paukunnawaw*. Mather was delighted, because he thought the Indians miraculously knew the European name for the constellation of the Great Bear. What he didn't realize was that they were telling him about the elder god who came from the stars and devoured them.

"Some Indians called him a long unprounounceable name which means The-Being-Without-Shape of-the-Estuaries. But I guess the most widespread name was Ka-tua-la-hu. It's hard to tell you what it means exactly, just like those hieroglyphs are hard to translate. The Sioux say it means 'he who lurks in the deepest lakes.' "

Harry said, "I think I'm going to go for some fresh air. This is like holding a seminar in a subway train."

Neil chimed in, "I'll join you."

Singing Rock held out his hand to Professor Thoren. "I must leave, too. We have a crisis on our hands to-night. But please understand how much you have helped us. When this is finished, we will return, if that is possible, and I will tell you everything I know of Ka-tua-la-hu. You deserve to know."

Professor Thoren gave a lopsided smile. "From what you say about him, I don't know whether I do."

They shook hands, and then Singing Rock turned and made his way back along the lighted tunnel into the darkness of the Petrified Forest.

"Well?" said Harry, as he emerged.

"It's much worse than I thought," said Singing Rock. "Ka-tua-la-hu was always the most grotesque and bloodthirsty of the elder gods. He was so feared that his name outlived the religion itself, and you can still hear some of the coastal Indians call someone they fear 'a ka-tua.' "

225

Neil said, "I don't really understand. You mean that Misquamacus is going to raise this god?"

Singing Rock nodded. "That was the second reason he chose this region for the day of the dark stars, apart from the strength he could draw from the old Wappo victory over the white settlers. Lake Berryessa is deep and wide, and an ideal place to call for a manifestation of Ka-tua-la-hu. You see, when Misquamacus banished him under the waters, he banished him under *all* waters, not in any particular spot, so he can raise him from any lake or reservoir or estuary or whatever he wants. It just has to be a big enough stretch of water to re-create the greatest and most horrible demon that ever was."

Harry sniffed. There was something in these dark woods to which he was allergic. He said, "What about Nashuna and Osso-bucco and all the rest of the demons?"

Singing Rock told him, "Demons and gods have to be summoned according to a hierarchy. First they summoned Sak, the guardian of the gateway, and with Sak's help they're going to summon the lesser demons. Then they're going to call Ossadagowah. For any kind of revenge, I would have thought Ossadagowah would have been quite terrible enough. But Misquamacus is obviously hell-bent on using Ossadagowah to call on Ka-tua-la-hu, and that's going to be devastation time."

Neil said, "We'd better get back there, huh? Back to the bus? I know this stuff is really important, and all that, but Toby—"

Harry put his arm around Neil's shoulders. "We're going to do the best we can, Neil, and a little bit more besides."

They made their way down the gloomy path of the Petrified Forest, down a flight of rough, log steps, until they reached the turnstile and the gift shop again. The girl was waiting for them anxiously, and she was obviously relieved that they weren't trying to bust their way out with a petrified tree under their arms.

"Did you see the professor?" she asked.

"Sure," said Harry. "Everything's fine."

"Did you enjoy the forest?" she asked.

Harry shook his head. "No. I was petrified."

They drove cautiously back along the highway to Lake Berryessa, but they needn't have worried about being intercepted by the Highway Patrol. The bridge across Pope Creek and its immediate surroundings were in chaos. Floodlights now illuminated the bridge from all sides, and there were police cars and press cars and armored half-tracks from the National Guard parked all over the road. Helicopters clattered in and out, bringing television teams and police officials, and there was a constant echoing blare of amplified comments from a loudspeaker system.

The night was still warm, but it was unusually dark already, and the air still trembled with the vibrations of a coming electric storm. Along the hills on the opposite shore of Lake Berryessa, across the deep, troubled waters, lightning forked like the fangs of a poisonous snake.

A cop held his hand up as Harry and Neil and Singing Rock slowly approached the bridge area in their pickup.

"I'm a parent of one of the children," said Neil, and produced his driver's license again.

"Okay, okay," said the cop. "Just pull over there and keep your head down. We'll let you know if anything changes."

Neil parked, and they climbed out of the truck. This time, Singing Rock took his suitcase with him, and they walked along by the side of the road until they reached the edge of the creek. There they stood against the railings and tried to see what had happened since the Highway Patrol had sent them away.

The school bus was still parked across the middle of the bridge, but now, even brighter than the arc lamps from either side of the creek, it was shimmering with a white, unearthly light of its own, and producing a constant high-pitched whine that set Harry's teeth on edge.

Neil said, "What's happening?"

Singing Rock set down his suitcase. "They are almost finished preparing the gateway. As soon as the moon goddess appears, they will emerge in their real form."

"What's the time?" asked Harry. "I think my watch died of claustrophobia in that tunnel."

"There's about a half-hour to go," said Neil.

Singing Rock opened his case and took out a small spherical cage made of curved bones bound together with human hair. He set it carefully on top of one of the uprights of the fence, and then hung strings of beads and ribbons around it.

"Is it rude to ask what that is?" said Neil.

"Not at all," smiled Singing Rock. "It's a caged spirit that's particularly sensitive to the presence of other spirits. Rather like a canary that miners take down the mine shaft to detect the presence of methane. When that cage starts rattling, we'll know that the first demons are drawing near to the bridge."

Neil peered at the cage worriedly. "A spirit? What kind of a spirit? A human spirit?"

Singing Rock laughed. "No. It's the spirit of a wolf. I borrowed it from one of the elders."

Harry said, "What about a medicine circle? Can you do something to hold those medicine men inside that bus? The way you did the first time Misquamacus appeared?"

"I don't think there's a chance," said Singing Rock. "Apart from the fact that it's physically difficult to get out there and draw one, your policemen will try to stop me, and so will Misquamacus. I think I prefer to conserve my energy for the battle itself."

There were now only ten minutes to moonrise. A little way away, just beyond a cluster of NBC television reporters and cameramen, Captain Myers of the Highway Patrol had set up a radio link post. He had obviously been outranked by the arrival of two police inspectors and a colonel from the National Guard, but he was tenaciously keeping in touch with the siege, and sending his men here and there to bring him news of what the military and the FBI were doing.

In the tense, warm night, under the unnatural brilliance of the floodlights, a burble of military voices came over the radio as the National Guardsmen were deployed along the hills overlooking the bridge, punctuated with occasional terse comments about the state of the school bus.

"She's still glowing. No brighter now. But still glowing."

"I don't know why the goddamn gas tank doesn't blow, the way that's shining."

"It doesn't blow because it's cold out there. Do you know how cold it is out there? That's ice on the handrail. You see it? That's ice."

"Crosby and Margolies in position, sir. We got a good view of the bus door."

"Where's that half-track? I want that half-track across

229

the road. I don't want anybody entering or leaving unless we say so."

"Do you think the children are dead?"

"Who knows? Who knows what the hell's going on?" Singing Rock lifted his eyes to the thunderous sky. "We won't see Nepauz-had when she appears," he said quietly. "How long is it now?"

"Two minutes," said Neil.

A Marine helicopter appeared from the southwest, and hovered around the bus for a while, taking reconnaissance photographs and trying to see into the iced-up windows. The draft from the helicopter's rotors washed fiercely around them, and Singing Rock's ribbons and beads flapped from the fence like the wings of ominous birds. Clouds of dry dust rose from the creek bed, and then gradually settled again as the helicopter sloped away southwest again, and disappeared.

"About a minute," said Neil.

"Then it's now," whispered Singing Rock. "Now is the moment."

The keening whine from the bus suddenly died away. The police and the troops didn't notice at first, but then gradually the hubbub from both sides of the creek diminished and sank into silence. Everybody turned and stared at the bus. There was total quiet under the floodlights, as if they were all waiting for the first take of a movie sequence.

Over the radio transmitter, a voice said, "What's happening now? All of a sudden, it's like a graveyard around here."

The school bus, in absolute silence, exploded. An intense ball of fire rolled right out of the middle of it, and pieces of debris flew into the darkness and littered the roadway.

"They've killed them! They've killed all the children!" yelped an NBC reporter. "The bus just exploded right in front of our eyes, and it must have killed everyone in it!"

A circle of fire still blazed on the roadway, and billows of smoke obscured their view. But then Singing Rock touched Harry's arm and said, "Look."

In the flames themselves, standing in a circle, were the tall figures of the twenty-two greatest Red Indian medicine men who had ever lived. They were dressed in their full ceremonial robes of buckskin and buffalo hide and elaborately woven robes, and their headdresses were decorated with horns and feathers and the tails of cougars.

Among them, in a robe of black and red that shimmered with gold and silver threads, with a headdress of outspread eagle's wings and carrying a mystical, carved staff, was the greatest of the greatest, the wonder-worker whose name was still whispered by the grasses and the trees of the wide American continent. His high cheekbones were painted with blue and yellow and white, in the war decorations of the Iroquois, and his deepset eyes burned with pride and with a desire for righteous vengeance.

Neil, with a feeling of breathlessness and fear, knew that this was the being who had possessed and overwhelmed his son; who had come to life as a man of wood and tried to destroy him. It was Misquamacus.

Singing Rock said, "Gitche Manitou, protect us. Gitche Manitou, aid us. Gitche Manitou, see that our desire for peace is good, and guide our hands."

He was about to cast the powders in front of them for protection, when Harry tugged at his sleeve. "Singing Rock—for Christ's sake! Look what they're doing!"

Through the barricade of police cars and armored trucks came a squad of ten National Guardsmen, young and fresh-faced under their khaki helmets. They formed a line across the road, and then knelt down, aiming their rifles at the medicine men.

Singing Rock, almost desperate, shouted: "They mustn't! Don't let them shoot! *They mustn't!*"

But over the transmitter the order snapped: "Aim— *fire!*"

NINE

There was a sharp rattle of gunfire. But it was only because they knew what was going to happen that Harry and Neil and Singing Rock could follow the fatal action of the next split second. Misquamacus swept his arm across in front of him, dismissing the manitous of each bullet, and returning them to where they came from.

Unprepared, unprotected, the ten young guardsmen were shot down where they were kneeling—killed by their own bullets. They died on the road in dark stains of blood, twisted and crumpled like sleeping children. There was a stunned silence over the bridge and its surroundings, and even the news reporters stared without speaking. A brief sharp odor of gunpowder drifted away on the unsettled wind. The echoes died away.

Singing Rock bowed his head. "They never listen," he said softly. "They never, ever listen. O ancient gods, protect us."

It was too late now. A further detachment of National Guardsmen was running forward with rifles and rocket launchers, and making their way through the fallen bodies of their comrades. They knelt on the road-way and aimed their weapons, while corpsmen ran out with stretchers to collect the bodies.

In the middle of the bridge, Misquamacus was spreading his arms, and he was beginning to recite the words of the summoning of Nashuna and Pa-la-kai and Coyote. His voice was deep, and it rumbled with the same timbre as the wind, and the vibrations that shook from the storm across the lake. The other medicine men turned inward to face each other, and spread their arms too, ignoring the intense line of guardsmen who were aiming their weapons at them.

"Pick a target carefully," instructed the National Guard colonel. "Then shoot at will until you've brought it down."

There was a nervous pause. Then: *"Fire!"*

The second holocaust was worse than the first. Both Neil and Harry dropped down to the dusty roadside as a shrieking, sparkling hail of automatic rifle fire burst over them in all directions. The NBC news reporter beside them was hit in the face, and keeled over backward in a spray of blood. Police and soldiers and spectators twisted and fell, and bullets shattered automobile windows and pierced gas tanks. Four Highway Patrol cars exploded and burst into flames, and the night was lurid with orange fire and the rank odor of blazing gasoline.

The National Guard colonel still couldn't comprehend that the guardsmen's own bullets were being turned against them, and he ordered another detachment of sharpshooters forward. Harry, crouched on the ground, said, "For God's sake, Singing Rock, you've got to tell them!"

Singing Rock said, "There's only one thing I can do.

I have seen it done by a great elder of my tribe, and I have heard it said that Crazy Horse could do it."

Harry said, "Don't take any stupid risks! Just go tell the National Guard that they're decimating us!"

They heard another order to fire, and there was another sharp crackle of rifles. Instantly, Singing Rock flung back his head and stretched wide his arms.

It happened so fast that Harry couldn't really see what was going on. But the entire salvo of rifle fire flashed in a wide curve away from Misquamacus and headed for Singing Rock. Singing Rock spread his fingers, and the bullets sprayed off his hands in a screeching, whining burst of fire and hot lead. Then there were nothing but echoes, and they were gone.

Harry stood up. Singing Rock was silent and pale, and there were beads of perspiration glistening on his forehead.

"You deliberately attracted those bullets," said Harry, hoarsely. "You dumb Indian, you. What would have happened if Crazy Horse's spell hadn't worked? They would have blown you away. Straight to the happy hunting grounds with no stop for lunch."

Singing Rock wouldn't look at him. "I have to trust my spells," he replied quietly. "If I lose my faith in my magic, what do I have left?"

Harry let out a long breath. "Okay. But next time, why not just duck when the bullets start flying? All right?"

Singing Rock nodded. There wasn't time for any more banter. The night was crisscrossed with flashing spotlights, and hideous with the whooping of sirens, but over it all they could still hear Misquamacus as he completed the incantation for calling down the first of the Indian demons. They could feel the rumble of thunder through their feet, and the lightning that had stalked the distant hills was now flickering closer.

"Listen," said Singing Rock. "Between them, those medicine men are calling down Nashuna and Pa-la-kai and Coyote. The demons won't be able to resist their summons, because they're too powerful, all together like that."

Neil, wiping a smudge of dirt from his face, said, "What are we going to do if they do call the demons down? How can we possibly fight them?"

Singing Rock took a look at the spirit cage he had left on the fence. So far it was quiet, and showed no signs of activity. He rearranged the ribbons and beads, and finished casting the powders he had brought with him.

Then he said, "What you have to remember is that almost every demon can be appeased. Some demons want blood, others want manitous. If you can offer a demon what he needs to survive and maintain his strength on the great outside, then you can usually succeed in dismissing him."

"Usually?" asked Harry. "How often is usually?"

"More often than never," replied Singing Rock. "And right now, we're clinging on to every straw we've got."

There was an earsplitting burst of thunder, and they looked in fear up at the sky. All the way down the dark length of the lake, huge trees of forked lightning sizzled and crackled, and the air reeked of electricity. Then darkness swamped them again, and the heavy clouds rolled over the mountains and blotted out the stars and the moon and the night sky.

Misquamacus was calling now, at the top of his voice. "Nashuna, we summon you! Nashuna, we command you! Nashuna, god of darkness, we summon you!"

Above the circle of medicine men, a hundred feet in the air, a roiling knot of darkness appeared, darker than the clouds. Out of its threatening, amorphous midst, Harry could make out scores of what looked like red glittering eyes, evil and ravenous, and from beneath its cloudy bulk, dark smoky tentacles trailed toward the ground. The spirit cage on the fence began to rattle and shake as if it were being worried by a mad dog.

There were heavy bursts of gunfire from police and soldiers on both sides of the bridge, and again both Highway Patrolmen and onlookers were cut down by slicing bullets. Over the transmitter, Harry and Neil could hear the National Guard colonel insisting on a cease-fire, and phoning Travis Air-Force Base for an air strike.

Singing Rock, though, was totally preoccupied by Misquamacus, and by the huge bulk of Nashuna the demon of darkness. He stepped forward now, through the lines of police cars, and walked to the end of the bridge. Harry, from where he was crouching, was sure that he could see Misquamacus bare his teeth and smile. Singing Rock was caught in the floodlight, one man alone against twenty-two, and against all the terrible powers of the elder gods, and Misquamacus was at last going to get his revenge.

Misquamacus raised one arm. Singing Rock stopped, only thirty or forty feet away from the circle of wonder-workers.

In his distant, strange, echoing voice, Misquamacus called: "Why do you fight me, little brother? Why do you defy me?"

Singing Rock didn't answer. Instead, he lifted his

medicine bones and beat them together over his head in a complicated rhythm. Then he pointed one bone up to the sky, up toward the dark bulk of Nashuna, and spun the other bone in his free hand.

Misquamacus suddenly understood what Singing Rock was doing, and raised his own arm toward Nashuna. But he was moments too late. Singing Rock's incantation was completed, and he abruptly pointed his second bone toward Neem, the bringer of thunder, one of the most celebrated wonder-workers of all time.

There was a roaring, grinding, screeching sound like a cliff collapsing. Neem, a muscular Indian in a buffalo-horn helmet, crossed his arms in front of him to prevent Singing Rock's spell from reaching him. For almost a minute, the two of them struggled against each other, with Misquamacus powerless to intervene. Branches of lightning spat and fizzed around them, with sparks showering across the road surface. From where he was standing, Harry could see that Singing Rock was hunched forward with effort, and that the arm which was still raised toward the grim shape of Nashuna was trembling with effort.

Suddenly, there was a horrendous scream. Neem, the bringer of thunder, had fallen to his knees. Singing Rock was almost standing over him now, pointing one bone toward his body and keeping the other bone directed at Nashuna. The rumbling noises were deafening, and Harry felt sure the whole bridge was going to collapse.

"Nashuna, demon of darkness, I give you this being's darkness for your stores of night!" called Singing Rock, in a high, strained voice. "Take his darkness as my sacrifice, and go back to the great outside!"

Neem fell to the road. He tried once to claw his way

toward Singing Rock, but he knew that he was defeated. Singing Rock had been too quick, too direct, and had used one of the most powerful sacrificial spells. Dying, the thunder-bringer shrieked in agony, as his skin peeled away from his body, transparent layer by transparent layer, and as his muscles and membranes and bones were bared. He fell apart like a dissected flower, while his inner darkness, the secret shadows inside his body, were drawn through Singing Rock's steadily pointing bone and funneled into the black knots of Nashuna's maw by the other, upright, bone.

There was another peal of thunder, and Nashuna was gone. Singing Rock stepped away from the spread-out remains of Neem the medicine man, warily watching Misquamacus. No emotion showed on Misquamacus' face, but he kept his arms raised as a protection against Singing Rock's magic.

"You have defied me," said Misquamacus. "Not for the first time, but for the second time. You will die for this, and your manitou will wander the great outside forever, in constant agony of mind and body. I, Misquamacus, promise you this!"

Singing Rock said nothing, but abruptly turned his back on Misquamacus and walked off the bridge. He came back to Harry and Neil and set his bones back in his case with almost casual professionalism. It was only when he turned to look at Harry that the strain on his face really showed. He was white with effort, and his eyes seemed to have lost all expression.

"How can you turn your back on him?" asked Neil. "Why doesn't he strike you down?"

Singing Rock dabbed at his forehead with his handkerchief. "He let me go because we've declared this a kind of contest. There are rules to any contest, and the rules to this one are that you don't unleash your medicine on anyone whose back is turned."

Captain Myers came across from the protection of his Highway Patrol car. He said briskly, "I thought I told you jokers to stay out of this. I thought I specifically ordered you out of here."

"It's just as well you didn't," Harry told him. "You'd all be lying around like cut-up frogs by now."

"I demand to know what's going on here," said the captain.

Singing Rock sorted through his case. "What's going on here is that I'm saving your life," he said brusquely. "Now, if you know what's good for you, you'll stay out of my way and let me get on with it."

"But what the hell did you *do* out there?" demanded Captain Myers. "What was all that stuff with the bones?"

"It's very easy," said Singing Rock, taking out two leather pouches of powder. "Nashuna is the demon of darkness, and darkness to him is like a blood transfusion. Everybody has inner darkness, physical and mental. I gave Nashuna the inner darkness of Neem, that medicine man there, and Nashuna was satisfied and went away. I'm afraid you have to understand that the inner darkness of a great medicine man is worth a great deal more to Nashuna than that of a captain of the Highway Patrol. He might have had to dissect a few hundred policemen to achieve the same result."

"Listen, you refugee from a traveling sideshow," snapped Captain Myers, "I'm ordering you off this area at once. If you try to make your way back again, I'll personally make sure that you're shot."

Singing Rock said, "If you make me leave, then I assure you that you won't be here to shoot me."

240

On the fence, the spirit cage began to rattle and shake again. Singing Rock turned around to listen to it, and then said, "It's Pa-la-kai. Misquamacus has summoned down the demon of blood."

"The demon of blood?" asked Captain Myers. "This sounds like a goddamn horror comic."

There was more thunder and blinding lightning, and for a few seconds Misquamacus and his medicine men were silhouetted by what looked like floating globes of light, intensely brilliant suns that swam above their heads. Harry, his hand raised to shield his face, could just make out the blue-white outline of *something* within that intense light source before the bridge and the creek were plunged into darkness again, and all he could see were red and green spots in front of his eyes.

Singing Rock went forward again, and stood in the gloom facing the bridge where Misquamacus had formed his circle. He called, "O spirits of wind, I call you now to help me. O spirits of the storm, give me your strength. I call upon you, hurricanes and whirlwinds, to give me your power."

Captain Myers said, "What the hell is that idiot doing? Doesn't he know he's going to get himself killed?"

Harry held the captain back. "Don't go after him. Give him a chance. He knows the risks better than you do."

A faint breeze began to disturb the grass around them. Then the breeze rose to a soft wind, and whistled through the fence, and through the bones of the spirit cage. In a few seconds, the wind had whipped up even harder, and clouds of dust were blown up from the sides of the highway. In a minute, it had become a shrieking gale, and they couldn't even hear themselves speak.

Behind Misquamacus, in the center of his medicine circle, the swimming globes of Pa-la-kai, the demon of blood, flared up again. They were brighter than the sun, brighter than anything Harry had ever seen before. In the end, he found it impossible to look. The dazzling globes were slowly floating together to form one shatteringly brilliant sun.

With his eyes screwed up against the light, Harry watched Singing Rock anxiously. He could see that the Indian was already tired, pitting his magic against Misquamacus and twenty other medicine men, any one of whom was more experienced and more powerful than Singing Rock could be in three lifetimes. And as the demon shone and shone, and slowly brought himself together into one supremely evil and unconquerable shape, Singing Rock's head fell onto his chest, and his arms gradually dropped.

The gale-force winds, which had sprung up so quickly, began to die away.

"Come on, damn you," whispered Harry. "You can't let him beat you now. Come on, damn you. Come on!"

But Singing Rock was exhausted. He sank down on one knee, and held his hands to his head to concentrate on the spell he was trying to work. And meanwhile Pa-la-kai, in all his ravenous majesty and brilliance, swelled larger and brighter and ever more devastating. Out of his dazzling maw came a cacophony of gruesome howls and shrieks of bloodlust, and he rose again, high over Singing Rock, to take his sacrificial due.

Singing Rock raised his eyes. Harry could see that he was almost blinded by the light of Pa-la-kai. Neil, standing close by, said, "He's finished, Harry. He can't fight that. He must be finished."

Singing Rock spread his arms. Only a few feet away now, Misquamacus stood over him in his eagle-winged headdress, tall and triumphant and vengefully straight-backed. Behind Misquamacus, in a silent semicircle, stood the greatest of the Indian wonder-workers.

"Pa-la-kai!" howled Misquamacus. "I give you this traitor's blood! I give you every drop that flows in his veins, every ounce in his heart! This is your sacrifice, Pa-la-kai, master of death! This is your reward, Pa-la-kai, god of blood!"

Singing Rock, instead of collapsing, staggered to his feet and sprayed his medicine powders in a crisscross pattern. His eyes were wild, and his whole face was contorted with the effort of what he was doing. In a stentorian voice, he called: "Ossadagowah! By the commands of the elder gods, by the forbidden words of Sadogowah, by the thousand deaths and the thousand lives, I bid you to appear!"

Misquamacus paused, taken completely by surprise. He stared at Singing Rock in disbelief. Singing Rock had actually dared to summon the demon whom no Indian medicine men ever dared to summon, the beast in no human shape whom Misquamacus had been intending to use himself to call up Ka-tua-la-hu, the one who slept beneath the waters.

Even though Ossadagowah was dangerous to any human, no matter how many sacrifices were placed before him, he was almost always inclined to favor those who summoned him from the great outside, and for a while, anyway, he would do their bidding. This time, in this manifestation, that meant Singing Rock's bidding.

Singing Rock had scarcely spoken when a strange cold cloudiness began to form over the bridge. The cloudiness widened and slowly settled downward, misting the bright globes of Pa-la-kai and making them shine with dim opalescence. In a few minutes, the fires of Pa-la-kai had died and dimmed, and there was nothing over the bridge except that chilly white miasma of evil.

"Ossadagowah, most revered son of Sadogowah, hungry one from the great outside. I offer you these wonder-workers," called Singing Rock. Again, he cast his powders. "I give you their blood and their brains and their very spirits to grind between your teeth. I give you their essence to absorb in your selfness. I give you this and offer you my prayer."

The white cloud coiled and twisted like fat transparent white maggots. It uttered a *noise*, too, like nothing Harry had ever heard. A doleful, hideous groaning sound, that made him feel cold all over. The sound of a being who was without pity, without emotion, without any recognizable soul. Harry knew what Singing Rock had risked, summoning Ossadagowah. He had risked himself, and everyone else around them, and maybe thousands of others. Only a great wonder-worker could seal Ossadagowah back on the great outside, and there were only two wonder-workers living who were capable of doing it. Singing Rock, if he was at the peak of his strength, which he wasn't; and Misquamacus.

Misquamacus knew that, too. He knew that Singing Rock had outwitted him. He paused for a moment, his face lifted toward the cold, waving tentacles of Ossadagowah, and then he reached into his costume. He produced a small gray tablet of stone, and held it toward Ossadagowah. At the same time, he started to chant and sing, quickly and loudly, and—Harry thought—almost desperately.

Ossadagowah groaned again, and his groaning shook

the earth beneath their feet. His cloudiness seemed to spread wider, and his tentacles thrashed the air. Then, very gradually, the coils of his amorphous form started to fold in on themselves and disappear, and within a few moments his whole being had vanished.

Now Misquamacus faced Singing Rock alone. But the ancient wonder-worker turned his back on Singing Rock contemptuously for a while, and raised his arms to address the other medicine men. They spoke among themselves, their faces grim and vengeful, and then, when they had decided on what they were going to do, they turned and faced Singing Rock again.

Misquamacus and Singing Rock spoke to each other for a while. Harry tried to catch what they were saying, but they were talking quietly and with little emotion, and when he did catch an occasional word, it sounded as if it was in some Indian language. It could have been a challenge from one medicine man to another. It could have been a demand from Misquamacus that Singing Rock should leave the side of the white men and fight instead for his blood brothers. Whatever it was, Singing Rock shook his head at the end of it, and walked back through the lines of police cars without another word.

"What's happening?" demanded Captain Myers. "What's going on out there?"

Singing Rock knelt down by his case and put away his powders and his amulets. Then he stood up and looked from Harry to Neil to Captain Myers.

"What you saw just now was just a skirmish," he said. "I caught Misquamacus off-balance, and I managed to prevent him from unleashing those demons on the countryside. But, as you can see, he is scarcely tired, and I am exhausted. He has twenty other wonder-workers to back him up, and twenty other wonder-workers to call up the most terrible of gods from elder times. He says that even without Ossadagowah, he will raise Ka-tua-la-hu from the waters, and that will mean the end of us all."

Captain Myers bristled with anger. "What is this?" he snapped. "This is a whole bunch of clouds and optical illusions and stuff like that, and you're trying to tell me it's dangerous? The only thing that's dangerous around here, fellow, is that gang of terrorists out on the bridge there."

"Terrorists?" queried Singing Rock. "You really think they're terrorists?"

"They stole the school bus, kidnapped the kids, blew the bus up. Then they shot down thirty people. What else would you call them?"

"Captain," said Singing Rock, "if all that is true, then where are the children's bodies?"

"Blown up, I guess," said the captain grumpily.

"And where are their weapons, those terrorists? Can you see any of them carrying a gun?"

"They're concealed. Russian-made concealed weapons."

"Concealed where?" asked Harry dryly. "In their hats?"

Captain Myers didn't answer.

Singing Rock said, "I tried to tell you before, captain, and you just wouldn't listen. Those men out there are reincarnated medicine men from many centuries past. In a while, they will raise from Lake Berryessa a god known as Ka-tua-la-hu, and Ka-tua-la-hu will kill all of us."

Captain Myers pulled at his ear. "Ka-tua-la-hu, huh?"

"That's right. A beast in no human shape. The most

terrible and feared of all the elder gods. The spawn of the Great Old One himself."

Captain Myers looked perplexed. He walked a little way away, and then he came back and said, "Ka-tua-la-hu?"

Singing Rock nodded. "If you look out on the bridge, you can see that they're beginning to call him already."

The captain shaded his eyes from the floodlights, and squinted for a while at Misquamacus and his medicine men. Then he stalked off to make a report over the transmitter.

Singing Rock pressed his fingers to his eyes. Harry watched him for a while, and then said, "Is there anything I can do?"

Singing Rock shook his head. "This is turning out to be a duel. The only trouble is, there are twenty-two of them—well, twenty-one now, if that makes any difference—and only one of me. I can't fight them very much longer."

"What about Ka-tua-la-hu? What can we do against him?"

Singing Rock shrugged. "I really don't know. And even if I did, I don't think I'd have the strength to do anything about it."

Neil said, "You can't give up now. If you beat them, I'll get Toby back. Please."

Singing Rock said, "I'm doing whatever I can, Neil. I promise you. But you mustn't hold out too much hope."

Neil said, "I've always had hope. Dammit, I've had hope when there was nothing else. When everybody thought I was crazy."

"But, Neil—" said Harry.

"But nothing," interrupted Neil. "The point is that white men beat the Indians once, including their medicine men, and if they did it once they can do it again. If Misquamacus was so great, how come the prairies are all farms now, and all the buffalo are dead, and the elder gods are all forgotten? How come the Indians are all living on reservations?"

Singing Rock tiredly ran his hand through his hair. "The Indians lost because they lost faith in their magic," he said. "It wasn't anything to do with the power of medicine men like Misquamacus. It was just that the medicine men couldn't do anything without the support of their nations."

"I don't believe it," snapped Neil. "I believe the white man won the West because he worked harder and fought harder and because he wouldn't ever give in."

"Neil," said Harry, trying to calm his down.

"I don't believe the Indians lost faith," repeated Neil. "I just believe that the white men were stronger, and that was all."

There was a rumbling noise from the direction of the lake. A humid wind blew for a while, and then died away. It left a strange smell behind it, a smell of fish and cold fog. All along the shores of Lake Berryessa, the water began to foam and grow agitated. A small tidal wave even washed into Pope Creek, below the bridge, in a swill of muddy froth.

Singing Rock turned and stared at the bridge. He could see Misquamacus, illuminated by the police floodlights, swaying from side to side and singing in a piercing, high-pitched tone.

"He's nearly finished calling the old one," said Singing Rock. "When all twenty-one of them recite the summoning together, then the waters will open and you will see Ka-tua-la-hu. Well, I hope you won't. Neil, Harry, you'd better get in that pickup and burn it on out of here. We're not going to stand much of a chance now."

"John," said Harry, "I'm not leaving you here."

"You have to," insisted Singing Rock. "You're no damned use to me anyway."

"John—I'm not going, and that's final."

Singing Rock looked at Harry for a moment, and then offered his hand. "All right," he said, softly. "I appreciate your staying. But don't say I didn't warn you."

Out on the lake, a huge, cold fog was rising in the darkness, and the waters were gurgling and seething in horrible anticipation. The earth cracked beneath their feet, and the temperature dropped lower and lower with each passing minute. Around them, police and reporters ran around in confusion. Only on the bridge itself was there any calm at all, an eye in the storm, as Misquamacus began to make slow beckoning gestures toward the lake, summoning Ka-tua-la-hu, the terrible elder god.

"I guess this is almost our last chance," said Singing Rock. "Misquamacus is really preoccupied now. It's going to take all of his strength to raise up Ka-tua-la-hu without the help of Ossadagowah, and all the strength of his friends as well. I'm going out there again."

He opened up his case and took out two war axes, each one decorated with scalps and feathers. Then he gave Harry one last look, and made his way back through the barricades toward the bridge.

Harry called: "Take care, will you?" But he wasn't sure if Singing Rock had heard him.

Now, hundreds of feet above the churning surface of Lake Berryessa, the grayish fog rose in the dim and terrifying shape of the elder god. It was so dark that Ka-tua-la-hu's writhing form was scarcely visible, but as he

249

strained his eyes, Harry could see something that looked like a nest of wriggling, repulsive serpents; something that disturbingly reminded him of every nightmare he'd ever had. *It was the raw essence of fear and repulsion; the loathsome horror that crawled on the fringes of the night. It was the ancient lingering memory that still makes men afraid of things that creep and things that slide, even though they have consciously forgotten why. It was Ka-tua-la-hu, the spawn of the Great Old One, the most hideous god of madness and fear.*

All twenty-one medicine men on the bridge had now raised their arms in obeisance to the elder god, and were singing a low, warbling incantation. They stood in their oweaoo, their circle, and they drew the overwhelming fog cloud nearer.

Singing Rock reached the end of the bridge and stood there alone for a moment, swinging a war ax in each hand. Then he whooped out a long challenging call, a mocking call that ridiculed Misquamacus and every other medicine man, a call that any Indian with any pride could not ignore.

Harry could see Misquamacus waver with indecision. But then the wonder-worker turned and left the other twenty medicine men to continue their call to Ka-tua-la-hu, who now loomed over them all in an immense boiling bank of evil clouds, and he faced Singing Rock with an expression of burned-out patience and deep revenge.

Singing Rock took two or three steps forward, and then he began to whirl one of the axes around and around until it was a blur. Misquamacus crouched down slightly in anticipation, but his eyes never left Singing Rock's face, and he looked confident and contemptuous. Harry, over by the fence, found that he was digging his fingernails into the palm of his hand.

The magical ax flashed from Singing Rock's hand and flew toward Misquamacus, turning end over end. But even before it was halfway there, Misquamacus gave a quick sweep of his arm, and the ax seemed to burst and turn into a black owl, which screeched once and then flapped away on the wind.

Singing Rock swung the second ax, faster and faster, and he threw it at Misquamacus with a hoarse cry of warlike vengeance. But Misquamacus was quicker, and stronger. His arm swept across his chest again, and the ax turned in midair and flew back toward Singing Rock. Harry watched in horror as Singing Rock tried to dodge it, but the speed and power of Misquamacus' magic made it unstoppable and unavoidable. With a sharp chopping sound that Harry could hear from seventy feet away, Singing Rock's head was knocked from his shoulders.

For an agonizing second, Singing Rock's decapitated body stood alone on the bridge, with a fountain of blood spraying from his severed neck. But then he twisted and collapsed beside his own head and lay still.

Harry turned away, his stomach heaving. He felt totally stunned, totally shattered. Without realizing it, he dropped to his knees, and stayed there while Misquamacus stalked back triumphant to his circle of medicine men, and joined his strength once more to the summoning of Ka-tua-la-hu.

Neil said, "Harry—what the hell can we do now? Harry!"

Harry looked up. His eyes were watering from retching. He said, "I'm damned if I know. Singing Rock was the expert."

"Harry—we've got to do something! Look!"

Behind him, the writhing cloud of Ka-tua-la-hu was

almost at the bridge itself, and its pale slimy tentacles were lashing out at the foam-wracked shores of the lake. The whole grotesque god was trumpeting now, trumpeting in evil and hungry delight, with a noise that sounded like dozens of tortured whales. Across on the other side of the bridge, Harry saw three National Guardsmen running as a tentacle lashed toward them. It caught them all, and dragged them shrieking into the boiling lake.

"We've just got to get out of here!" shouted Harry. "That thing's going to kill us all!"

"But we can't!" Neil insisted. "What about the children? What about all the people who are going to die?"

"I'm not a goddamned martyr!" Harry yelled back. "I'm a goddamned mystic!"

Already, policemen and soldiers were running past them and scrambling up the loose dirt and rocks of the hillside. A cold, foul wind was blowing—a wind that stank of silvery fish skins and fetid flesh. Out of the mass of serpents, another tentacle flailed toward the shore, and a policeman was crushed and pulled into the water.

There was a high-pitched screaming sound, and suddenly five Air Force jets, all flying in tight formation, came streaking northward along the length of the lake. They passed the cloudy bulk of Ka-tua-la-hu, and Harry saw the hot scarlet-blue flames from their tail pipes as they used reheat to climb and bank and circle away.

Ka-tua-la-hu screeched and groaned, and another roiling mass of tentacles appeared from the upper clouds.

Harry and Neil could hear what was happening over the abandoned transmitter. The National Guard had pulled back a half-mile, and their colonel was trying to direct the air strike from Dyer Creek.

"Air strike to ground. What do you want us to sap?"

"The bridge there. The Pope Creek bridge. You see where that kind of gray fog stuff is?"

"We're coming back for another run there. We don't see the bridge too clearly."

"Where that gray fog stuff is. That stuff with all the tentacles like a damned octopus."

"An octopus? What is this? We don't see any octopus."

Harry and Neil could hear the jets rumbling behind the hills. Then they flashed into sight again, still flying tightly together, and made a curving pass over the bridge and off into the clouds to the south. They were followed by a sharp sonic bang.

"We see the bridge and the cloud mass. You want the bridge knocked out?"

"That's right. Knock out the bridge, and see what you get when you fire a few rockets into that fog."

"Okay, ground. We're coming in for a trial run, then we'll get at it."

Again, the whistle of the jets came nearer. But as they appeared over the hills, there was an abrupt garbling of sound over the transmitter, and a chilling, screaming noise.

"What's happened? I can't see! I can't see anything!"

"Oh, Christ, my eyes are gone! My eyes!"

The five jets thundered overhead, but this time they were wildly out of formation. Two of them collided almost over the creek side where Harry and Neil were crouched, and there was a monstrous explosion and a rolling ball of fire that spun across the valley and

253

crashed onto the hillside opposite. The other three tumbled out of sight, but Harry and Neil heard three dull thumps in the distance and saw the flash of igniting fuel.

Harry wiped sweat from his face and looked up at the towering bulk of Ka-tua-la-hu, white and heaving and infinitely evil, a mass of wriggling tentacles and cloudy horror.

"Well, Neil, I guess we're on our own."

Neil slowly shook his head. "We're not on our own. We never have been. These Indians have called up all their old spirits and demons and ghosts to help them, why the hell don't we call up *ours*?"

"What are you talking about?" said Harry. "Are you crazy?"

"That's exactly what I'm not. I've been stupid, that's all. Dunbar helped me once and he'll do it again. That's what he was trying to tell me. The Indians may have massacred those white settlers up here at Conn Creek, but they made a mistake when they chose to use that massacre as a focusing point for all this. They disturbed the spirits of the settlers, right? They disturbed Dunbar's ghost. And what I said about the white men licking the Red Indians is true. They licked them because they were stronger, and better armed, and better organized, and in the end they were more determined."

"Greedier, too," said Harry.

"Sure they were greedy. But their greed was what made their determination even stronger. And they're not only determined, they're *here*. They must be. They're just waiting for us to call them, like that monster was waiting for the Indians to call him."

"You're going to call them?" said Harry. "Now I know you're out of your mind."

Neil stood up. "You bet I'm going to call them. We're going to win this time, Harry. We won in the old days and we're going to win again. My ancestor started all this, and it's up to me to set it right."

Harry tried to grab his arm, but Neil ran off through the lines of deserted police cars, ducking and weaving. The ravenous cloud of Ka-tua-la-hu was almost over them now, its tentacles blindly searching for human flesh. Harry saw one white serpent slither across the ground and catch an unsuspecting jackrabbit, instantly tearing it into a bloody rag with a crushed skull and bulging eyes.

Neil made it to the bridge. The twenty-one Indians were still standing there in their magic circle, using all their powers now to bring Ka-tua-la-hu out of the lake and across the countryside, to devour and ravage and take revenge on the white man. Misquamacus was standing in the center of the circle, his head back and his eyes closed, his fists pressed against his chest. Out of his mouth came an endless howling ululation, a sound as ancient and timeless as the first man who ever called on the elder gods to wreak death on his enemies.

Neil, alone, shouted: "Dunbar! Dunbar! I need you!"

His voice sounded pitifully small amid the screeching of the Indian medicine men and the astral moaning of Ka-tua-la-hu. But he called again and again: "Dunbar! Dunbar! Dunbar!"

Harry yelled: "Neil! It's no damned good! Get out of there!"

"*Dunbar!*" howled Neil. "*Dunbar, for God's sake, help me!*"

Harry rubbed dust from his eyes. He wasn't sure whether he was imagining things or not, but there seemed to be more people on the bridge. Their figures were faint at first, almost invisible, but as Neil shouted *"Dunbar!"* over and over again, their shades seem to gather substance and shape.

They didn't take on complete solidity. Harry could still see the shadowy railing of the bridge through their bodies. But they were solid enough to recognize. Twenty lean, rangy men in mackinaws and buckskin shirts and long dusters, with beaten-up hats and drooping mustaches. Twenty hard-bitten old-time settlers, with rifles and guns. And a little way behind them, on the hillside, stood twenty women in bonnets and capes, and a group of silent, unmoving children.

They were the ghosts of the Wappo massacre at Las Posadas, the spirits of 1830 returned. The people whom Bloody Fenner had led to their deaths, and whom his descendant was now calling to take their revenge, the white man's revenge on the Indians.

The medicine men lowered their arms, and stood facing the ghostly white settlers in cautious bewilderment. But the settlers didn't step forward. They simply raised their rifles, took aim at the medicine men, and fired. There was a flat, unreal report, and smoke appeared to drift away on the wind. The medicine men collapsed to the road.

At the same time, as the incantations of the medicine men ceased, a deep, groaning sound emerged from the shape of Ka-tua-la-hu. The ground shook again, like a huge earthquake, and the night sky was ripped with lightning and peal after peal of shattering thunder.

In a final devastating burst of noise, the elder god rolled back into the lashing waters of Lake Berryessa, and sank in a turmoil of foam beneath its surface. It left behind that cold stench of the deep and dark waters that lapped and splashed and lapped again, but the god was gone.

Harry ran up to the bridge. Neil was still standing there, exhausted and alone. The bodies of the medicine men were strewn everywhere, their painted faces against the asphalt, their costumes bloodied and torn. Harry circled around them gingerly, looking for Misquamacus. Neil followed close behind.

Then Harry heard a voice. He looked up through the drifting powder smoke, and there at the end of the bridge stood Misquamacus, with Broken Fire, the Paiute medicine man, beside him. Both of the wonder-workers had been wounded by the ghostly bullets of Dunbar's settlers. Misquamacus' right arm hung beside him, dripping with blood, and there was a dark stain on Broken Fire's breeches. But Misquamacus' face was still deeply marked with anger and revenge, and he fixed Harry with eyes that glittered and burned.

"You think you have defeated me, white man, but I shall destroy you, too, just as I destroyed your traitorous friend. First, though, Broken Fire will burn the man Fenner, so that you may see what I have in store for you."

Broken Fire raised his hand, just as Andy Beaver had done, and pointed it toward Neil. Harry tried to take a step forward, but Misquamacus made a sweep of his left arm, and Harry felt as if he was paralyzed, unable to move another step. Broken Fire chanted the ritual words to create fire, and gave a low, penetrating cry.

As he did so, however, there was a curious vibration in the air between him and Neil. For a brief moment, Harry was sure that he could see the outline of a young man, with one hand raised, protecting Neil from the magic that projected from Broken Fire's outstretched finger.

There was a roaring gout of flame from Broken Fire's hand, but it flared up against the ghostly outline of the young man, and enveloped Broken Fire instead. The medicine man screamed in agony as the fire seared his face and his bare chest, and he dropped to the road in a struggling, twisting mass of flames. After a while, he lay still.

Misquamacus turned to Harry.

"Your legacy has always been one of death and destruction, white man. You have slain my people and raped my women and destroyed my prairies and forests. Now you have dismissed even my greatest gods. I sought revenge on you and the one called Singing Rock, and on all white men and their running dogs, but revenge has sought me instead. This is my last life on this earth and I must now go to the great outside unfulfilled.

"I could kill you now, but I shall not. I want you to remember me instead for the rest of your moons, that you knew and fought against Misquamacus, the greatest of the wonder-workers of ancient times. I want you to know, too, that even on the great outside I shall seek a way to revenge myself for what you have done, and that you will never be safe from my anger."

The medicine man raised his hand in the Indian sign which means "so be it," and then turned away. All Harry and Neil could do was watch him disappear into the smoke and the darkness.

But even as they stood there, they heard voices behind them. Small, young hesitant voices. They turned, and there on the bridge where the bodies of the medicine men had been lying were the children of Bodega school. Linus Hopland, with his scruffy red hair, Petra

258

Delgada, Ben Nichelini, Debbie Spurr, and Daniel Soscol. Even old Doughty was there. They turned again, and where the burning body of Broken Fire had been stood Andy Beaver, dazed but alive. And out of the smoke into which Misquamacus had walked, shyly at first, but then with a rush, came Toby.

Neil knelt down and flung his arms around Toby and cried openly. Harry watched him for a while, and then went to the parapet of the bridge, took out a cigarette, and lit it. He didn't want to go look at the body of Singing Rock. He wanted to remember his Indian friend the way he always had been before—dignified, wise, tolerant, and humorous. What lay on the bridge were only mortal remains, after all. Singing Rock's real self, his manitou, was now on the great outside, in the magical hunting grounds where the wonder-workers prepared themselves for each fresh incarnation.

He took a long drag at his cigarette and then brushed tears from his eyes with the back of his hand. He thought he must be getting old. The wind always seemed to make him weep.

They sat in the kitchen at Neil's house, polishing off the remains of one of Susan's cheese-and-bacon pies, with fresh broccoli and red potatoes. Then Neil brought some more beer out of the fridge, and they drank a quiet toast to survival, and maybe to Dunbar, too.

Harry said, "It was too near this time. I don't ever want to meet that goddamned Misquamacus again as long as I live."

Susan gave him a gentle smile. "The best thing you can do now is forget it. It won't happen again, will it? Not like this."

259

"I don't think so," said Harry. Then he added, "No, it won't."

Neil drank beer and said nothing. Toby, at the other end of the table, was playing lumberjacks with the stalks of his broccoli, cutting them up and floating them downriver on the cheese sauce.

Harry said, "I still don't know what happened with Broken Fire. I thought he was going to burn you up like a cheap hamburger out there on the bridge."

Neil lowered his eyes. "I don't know, either. But I've got a kind of hunch. I don't know whether you saw anything in the air between me and that medicine man, but I could swear I glimpsed my dead brother Jimmy for a moment. It was as if he was acting as a shield between me and that fire."

Neil set down his glass. "You remember what Singing Rock said about Broken Fire? His magic didn't work too well against the spirits of people who had been killed by white man's technology. Well, that was how Jimmy was killed. We were out working on our car, him and me, and I accidentally let the jack slip and he was crushed."

There was a pause. Susan and Toby and Harry all looked at him in silence, and let him come to terms by himself with what had happened.

"What I learned out there," said Neil, "was that Jimmy doesn't blame me. He protected me, and saved my life, just like the spirits of all those settlers protected the American heritage that they'd help to found. I believe the spirits of the past are with us all the time, whether they're good or whether they're evil, whether they're fancy and frightening or whether they're plain and helpful. I still don't understand it all, and I don't

260

suppose I ever shall, but I thank God that the world is made the way it is."

Harry Erskine finished his beer, wiped his mouth, and stood up. "I'm going to have to make a move," he said, "or else I'm going to miss that plane."

"How long are you going to stay in Dakota?" asked Susan.

"Just long enough to make sure that Singing Rock gets buried the way a great medicine man should. Then it's straight back to New York."

Susan smiled. "Well, you call and see us again, you hear?"

Harry nodded. "Thanks for the lunch. It was terrific."

They walked out to Neil's pickup and Harry threw his suitcase in the back. Susan and Toby stood by the kitchen door waving as he climbed into the passenger seat and closed the door.

"So long," called Harry. "And stay away from Indian medicine men from now on."

Toby grinned and lifted his hand for a second in the same sign that Misquamacus had made before he vanished. The Indian sign for "so be it." Then the sign was gone, and the boy was simply waving.

Harry looked at Neil and tried to appear cheerful.

"Nice boy you've got there," he said, and reached for his cigarettes.

Evil does not die . . .
It waits . . .
To be re-born!

THE MANITOU

GRAHAM MASTERTON

☐ P40-233-3 $2.25

"Masterton has concocted a tale that just won't let go, and will have them screaming for more. Highly and memorably visual, *The Manitou* aches for translation onto film; the special effects possibilities are virtually never-ending . . . word-of-mouth could make it this year's rage!" —*Bestsellers* magazine

This multimillion-dollar film spectacular from Avco Embassy Pictures is the terrifying tale of the reincarnation of an ancient Indian medicine man. *The Manitou* is a powerful novel of horror, vengeance, and sorcery.

PINNACLE—BOOK MAILING SERVICE
Box 690, Rockville Centre, N.Y. 11571

Please send me the book I have checked above. I am enclosing $ _____ (please add 50¢ to cover postage and handling). Send check or money order—no cash or C.O.D.'s please.

Name _____

Address_____

City _____ State/Zip _____

Please allow approximately four weeks for delivery.

Two Soul-Chilling Excursions Into The World Of

GRAHAM MASTERTON

THE SPHINX

☐ 40-189-2 $1.95

The terrifying tale of a beautiful woman—an exotic combination of American and Egyptian blood—and a secret so frightening and horrible that it would turn her husband's life into a nightmare . . .

THE DJINN

☐ P40-061-0 $1.75

"Masterton builds up the suspense little by little until a shattering ending totally captivates the reader."
          —*West Coast Review of Books*

The spine-tingling story of a bizarre suicide, a mysterious young woman, an ancient Arabian jar, and a life-and-death struggle against unspeakable evil.

PINNACLE—BOOK MAILING SERVICE
Box 690, Rockville Centre, N.Y. 11571

Please send me the books I have checked above. I am enclosing $ _____ (please add 50¢ to cover postage and handling). Send check or money order—no cash or C.O.D.'s please.

Name _____

Address_____

City _____ State/Zip _____

Please allow approximately four weeks for delivery.

"An excellent piece of work:
swift, wry, readable,
and terrifyingly pertinent."
—Frank DeFelitta,
author of the
national bestseller, *Audrey Rose*

P.J. O'Shaughnessy

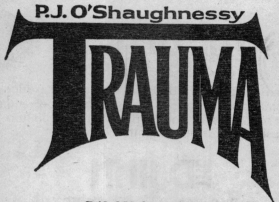

P40-359-3 $1.95

Combining the best of *One Flew Over the Cuckoo's Nest*,
1984, and *Brave New World*, *Trauma* is the frightening
story of Sebastian Cant, a man who had everything he
could want, except his freedom—and his refusal to pas-
sively accept his fate.

PINNACLE—BOOK MAILING SERVICE
Suite 1000, 2029 Century Park East, Los Angeles, CA 90067

Please send me the books I have checked above. I am enclosing
$_____ (please add 50¢ to
cover postage and handling). Send check or money order—no cash or
C.O.D.'s please.

Name _____

Address _____

City_____ State/Zip_____

Please allow approximately four weeks for delivery.